PIZZA
WARS

BY
AHMED DEBANI aka IAN NEWTON

The
X
Press

Published by
The X Press
PO Box 25694
London N17 6FP
Tel: 020 8801 2100
Fax: 020 8885 1322
E-mail: vibes@xpress.co.uk
Website: www.xpress.co.uk

First Edition 2004

Copyright© Ian Newton/Ahmed Debani 2004

Printed by Bookmarque Ltd, Croydon, UK

Distributed in the UK by Turnaround Distribution
Unit 3, Olympia Trading Estate, Coburg Road, London N22 6TZ
Tel: 020 8829 3000
Fax: 020 8881 5088

ISBN: 1-902934-38-5

www.xpress.co.uk

It is the most powerful weapon in Western liberal democracies. In skillful and clever hands it can be used to control men, make money, or to have fun.

To understand its nature is to take power over your destiny. Yet it is no more than a game like chess or monopoly. The game is politics...let us play. But a note of caution before we begin, all is not what it seems in this world.

This book is dedicated to the memory of: Allan John Bryan.
Just a mate, and friends like him you count on one hand.
Always, too much was never too much to ask.
Never far from our thoughts.

ONE

The night rain had almost relented. Inside the small pizzeria, the two Iranians took one last look around as they shuffled on their coats and turned out the lights. It had been a long night. They stepped out into the damp cold air and locked the door behind them, the older of the two carrying a large sports bag, which held, among other things, the night's takings.

Babbling away in Farsi and laughing as they walked the few yards to the car, a sudden rush of scrambling feet surrounded them as shadows emerged from the darkness. A sickening crack could just be heard over the whistling cold wind. Wood crashing into human bones. The two men crumpled to the glistening wet pavement, blood gushing from gaping face and head wounds. The gang of violent shadows mercilessly tore into the defenceless men with a flurry of ferocious kicks. Groans and moans turned into silence. Eyes bulging and mouths open, the bodies of the two men lay frozen as slow pools of steaming blood encircled them.

From out of the darkness a night blackened figure walked without haste toward the demonic silhouettes that towered over the two bodies. The man stood for a moment looking down at them. Indifferently, he poked at the head of the older man with his foot, positioning it so that the macabre glare of inflicted violence stared openly back at him. A mocking voice whispered in Farsi what could have been a foreign incantation or curse: "*Salem alicome* my Iranian brother!! In business you have to do these things."

Gloved hands snatched a baseball bat from an outstretched

hand and inflicted yet more frenzied blows upon the defenceless bodies. In a gesture of contempt, he threw the bat down beside the men— it's job finished. In sudden pain, the figure then clutched his awkward left arm and winced in agony. He kicked at one of the men on the floor. The sound of footsteps faded into the night.

§§§

Goldthorpe was a sleepy market town on the fringes of the Leeds' suburban sprawl. It was quiet haven for the middle and upper classes to escape the harsh realities of city life. Here, people indifferently made their money during the day, and in the evening retreated to safe and comfortable sanctuary. With its expensive houses and big posh cars, Goldthorpe was cut off from the city by a lack of regular bus service. This ensured that it stayed out of reach and pocket of urban riff-raff.

Goldthorpe liked to think of itself as a different kind of town, but this snobbish self-delusion betrayed itself at the weekend. Like most places, the usually peaceful conservative dignity of the market square came to life in an explosion of weekend release. This Friday night was no different. The streets were thronging, the pubs were full to capacity and the cash register at the only local fish and chip shop in Goldthorpe merrily rang away much to the delight of its proprietor, Peter Hardcastle.

Six foot-two with hair cropped so short it made him appear bald, he was a man of giant muscular proportions, and a truly fearsome sight to any drunken customer who dared give him any lip. He had a notorious reputation for violence, but in his business, it was this reputation that had kept competitors at bay and his enemies silent. There was always a queue at Peter Hardcastle's Fish and Chips, and after the pubs called time on the last drunken reveller, the queue outside the shop would extend out of the door and down the street. The chip shop was a gold mine.

This Friday night was no different than any other—except for one thing. A smart, black, four-door BMW parked nearby. Inside, three men sat patiently watching the shop with interest. Seated in the rear of the car were two men of Asian origin. One was muscular and middle-aged , with a hint of grey hair. His name, Rashar Nuraman — an Iraqi. Next to him sat an old and seemingly frail man, respectfully known in the takeaway world as Amu Sultan, which in English roughly translates as Uncle Sultan. In the front driving seat sat an almost hauntingly good-looking white man with a slightly olive complexion. In his early twenties, he had unusual, piercing green eyes and almost teutonic blond hair. In English circles he was known as Tony Debani but his appearance masked his true origins.

Tony was two sides of an ethnic coin. In the English world he was called Tony, while in the other he was called Ahmed, his middle name. He was half-caste, the name on his birth certificate matched his family history: Anthony Ahmed Debani. Tony was the product of a marriage between a local girl from the port city of Kingston-Upon-Hull and a Yemeni merchant seaman. Growing up on the hard streets of Hull's notoriously tough Hessle Road, Tony had never forgotten the lessons learned on that street. Because his father was a different colour and therefore different, he had never been allowed to forget that he was a WOG in a white man's world. It was a name that others would learn quickly never to call him to his face.

He learned to fight and steal on the streets, and learned just as quickly the consequences of petty crime, as one by one his friends disappeared to Borstals and prisons. Like most working class kids with a few brains, he was drawn into Socialist politics, the trade union movement, and later in a minor way– journalism.

As a young shop steward he developed a curious way of dealing with industrial disputes. It was a tactic that some might describe as blackmail, when put more simply. In the end, how he got the right result mattered little to him because the powerful men he was up against would just as quickly do to him, what he was doing to them, if they got the chance. It made him one of the most successful shop stewards in Hull and made him popular with the rank and file. But to others with less imagination and different ambitions within the union, it made Tony something else— a dangerous man to both union and employers. And he was a wog, with a white face perhaps, but a wog none-the-less and this union was not ready for that yet, particularly from an Arab. In this man's union such men should rarely be seen and never heard. And to seek industrial glory over their betters in their own country, well that was a sin. On both sides of the union and employer divide, men in the echelons of power were already conspiring to plot his downfall.

Of the four shop stewards that sat on the committee, three were suddenly promoted to shift managers. Only the fourth shop steward, Tony, was singled out. The old tried and trusted games were brought out of the political trick box and the redundancy trap was laid and sprung. It was not long before Tony found himself out of the union, out of a job and out in the cold. People he had defended and had once thought of as friends, took no time in forgetting their debt. Some, who had been ready to betray their fellow workers behind closed doors, now took the glory for themselves.

If Tony was anything, he was a survivor and he had learned the ways of the world. This was nothing more than another lesson to be learned, heeded and forgotten at his peril. Unlike many others who had been set up in the same way, Tony had not been completely blacklisted. He had friends in his other world and there his reputation had not gone unnoticed; Anthony had something they needed. He knew how the British political system worked inside and out and he had the contacts to use it.

Anthony was the politician of the trio— the Mr Fix it. Six foot-two with blond hair and fluent in Arabic, he'd become a curious figure in the ethnic community. Endearingly he was known as The White Arab. This morally bankrupt world of twilight business on the fringes of legality was not something he would have chosen for himself. But now he found himself an integral part of the heartless business mincing machine that kept the poor in poverty, the repressed in fear, and those in control in great luxury at the expense those imprisoned in the invisible world of fast-food takeaway.

Anthony consoled himself with the fact that the world he had been born into had given him no choices. This white man's world had tried to sentence him to a life of struggle just because he had been born with an Asian name and an Arabic father. It was not he who was guilty but them. For Anthony, there was no choice. He had tasted poverty— and wealth without morality, though bitter, tasted much better. One day he would get out of this game he

8

detested so much. He harboured secret ambitions of going to university and finding a place in the world that would give him dignity and the type of respect that came without fear.

"Well," said Tony quietly. "What do ya think?"

"How much does it take?" asked Amu Sultan in a smooth barely accented voice.

"I've had someone watching it all week," said Tony, "I'd say about twenty five grand. He does delivery from the back, four vans that never stop all week."

Amu Sultan smiled. "Four vans from the back you say. What V.A.T. does not see eh?" He laughed quietly to himself.

"Well?" asked Tony waiting.

Amu Sultan looked at Rashar and indicated his approval with a nod of the head.

"It's good I think." Rashar's eyes were locked onto the white giant serving behind the counter. "What do we know of this man?"

"Local hard case, very hard. A psychopath I think. He doesn't fuck around. A few years ago a Pakki tried to open a takeaway up the road from here. He ended up in hospital after someone poured petrol through his door and burned his house down. No one's tried since."

"Problems, always problems," whispered Amu Sultan heavily.

"You don't get anything for nothing. You should know that Amu Sultan," Tony answered.

"Don't worry about him," Rashar said casually. "We give the job to the Sheffield Yemenis."

"No, no, I think we leave the Yemenis out of this for now," said Amu Sultan thoughtfully. "They spill too much blood. That is not only expensive but I think could cause problems here. I think you can deal with this Ahmed?"

Rashar was seething. "I know what this man needs!" Rashar opened up his jacket with smile. He was wearing an automatic pistol under his arm. Rashar liked his toys and liked to show them off; it was all part of his endless games. And in a curious way– an Arab way– Rashar was threatening Amu Sultan and Tony without words, and they knew it.

Anthony shook his head and laughed without humour, "One day Rashar, you're gonna get us all in prison wearing that thing.

This is England not Iraq."

"Put it away," said Amu Sultan quietly, "...there are times for such things, and this is not that time or the place. We go gently, gently first." Amu Sultan then turned to Tony with a smile and satisfaction in his voice. "What you have seen here is good work Ahmed, you have done very well and I am well pleased, but what about the shop?"

For an answer, Tony turned around and pointed through the rear car window to an empty shop across the square. "Just there. The position is just beautiful, and the shop inside is massive. We could probably get seating for six put in and still have plenty of spare room for standing customers. There's also road access at the back for doing deliveries. To start with we'll need at least three drivers, even if we only half Hardcastle's customers."

Amu Sultan was now smiling with anticipation. Just as always, Ahmed had done his homework, leaving nothing to chance. "And what of politics and planning permission?"

"Should not be a problem," answered Tony confidently. "The council's Conservative controlled. The main man is a councillor called Bob Ronson. Nothing gets through without his approval. Hardcastle is probably giving him a back-hander to keep other people out."

"Then he might change sides for a price then I take it?" anticipated Amu Sultan.

"He should come cheap," said Tony with wry smile.

"And just how much is cheap?"

Tony took out a small notebook from his jacket pocket and flipped it open. "Very cheap I think; I checked him out." He referred to his notes, giving a run-down on Ronson with an efficiency to which Farida had long been accustomed. He often wondered where Tony came by his information and his sources, but he knew better than to ask. "Ronson has a history," Tony began. "A very interesting history. His real name is Michael Burgess. He's from down south, been up here for years," Anthony paused with a smile. "Our Councillor Ronson it seems, likes children. He served six years in Strangeways Prison for a string of child abuse offenses in the sixties."

Amu Sultan smiled to himself. "How respectable our British politicians are," he said mockingly.

"I don't think planning permission will be problem," said Anthony confidently.

Amu Sultan was well pleased. "Good. You have done well, as always. Unlike others," he added with disapproval aimed at Rashar sitting next to him. "I have enough problems, and speaking of problems..." he turned to Rashar, "I thought I told you I wanted those Kosovan asylum seeking bastards out the house in Hull. They have paid no rent for two months and the place is a pig house. Bastards come to this country and think they can do what they want."

"Oh don't worry," whispered Rashar intensely. "It is taken care of as we speak."

Tony sighed to himself. He knew all too well what Rashar meant.

Amu Sultan smiled to himself, detecting Tony's disapproval. In Farida's book, if Tony had one weakness that was it.

"I see you do not approve Ahmed," said Farida.

"What you do is your business Amu Sultan," Tony replied.

"I know my own people Ahmed and you must learn them, too. You must also learn, Ahmed, weakness breeds disrespect and for us that is dangerous. You should not feel too badly, in business you have to do these things."

"I'll go see this Councillor Ronson tomorrow," said Tony changing the subject.

"No, not tomorrow," Amu Farida answered curtly, "...see to it when you get back."

"Why, am I going somewhere?"

"You are busy for the next five days." Amu Farida had a diplomatic way of making an order sound like a request when dealing with Tony. He was English after all.

"I am?" he answered curiously, "With what?"

"I want you to accompany Rashar collecting."

"Why me?" Tony protested. "I don't do that anymore Amu Farida."

"You do as I say," Amu told him firmly. "Rashar does not have your flair with the words." Amu Farida was now looking straight-faced at Rashar, his voice sarcastic and scathing. "Last month he put three managers and two chefs in the hospital. You need to show him other ways to do this thing."

11

"I don't need Ahmed or anyone telling me my job. We all work for the Company. We all own the Company," Rashar answered angrily. "The people are different since he did the collecting. They get clever and don't want to pay. I always get the money. I don't need him!"

Amu Sultan looked at Rashar without compromise. "I am the Company Rashar. Don't forget that. You do as I say Rashar. You are too eager with your fists. Ahmed will speak with them first, then if he has problems, you may speak with them in your own way. "*Anta tefham?!* –You understand?!"

After a pause Rashar swallowed hard and replied, "*Iowa* –Yes."

Just every now and then Rashar liked to push the boundary. It was a sort of challenge to test Amu Farida's authority. Amu Sultan recognised this. There were always those in his world probing for signs of weakness, anything they could use against him to push him out. It was almost a tribal-like survival, a constant challenge, where those seeking advantage showed no mercy and gave no quarter once weakness had been found. But Rashar found no weakness here, only a humiliating slap-down that left him in no doubt about who was boss.

In the car mirror Tony looked at the two and could almost feel the tension and anger straining in Rashar's face, begging to be released. In the sudden silence, the atmosphere in the car closed in like oppressive humidity. One day Tony knew that there would come a time when Rashar would not back down, when Amu Sultan's weakness would be found. He hoped by then that he would be out of this game and long gone. Tony raised his eyebrows and without a word turned on the engine. The car silently slipped out of the square.

§§§

The smell of Albanian cooking permeated the walls of the old house. To the four Kosovans sitting on the floor ready to eat from a communal plate of fried chicken and rice, so far life in England had been all they had hoped. They had money for food, graciously provided by the British State and money to live, also graciously provided by the British State. The little extra money they earned working illegally for miserly takeaways owners, they spent down at the local pub. As a community, their numbers had so swamped the regulars that they had ousted the locals, who now drank elsewhere. An influx of local prostitutes had also moved in to serve the needs of this new foreign customer, and business was booming. Any antagonism met from locals was no problem for them to cope with. The spite of a few words shouted across the street was nothing compared to life in Kosovo, where words came out the barrel of an AK47.

As they leaned forward to take food, the front door came crashing off its hinges and six masked men rushed into the room, and laying into them with baseball bats. There was no fight and it was over in seconds. The four Kosovans lay groaning in a bloody heap about the room, their food splattered across the walls and threadbare carpets.

The six masked men stood towering over them. One of the men knelt down and spoke fiercely into the ear of one the moaning Kosovans. Although the language was English, they recognised the accent as Arabic. "We will be back in one hour; *ache wallah*-be gone." The masked man grasped the Kosovan by the throat and tightly squeezed. "You understand?!!" It was not a question.

The bloodied Kosovan nodded as he gasped for air. The masked man slammed the Kosovan's head into the floor and stood up. "Remember, one hour!!" He turned to the other men. "*Yellah!!*- Let's go!!" As quickly as they had come and the six men were gone.

13

TWO

If there was one job that Tony hated it was collecting. It was five days of non-stop motorway mileage from one end of the country to the other. In total, the Company owned–one way or another– thirty pizza takeaways, from as far north as Glasgow and as far south as Luton. They were all franchised out to managers from the local ethnic community and were effectively fronts unlinked to other takeaways in different cities. Once a year the owner would shuffle his name in such a way that to Customs and Excise it would look like someone new had taken over the business. In this way, each takeaway received the maximum VAT allowance of forty grand a piece on turnover. There was also less danger of any former managers taking up grievance with the VAT office, since they too, would be up to their eyes in the fiddle.

On average, each takeaway turned over about six grand a week. In theory, that usually worked out to about forty percent overhead, a tiny percentage VAT, and the rest pocket. It was one hell of a lot of cash to collect once a month but it never went according to plan. In a cash business there are always managers who skim off the profits or a delivery driver who upped his miserly pay by a tenner or so a night. It was all taken into account in the calculations.

As long as the Company made near enough their regular bundle, nobody complained. Amu always allowed some leeway on the fiddling. It was when the fiddle got out of hand that Amu usually put his foot down, then the blood and snot would be sliding down the walls. That was the other part of the job that

Tony hated. Whether the managers were Arab, Pakistani, Iranian, or other, it always took persuasion to get the money. Excuses, they had a million of them and Tony had heard them all, but one way or another they got their money.

The monthly collection usually brought in around ninety thousand pounds cash after deductions. The people fronting the shops received a ten percent monthly bonus straight off the top, as well as very good weekly wage. Amu Farida was a great reader of human nature— as long as they were well looked after it, was in their interest to look after Amu Farida. Of course it still did not satisfy all of them; some arms still had to be twisted.

In many respects, getting the money was the start of another problem. It was a lot of cash to get rid of and it was not as though you could put it in the bank. The tax people would have been on them like hot shit off a stick. But there were ways. Farida, being an Iranian, would often simply take a suitcase full of cash home to Iran every three to four months. Crude, but it worked. Or sometimes he would use the Pakistani money brokers dotted around the country to get it wired to an Iranian bank. It was simple and efficient, and because it was based purely on trust there was no paperwork for VAT or revenue to get their hands on.

Tony had similar problems to Amu Farida but on a smaller scale. He had a string of family members holding bank accounts with substantial sums in. What Rashar did with his share was a mystery, and he never talked about it. Amu and Tony joked that he probably kept it under his bed and counted it every night. He was that type of man— a real greedy bastard.

It was a tacky twilight business and very dangerous at times. If you wanted self-respect or had a social conscience like Tony, it was made harder by the fact that sometimes people had to be hurt.

Rashar had arranged to meet Tony at nine o'clock in the city centre of Hull just near the golden statue of King Billy. Tony sat there impatiently waiting and staring at the hapless human flotsam and jetsam going in and out of the nearby dole office. Maybe he should be thankful for what he had. If fate had dealt him another hand it could have been him walking into that dole office. For just a second he was distracted, as a young, very sexy blond girl passed his car. For a moment or two their eyes met and locked in mutual attraction, then suddenly the girl looked away and hurried down the street. Tony watched her shapely figure disappear around a nearby corner.

"Would I?" he said aloud to himself.

What he did not see was the young girl climb into the driver's seat of a metallic silver Golf GTI that was parked waiting for her. Inside sat an older with a long-lens camera perched on his lap.

"Did you see where he went?" asked the man.

"He went into the benefit office," she answered in a raw Geordie accent.

"Bloody typical," said the man seething.

"I think someone's waiting for him. That blonde one, Ahmed, is parked just across the road."

"Ah yes, he's the clever one. The one they call The White Arab. Now that's interesting," he said intently. "He doesn't usually go with him. If he does the collecting with him then we'll get all three of the bastards together. It might be our lucky day."

Still waiting, Tony looked at his watch. He was parked on double yellows and getting impatient and had spotted a meter attendant coming up in his rear view mirror. When Rashar finally appeared, he was coming out of the door of the dole office. He was dressed in a smart blue suit and as usual wearing his Gucci shades. Rashar liked the mafia look. He was carrying a holdall and a newspaper.

Tony shook his head. "Fucking hell! The bastard's signing on," he said aloud to himself.

Rashar jumped in the car and threw the holdall on the back seat.

"What the fuck are you doing in there? Are you crazy? If you get caught by the dole people, you risk all of us. Just for a few fuckin' quid!!"

"If I don't sign on, what do I tell the tax man? I don't have two passports like you."

What Rashar was referring to was the way Tony dealt with the tax man. As a dual national he had two passports—one British, one Yemeni. It had been simple to get a Yemeni entry stamp in his passport showing that he had been out of the country and in Yemen most of the tax year. It worked like a charm.

"Anyway never mind that," said Rashar, his tone suddenly

changing. He threw the newspaper under Tony's nose. "Have you seen this?" The headlines hit Tony slap in the face.

"VICIOUS ATTACK. TWO SERIOUSLY INJURED."

"It's Hijan and Husseini. Somebody seemed to have sorted them out last night."

Tony's head was glued to the headlines. "Who?"

Suddenly the meter attendant was tapping on the car window. "Just drive!" said Rashar hurriedly.

What Anthony and Rashar did not notice as they pulled away, was that the metallic silver Golf GTI had also emerged from around the corner nearby and was following some distance behind them. Angela Carrick intently watched the car up ahead as she drove. The smartly dressed man that sat in the passenger seat next to her was much older. His name was Tom Bradley. They were both VAT investigation officers but of the two, he was more senior in rank. As they continued in pursuit, Tom snapped numerous photos of Tony's car just ahead.

"Drop back a bit," Bradley instructed her, "…you're getting too close."

"I don't want to lose them."

"Don't worry about that. They're going where they always go first–Sheffield."

"I wonder why he is with him this time?" asked Angela curiously.

The man in the passenger seat gave a laugh that was almost a sneer. "Maybe someone wants both the bastards out the way." Bradley put down his camera and could not resist a quick look at Angela's legs, as her short skirt had ridden some way up her thighs.

Angela detected an acid tone in his voice. "You talk as though you dislike them," she commented awkwardly. She could see he was looking down at her legs and making no attempt to hide it. It was an uncomfortable moment and she made a feeble attempt to pull down her skirt, much to Bradley's amusement.

"And *you don't*?" he snapped back.

"It's my job," said Angela indifferently. "I have no personal feelings either way."

"Well you should have," Bradley snapped back in a voice that was almost angry. "People like them are the dregs of the earth,"

Bradley went on. "…they come to this country and from day one they milk it. It's mostly decent British people who always have to pay for what these bastards won't. They make me sick."

Angela was taken aback by Bradley's outburst. "You sound as though you don't like them because they're Arabs. I've dealt with white people who have fiddled us out of millions and just walked away after some clever lawyer has sweet-talked the judge. To me – black, brown, white, or whatever – they're all the same. No different to each other."

"When you have been in this job as long as I have, you see it all. But there is something insidious about these kinds of people. When they come to this country they just cannot believe what a soft touch we are. In their country, they would have their fingers sliced off for stealing a camel turd."

There was a long awkward pause of silence. Angela was reluctant to challenge Bradley further. After all, he was her superior. She pretended to look down the road ahead.

"Yes," Bradley sneered aloud, "If I had my way I'd send all the bastards back."

Once on the M62 motorway Tony put on the car radio. It was on the half- hour news. "A suicide bomber has killed sixteen people in Israel," announced the newsreader, "—and wounded another sixty. The Islamic fundamentalist terrorist organisation Hamas has claimed responsibility."

Rashar cursed at the news reader. "What does he mean, fuckin' 'terrorist.' When the French were fighting German occupation, they were the resistance fighters. They always have double standards with the Arabs."

"I never knew you cared Rashar," said Tony. "You never struck me as a political animal."

"Of course I care," Rashar snapped back. "The Palestinians are Arabs. Palestine is their land and they are fighting for it. Like any man would. The fuckin' Jews think they own the world."

Tony laughed. "They do."

"Not in the Arab world they don't. We throw them all out," said Rashar.

"Exactly," said Tony. "You threw out all the Arab Jews. And where did they go — Israel." Tony looked at Rashar with a wry smile. "That was real clever of the Arabs, eh Rashar?"

"Most of the Jews in Palestine are from the West," said Rashar. "They are the ones who cause all the trouble. Why do you think the Germans killed them all? Because everywhere they go, the Jews cause trouble and get too big for their boots."

"The Jews are just people like any other — no different," said Tony. "They are people who just want to get on with their lives, just like me or you. It's politicians that divide people."

"Then go and tell that to the Palestinians," Rashar answered. "Go and talk to the refugees in Lebanon, Syria or Jordan. Go and tell them that the Jews are just ordinary people. They will put a bullet in your head. Sometimes Ahmed you talk out of your arsehole."

"Jews and Arabs, what the fuckin' difference," said Tony. "I tell you Rashar, if I took twenty Jews and twenty Arabs, stripped them naked, put them in a line and then gave you a gun and said go down that line and shoot only the Jews, I wonder how many Arabs you would shoot by mistake?"

Rashar was laughing now, because he knew Tony was right. "What you say is clever. But if there is no difference between the Arab and the Jew then why are they fighting?"

"Oh there is a difference alright Rashar, but you can't see the difference." Tony pointed to his head and his heart. "The difference is in here and here and it is what gives the Jews so much power over the Arabs." Tony started to smile. "My old man told me the difference. I didn't know what he meant at the time, but I do now. Ya know what he told me Rashar? He said when the Jew climbs the ladder of life, as he climbs it, he holds onto the Jew who is following him to ensure he does not fall and helps him up the ladder. When he reaches the top, all those coming up behind him he will lend a helping hand. Now when the Arab climbs up the ladder of life, he will stand on the hands of those following him and do everything to kick them off the ladder. When he gets to the top, he will push the ladder away from the wall so no other Arab can use it."

The two men in car stared at each in silence for a second. Rashar took in a heavy breath and sighed with a half smile. "Your father sounds a clever man. I think perhaps he was right, but it does not help the problem for the Palestinians and the Jews. They are still killing each other."

"The problem Rashar, is created by clever men," said Tony.

"You mean clever politicians?"

Tony smiled and shook his head. "Politicians are not clever my friend. It is the people who put them there. Behind all politicians are the really clever men, especially in the West. They are the men you never see — the real enemies of good men. The ones who control the politicians and through them the ordinary masses. They are the real power, the ones who pull all the politicians strings."

Rashar was suddenly laughing. "You understand too much Ahmed. I know now why some say you are dangerous — you are a politician. Perhaps a dangerous politician," he said with a chuckle.

"That's what I get paid for," said Tony. "Politics is no more than a game like chess or poker. In the West it is the most powerful weapon in the world in skilled hands. More powerful than an atomic bomb. It is the mechanism by which people in the West are managed. It is also a game the Arabs need to learn to play with equal skill. Then there is no need for killing. Politics my friend, is the game of clever men. The game which has no end."

"What you say I understand," said Rashar, "...but the war in Palestine will go on."

"War and violence are the tools of the ignorant," said Tony, "...given to them by clever men who know that using politics will be to their loss. Those who turn to violence first have lost the political argument. You would do well to remember that."

"The bottom line in all arguments is power and fear. If you have that your enemy will respect you. The Israelis now fear the Palestinian, they fear Hamas," answered Rashar.

Tony sighed. "So you think suicide bombing and the killing of innocent people is the answer?"

"What do you want them to do?" Rashar argued back. "Since 1948 the Palestinians have been fighting to get their land back."

"And what have the other Arab states done to help since the Intifada?" asked Tony rhetorically. "Stood back and watched," he continued. "And in the wars they've had, the Israelis have kicked the Arab arse."

"That is because the Arabs are not fighting the Israelis," Rashar

20

answered fiercely. "They are fighting America. The Americans give the Jews everything— money, the best guns, the best aircraft. Let us see how far Israel gets in a war without their precious America. And now that Bin Laden has struck America, the Americans will know there is a price to pay. How long do you think America will support Israel now that Arabs have attacked?"

"You are right, Rashar. America will have to rethink its foreign policy in the Middle-East. That is one thing that Bin Laden has achieved. On September the 11th America suddenly had a big wake up call. Bin Laden made America pay, you might say. What Bin Laden did to America no one else has ever done, I suppose you have to respect him for that."

"You have an English saying," said Rashar with a wide smile. "If you play with the traffic don't be surprise if you get run over. On September 11th America was hit by a juggernaut." He started to laugh, "And an Arab was driving."

"Don't be too smug Rashar," Tony cautioned him. "The Americans are taking their vengeance in Afghanistan and now in Iraq."

"And now America struggles in Iraq, answered Rashar more smugly,"...and the body bags come home. But what fools are these? America destroys the man who hates fundamentalism more than they." He laughed. "I have no love for Saddam or America. And I care less for both equally," he added indifferently. Bin Laden gave America what it deserved. You play with fire and you will get your hands burnt. I think the only person who is dancing for this war in Iraq is Bin Laden. America gives him a birthday present."

Tony could not help a smile of cynical amusement. Like everyone else on September the 11th, he remembered exactly were he was and what he was doing. He also knew that when the initial pictures of the first plane hitting the first Tower came through, that it was no accident. Something inside told him that this was the long hand of Arab vengeance and hatred reaching out across the oceans. No more than a few hypnotic minutes of watching, and a second plane struck the second Tower. Suddenly Tony's phone was ringing and Amu's voice was screaming hysterically down the phone. He, too, had watched the same pictures.

Pizza Wars

If this was not enough there was more to come, as more dramatic and incredible television reports came live into living rooms. It was impossible to move away from the scenes of carnage being played out in front of him. It was almost unreal, like a Hollywood disaster movie being played out in real time. But this was no movie. Without speaking, Tony put down the receiver like an automaton, his eyes still transfixed on the TV. Again the telephone was ringing. Tony did not recall picking it up, but he remembered the voice screaming down the line with hysterical joy— elation bordering on the irrational. "They've hit the fuckin' Pentagon!! They've hit the fuckin' Pentagon!!"

Over the next few days a strange masquerade played itself out on the television screens as leading British Moslems and British Arabs stood side by side with the Prime Minister Tony Blair to condemn the events in New York. But what Tony remembered was the truth and the truth is rarely, if ever, seen. He remembered the hidden smiles of satisfaction on smug brown faces. The quiet whispers and secretive pride behind the artificial mask of consolation and sympathy expressed to the white native Brits, whilst behind backs they sniggered satisfaction for the new Moslem Robin Hood, Osama Bin Laden. The sympathetic brown faces the British establishment had so quickly mustered to display on national television, in fact represented no-one — nothing but their own fear.

The truth of September 11th was this: what goes around comes around. At last, someone had turned around and punched the giant bully on the nose and laid him out cold. If there was happiness for those around Tony it was a happiness that Tony did not share or understand. When the innocent die, what is there to celebrate — the victory of hatred over reason, life over death, violence over peace? Tony's two worlds were declaring war on each other. So what would he say when his English friends scorned and slandered the Arabs for what they had done? And what would he say to his Arab friends who wallowed in the foolish glory of victory over the defenceless?

Tony had bitten his tongue too many times when listening to Rashar's attitude. Tony had a golden rule that he rarely broke: Never argue with fools. On this occasion he decided to make an exception.

"You know, you amaze me Rashar," said Tony arguing back. "Here you are in England. You have money, you have wealth, and most importantly, you have the freedom to come and go as you please. And you are in this country because if you had stayed in Iraq, Saddam would have had you put up against a wall and shot. And now that he is in jail, you still don't want to go home. You sit there and slag this country, so if you dislike it so much, why don't you fuck off back to Iraq?" demanded Tony harshly.

"I go when I am ready!" Rashar snapped back.

Tony laughed at him, "But you hate it here?!!"

"So what!!" Rashar answered holding out hands. "This country is good for making money. It is a very rich country."

Tony shook his head and laughed. "But everything you admire in men are all the things that would destroy the Western way of life: Bin Laden, suicide bombing…"

"Bin Laden is fighting for Islam, for freedom of the Arabs," said Rashar proudly. "Bin Laden is a Prophet. He is the only Arab leader that delivers. He did what no other Arab could even dream to do. He struck The Great Satan."

Tony Laughed. "Oh yes, let's not forget the Great Satan America. But what is America to you Rashar?" Tony probed him.

"America is a thief who wants nothing more than to steal our oil and keep our people poor," Rashar answered blandly.

Tony shook his head. The conversation was becoming heavy going. "No Rashar, you must think about the question."

"If you are so clever then you answer it," retorted Rashar.

"America is a nation of immigrants," Tony began to explain. "It is made up from every nation on this planet. Black, white, brown, English, Spanish, Arab, Jew you name it — they are Americans. When you say he is an American, what you are actually saying is a 'native of the world'. And when any nation on earth attacks America, you are, one way or another simply attacking yourself." Tony paused. "Don't you see that Rashar?"

"Your argument is good and clever," conceded Rashar. "Then tell me this? Why do so many people hate them for their history, and their greedy selfish ways?"

"But that's simple," said Tony. "Why does anyone hate someone who is successful and likes to boast about? It's called jealousy. You're a businessman Rashar, how many people hate you because you have nice clothes and money?"

Rashar was now smiling because he had a clever answer waiting for Tony. "What you say is true about jealousy. But Bin Laden is not jealous of America. He gave up the riches of world and could have lived in comfort all his life. Yet he chose to throw it all away and go and live in cave and fight America for what they have done to the Arabs."

Suddenly Tony was silent with no quick answer for Rashar. Rashar knew it and was loving his moment of glory. "So what is your answer Ahmed? You seem to have no words. I have won, yes?" said Rashar with a clever smile.

"You are right Rashar," said Tony quietly. "Bin Laden did not attack America out of jealousy. But Bin Laden is more than a man…"

"— a Prophet!!" interrupted Rashar as if making a holy revelation.

"I suppose some might call him a Prophet," said Tony.

"And what would you call him?" enquired Rashar with emphatic interest.

Tony thought for a while then answered, "I would call Bin Laden *an idea*. I think it was inevitable that one day the Arab political soup would have produced such a man. He is an idealist who believes in his cause and his people. I think the Americans will have a great problem with him whether he is dead or alive. America may be the most powerful nation on earth, but an idea cannot be destroyed with weapons that will only elevate the name of Bin Laden into legend, and further spread the idea."

"Bin Laden will win," Rashar announced with pride. "He is blessed with the wisdom of a holy Prophet."

"Alright then," Tony conceded. "Let's suppose that Bin Laden defeats the West. Everything you ran away from in Iraq will be here in England. You would be the first Bin Laden would kill. To Bin Laden, people like you are the people he hates the most."

Rashar laughed. "No, no, you misunderstand Bin Laden. You read too much of what is in the British papers. If Bin Laden is so bad why do the people of whole Arab world love him? Even in Iran he is a hero to poor people, a fighter for Islam. And they are Shia Moslem."

"I will tell you something about religion, my friend. Religion takes people backward. God provides all the answers for the ignorant. When man cannot answer a question for himself because it confuses him, the answer is God."

"When your own father is a Moslem, in Islam that makes you a Moslem. So you should not say these things Ahmed," said Rashar a little outraged. "Allah will punish you. I should worry about your soul."

Tony laughed. "Let me worry about that. But let me ask you a pretend question and I want you to answer truthfully."

"Then ask it?" said Rashar.

"Right!" said Tony. "You have two choices of were you want to live, England or Iraq? Where do you choose?"

"That is easy," said Rashar. "I choose England."

"But why?"

"Because life here is good and I am free," said Rashar simply.

"Alright, fair enough. Now you have to make another choice," continued Tony, "…two choices again. And you have to answer truthfully." Tony looked at Rashar for a couple of seconds. "You have to choose which one of these two countries to live in: Palestine or Israel? Remember, you just told me why you like England. Which one of these two countries is most like England?"

A smile broke across both faces as they looked at each other.

"That's not a fair question Ahmed," contested Rashar.

"Answer the question Rashar!" Tony insisted.

"You know what I have to choose," said Rashar, a note of defeat in his voice.

"Exactly. If you want to live as you do in England, you have to choose Israel, because if you have lived in the West, who the hell wants to live under Arafat?"

"Your words and tricks are very clever Ahmed, but the Palestinians are your blood as well as mine and you should defend them," said Rashar.

"Look, I feel sorry for the Palestinians," said Tony, "I really do. But if the Arabs had used their brains they could have defeated the Jews without firing one shot and without one Jew or Arab getting killed."

"Then tell me how to work this miracle of yours?" said Rashar scathing. "How can you see so much that others have not?"

"Because I sit on a hillside," said Tony with a teasing smile.

"You speak in riddles," Rashar said irritated. "Just tell me what you mean."

"Isn't it obvious Rashar? From were I stand I can see the battle going on, and see what those in the battle cannot."

"And what is that?" snapped Rashar.

"The games of course," said Tony. "I can see the games being played and the men that stand in the shadows."

"And what can you do that the whole might of the Arab armies could not?" asked Rashar.

"You use your fuckin' brains Rashar," said Tony suddenly straight-faced. "The Jews understand the Arabs. They play them like an orchestra. The Zionists are very clever, but they have one weakness, and they know what this weakness is and they also know that the Arabs are not clever enough to spot this weakness, let alone know how to use it. They know the one thing that threatens the State of Israel is not war, but total and absolute peace. Israel is building a nation on conflict. Nothing binds a nation together more than conflict. Understand the Israelis and you understand their weakness."

"And what is this weakness only you can see?" asked Rashar with a mocking laugh.

"You can take the piss if you want Rashar. But you also know me. People come to me because I understand politics. Amu Sultan comes to me because I find the answers to problems that others cannot solve. Now how would I defeat the Israelis without firing a shot? Easy," said Tony.

"The Jews are greatest entrepreneurs the world has ever seen. They are the honey bees of a modern capitalist economy. In business no one can beat them. If the Arabs were to make total and absolute peace with Israel and open all its borders to free trade, within ten years the population of Israel would dissolve into the surrounding Arab nations to make business. It is in their blood. They would make the Arab nation one of the most powerful in the world. Can you imagine what the Jews would have achieved with all the money from Arab oil? Can you imagine the factories, the banks?"

Tony's voice dropped to a more critical tone. "And what do the Gulf Arabs do with the oil money? They spend it on expensive toys provided by the West whilst the rest of the Arab world starves. Oh yes, the Americans sell the Saudis the best aircraft, but can they fix them? No. The rich Arabs like to drive the sports car, but they do not want to fix it."

Rashar started to laugh. "You know Ahmed you are a very clever politician. You see things totally different to everyone else. And what you say about the Jews is probably right. You should take care that the Israelis don't find out, they will kill you. You should go and talk with Arafat," he said laughing.

"I don't think you understand me Rashar. What I am saying is just an idea. You know me; I like ideas, especially political ones. But don't get me wrong, I do not want to see the destruction of Israel. Israel is as important to me as it is any Jew. Israel is important for every member of an ethnic minority that lives in the west, not just the Jews."

"You are strange Ahmed," said Rashar. "You are half Arab yet Israel is more important to you than Palestine You do not make sense."

"Think about it," said Tony. "Israel was born out of the Holocaust. Six million Jews went to the gas chamber. Israel is a living symbol of what happens to ethnic minorities when political madness breaks out. It is a reminder to all people– especially in the west– of their guilt, of what hatred can do. I live in the west Rashar, so do you. As a half Arab living in a white man's world, the symbol of Israel protects me as much as it protects any Jew. I will tell you this Rashar, if Israel were ever to fall then so would civilisation. Because all evils that lie dormant in the minds of men in this so-called civilised world would suddenly be set free and they would come after us all — black, brown yellow you name it, not just the Jews. I tell you Israel is like a psychological damn in the white man's brain, it holds back all the evils that some men would like to bring down on any man that is different. If Israel ever falls, that dam would brake, and all the evil, jealousy and hatred it holds backs would descend upon all of us."

"You make things sound so complicated Ahmed," said Rashar.

Tony smiled. "Nothing is ever black and white Rashar, only to ordinary men. You more than any should know that Rashar."

A silence followed between the two men. So many of Tony's words had made a strange sense inside Rashar's head. As an

Arab his instinct to challenge what Tony had said and to defend his Arab brothers seemed to drain from his thinking and he was overcome with the realisation that Tony was probably right.

"Your words and thoughts are true I think," said Rashar with a forlorn expression. "But I think for me as an Arab what you say should cause me great insult but it does not, and I am not sure why. Perhaps because you are half Arab and your words do not come from the mouth of an Englishman, I let you say these things. I know you are a secret person and there are many things about you that only you know."

"And what about you Rashar?" said Tony with a wry face. "Is it not the same? You, too, have your secrets. I learned a long time ago that today's friends could be tomorrow's enemies. You keep your secrets to yourself and no one can blackmail or betray you."

Rashar was laughing at the comment he felt was aimed at him. "For someone who is half Arab you don't like Arabs very much. You seem to think better of the Jews, maybe you should become a Jew."

Toni started to laugh. "Once I did."

Rashar laughed and said in Arabic, "You are one crazy Yemeni."

"It was when I was working in the world of the English," Toni started to tell him. "My job meant that I had to go into the factory sometimes and talk with people in there if there was a problem. Ordinary English, they will always try to take the piss out of you. If you are fat, if you are black, even if your wife is ugly, they will take the piss out of anything. That is what it is like working in a factory. Anyway, when someone found out I was half Arab, they used to try and wind me up and take the piss about the Arabs."

"So what did you do?" asked Rashar.

"Simple," said Tony, "I became a Jew."

"But how?"

"A little hint here and there, a rumour spread about by myself," said Toni, "…very subtly of course."

"But why would you do this?" said Rashar, "I don't understand."

"Psychology Rashar," answered Toni. "As soon as the factory workers found out I was Jew, they started to take the piss out of me because I was a Jew."

"But you are not a Jew," said Rashar getting confused.

"Exactly," said Toni simply, "…when they took the piss because they thought I was an Arab, I always tried not to show it, but it made me angry. When they suddenly found out I was a Jew and they took the piss, it didn't make me angry inside, because I'm not a Jew. Simple psychology. I turned their piss taking on them. They went on for months taking the piss because they thought I was a Jew and they could not understand why it didn't wind me up."

Rashar started to shake with laughter. "You are fuckin' crazy Arab, Ahmed. But very clever."

Tony looked down the long motorway in front of him and sighed. "And anyway, it's not the Arab people I don't like," said Tony. It's the Arab leaders, the rich Arabs like the Saudis and the Kuwaitis and the rest of those oil-rich shit houses. They are frightened of their own people so they leave them in poverty and ignorance, because with education comes a free mind and free thought." Tony was on his soap box now and almost making a speech. "With education and freedom people want choice. They want democracy, and that is what all Arab leaders fear the most. Because with education and democracy all those *cuss um muck* 'motherfucker' Arab governments would be out on their fuckin' corrupt arses. Maybe that's the one good that will come out of Bin Laden. He should fuckin' kill all the corrupt Arab leaders for what they have done to the Arab world."

"That has always been the way," Rashar answered. "An Arab leader who has power will not give it up until challenged and defeated."

"But that's what I'm saying," said Tony. "You bang on about Bin Laden, but who would you rather ruled this world? Bin Laden or George Bush? Make your choice Rashar."

Rashar did not answer the question. He shook his head and laughed. "You are too dodgy for me Ahmed."

Tony smiled back cleverly. "That's not answering the question, is it Rashar?"

"Well that's politics and you are politician," Rashar laughed back him. "A good answer, eh?"

"A good answer," conceded Tony smiling. "You are learning."

They were no more than twenty miles out of Hull when they pulled off the motorway and stopped at a Little Chef restaurant. Rashar grabbed a cup of coffee and Tony got one of those breakfast meals that look more plastic than food. The place was full and they took a table near the window. Tony started once again to read the headlines in the local paper. Rashar could see that Tony looked worried. With so many ears nearby they spoke in Arabic.

"You look worried my young friend. Tell me what is in your mind," urged Rashar.

Tony slapped the paper with the back of his hand with frustration. "Things are difficult enough," said Tony. "But the last thing we need is the coppers sniffing around."

"And why should they bother us?"

"Because it starts with coppers, then it's VAT and tax, and you know it was Husseini who sliced Amu's arm," said Tony. "That gives them reason enough to come looking in our direction. He always said he'd get even."

"You think it was Amu Sultan?" said Rashar almost laughing.

"I don't know," said Tony. "But the coppers will still come round asking questions."

"Husseini is camel shit; he always will be," said Rashar harshly.

"Husseini is dangerous in more ways than one," said Tony.

"He is nothing but a thief," Rashar answered him.

Now that was rich coming from Rashar. "And we are not?" Tony laughed aloud to himself. "Sometimes I think we are no better than he is."

"You speak for yourself Ahmed," Rashar snapped back indignantly.

"Then tell me the difference between us," Tony challenged him.

Rashar poked his chest. "I have some honour, that is the difference," said Rashar. "I sometimes do bad things, but I have never lied to an honest man and I have only stolen from thieves."

Tony almost choked with laughter on his tea. "That's very good Rashar. I like that one. Where did you read it?"

Tony was now taking the piss, Rashar knew that much. He flicked his hand at Tony in a dismissive Arabic gesture. "Ahh, you English, always taking the piss. I am being serious now Ahmed. It is bad manners to do these things."

Tony put up hands in an apology. "You're right, I'm sorry Rashar."

"As I was saying," continued Rashar, "…I thought Husseini was my friend when I did business with him. I soon found out the truth."

"What Husseini does is not clever, is it? You say you thought he was your friend. You should know better Rashar, friendship and business is like trying to mix oil and water. That's how he works, he preys on friendship. To Husseini, friendship is not something to be valued, it is no more than a business opportunity. He gets your friendship and confidence and when you don't expect it, he knifes you in the back."

"Yes," Rashar agreed, "…but he makes a lot of money."

"He may make lots of money," retorted Tony, "…but he also makes lots of enemies. It is the easiest thing in the world to steal from a friend or someone who trusts you. What is clever about that? If I invite my friend into my house and while I am taking a bath he steals money from my wallet, that is not clever Rashar. And that is all Husseini does. It's not business and it's not clever. It's also very dangerous. One day you end up stealing from the wrong person and you end up just like Husseini."

"You are right Ahmed," said Rashar, "he has many enemies. He has robbed everybody he did business with. Even you, Ahmed. So you have a motive too. Even I have a motive. He took me for thirty grand." Rashar's voice dipped to a more curious tone as he asked Tony a question. "There are also many, Ahmed, who wondered why you did nothing when he robbed you." Rashar was now smiling at Tony. "You are half Yemeni — vengeance is in your blood."

Tony knew that Rashar was searching for that loose moment when his guard would come down, and in a moment of laxity he might confess to things that his wisdom and experience would advise him to keep secret. He was more than aware that a slip of the tongue in an innocent moment could easily come back to haunt him sometime in the future. In the world Tony was in, everyone had an agenda. You told people only what they needed to know, and what you wanted them to know — never the truth. In business and politics the truth was a phenomenon rarely heard or seen. To do otherwise, would be stupid, dangerous and an open invitation to both your visible and more importantly invisible enemies to use the information against you. "Maybe I was not totally robbed by Husseini," said Tony cryptically.

Rashar was intrigued. "What do you mean?"

"Sometimes things are not always what they seem Rashar," Tony baited him skillfully.

Rashar was suddenly pointing his finger at Tony with a big smile. "Ahhh!! Then you did do something to him. I knew it!!"

"I never said that Rashar," said Tony with a wry smile. "Maybe I got something from Husseini that he never even knew I took. You don't always have to take vengeance, Rashar. Learning from experience is just as important."

"And what did you learn Ahmed?" Rashar asked with a whisper.

"I learned what I paid for," said Tony giving nothing away. "It cost me thirty thousand pounds. Now Rashar, answer me this, why I should give you this expensive lesson for free when it cost me so much. If you want to know what it was then you have to give me thirty thousand pounds." Tony paused and started to laugh. "Then, I will tell you Rashar."

Rashar burst into a fit of laughter. "It is true Ahmed," said Rashar, "you are clever bastard!!"

What of course Tony would not tell Rashar, or anyone else for that matter, was that he had taken his vengeance from Husseini. He had waited with patience until Husseini had robbed someone else, as he eventually knew he would. Then using that as a smoke screen, Husseini had seen his pride and joy in the form of a thirty foot yacht, blown to pieces as it moored quietly in Hull Marina. Then just to rub some salt into the wounds, the insurance claim which followed was declared void by the underwriters, after an anonymous caller had pointed out to the loss adjusters, that for business protection reasons, the boat was registered in a name other than that of Husseini's. Unfortunately for Husseini, the insurance policy was in his name and therefore technically the boat was not covered.

Whilst some might have been tempted to brag about taking their vengeance, not Tony. In fact, Tony never viewed it as vengeance — it was simple justice. Tony wanted justice for being robbed by someone he had trusted, and the type of justice he wanted would not have been found in the courts. This way he was satisfied and no one was the wiser. And to let Husseini know what he had done just for the hell of it would have been the work of a fool, because it would have only have provoked him to seek more vengeance and Tony had neither the time nor the inclination to get involved in a vendetta.

The list of Husseini's victims was endless and now he was at least aware that one of them was dangerous. The fact that he did not know which one would be enough to make anyone quite nervous, and Tony liked the thought of that.

"I have often wondered how he gets away with it," said Tony curiously. "I thought by now the police would have done something about him."

"Who knows and who cares," said Rashar indifferently.

Tony shook his head with a deep curious thought. In the back of his mind something had always bothered him about Husseini. It was something that he could not put his finger on, but it had always been there nagging away at him whenever the name had been mention. It was like trying to remember an important name, or face that no matter how hard you tried, you just could not recall. Things happened like that with Tony. Little things that others might not notice would subliminally go into Tony's head and into a mental filing cabinet. If his instincts were right, then usually one by one the little things would start to add up, until eventually the lights would come on and like a sudden revelation, he would know what was going on. "There is just something about Hussein that bugs me," said Tony, "…something not right. I don't know what it is but there's something there."

"Forget Husseini," said Rashar. "Bastard has got what he deserves. He played with the most dangerous material in the world. He played with human emotions. *Wallah*- I swear by God, it was only a matter of time. Husseini and his own greed brought on this. There are many, many with motives for this. But you and I both know each other and if I wanted this, I do the whole job and just put ten thousand pounds into Iran, make a telephone call, and when he visits…" Rashar put an imaginary gun to his head and pulled the trigger. "Life comes cheap in Iran."

Tony laughed. "You can't tell that to the police, Rashar."

"Who cares about the police. I'm just saying. I know it wasn't me, and I know you don't work like that."

"And what if it was Amu Sultan?" said Tony.

"That is his business, and in business you have to do these things. What does it matter anyway, what is done is done," answered Rashar philosophically. "Somebody has wiped this piece of slimy green dog shit off our shoes for us and taught him a lesson he needed."

Rashar's metaphor was doing little to help Tony eat his already unappetising breakfast. Tony also got the impression that for some reason, Rashar was going over the top in his condemnations of Husseini and that made him curious. If Rashar had some hidden motive, Tony had no inclination to ask him; it would give away his suspicions and he didn't want to get Rashar's guard up. Also, but less importantly, if Tony's suspicions were wrong and he was going to be stuck with Rashar for the next five days, it would make their already difficult relationship, impossible.

"Do I care who? No!! They save me a fuckin' job Ahmed. He got what he deserved. You think sometimes, Ahmed, I am bad person, but after doing business with Husseini I feel I have been down a sewer with the shit piss and vomit."

Tony threw down his knife and folk and stood up. "*Yellah* – let's go, we have long days."

Rashar swilled down his coffee. "What's wrong? Not hungry?!!" He shrugged his shoulders, picked a sausage off Tony's plate and followed him out.

THREE

In the dim light from a single bulb, it was near enough impossible to recognise the features of the human being behind the mask of blood and bruises that covered the young man's face. The cellar was almost quiet now except for the miserable whimpers of the figure slumped in the chair and the occasional flutter of wings that came from the chickens imprisoned in the nearby cages. The old Yemeni Sheik, with his long grey Islamic beard, dressed in traditional robes, showed absolutely no emotion as he sat opposite this broken figure dipping bread crust into a bowl of lamb soup and rice. As his black and decaying teeth crunched into the hard bread, what might have been a smile crossed his weathered brown face and he stared at the broken figure across the table and shouted at him in Arabic.

"You are *cuss um muck* – a motherfucker. Allah has said I may take your hands off. This is the law and the judgement of God for a thief!"

The young face across the table tried to plead, but the Sheik's answer came with a swift nod of the head. Suddenly, the men who stood in the shadows of the cellar were again upon the seated figure and raining blows on him. The screams reached no further than the cellar door and were all but absorbed in the urgent flapping of the nearby chickens. A few moments passed, and again it was silent.

§§§

Pizza Wars

Burngreave, in Sheffield, is known locally as little Arabia. The area is old and decaying with long streets of grey terraced houses that go back to before the Second World War. It is hard to spot a white face. Most of the inhabitants are native Yemenis or their descendants, some are half castes— the result of many a marriage between a Yemeni and a local lass. In the Yemeni community there is no distinction made between the two. Such judgements are left to the local whites to make; they tolerate the community but do not like them.

The whole area is a strange, almost bizarre sort of subculture, as if a small part of Yemen had been grafted onto a Yorkshire town. These days there is little to do. With the loss of the steel making mills in which many of the Yemenis worked as labourers, few had found other work. They had few talents and resigned themselves to the monotony of life on benefit and watching Arabic satellite television in the many coffee-houses which only they frequented.

Tony's car pulled up outside Sheik Ishmael Yunis's coffee-house that lay on the fringe of Burngreave. In the streets outside, the kids played football like in any other British street except the language they shouted in was not English, but an odd combination of English and Arabic with a Sheffield accent.

Tony always had a foreboding sense of deja-vu when visiting this part of Sheffield. It was almost as if he was haunted by memories from his past. In his infant days he had visited many times with his father, and then, as now, he had always felt a strange confusion for this half-way house of a world. Tony also felt guilty that he should have so much and they should have so little. He wondered why time seemed to have stood still for them whilst he had moved and struggled on to a better life.

The kids playing football immediately stopped their game as Tony's BMW pulled in to park at the side of the road. As he climbed out of the car, one of them picked up the ball and stared at Tony without a smile. The children were looking at him as though he were an apparition. They were even more shocked when he spoke to them in Arabic.

"What are you staring at?" he asked the children.

Across the other side of the car, Rashar answered for them. "Have you ever seen a blonde Arab? They are curious!"

Tony smiled to himself and took a bundle of notes out of his pocket and offered it to the small gang of brown children that stood transfixed, staring at him. It was traditional to offer children money in Yemeni culture. Anthony remembered this from his own childhood days when many Yemeni friends of his father had given him money. It was gesture of magnanimity, of friendship. After a moment of hesitation, the children all smiled at each other, snatched the money and ran off towards the local sweet shop.

Rashar was not impressed. He shook his head with a sneer. "You know your problem Ahmed? You are soft. You think you know the Arab. You don't. You give them too much. They will only think you are weak when you do such things."

"Mind your own fuckin' business Rashar!"

Rashar laughed. "One day you will learn."

They walked the few yards up the road towards Sheik Yunis's Pizzeria which also seconded as a local coffee house. Rashar suddenly stopped walking and stared angrily at a fish and chip shop across the road.

"What's wrong with you?" said Tony.

Rashar gestured towards the chip shop. "That wasn't there last time."

"So what?"

Rashar shook his head and cursed under his breath. "I warned the Pakki bastard last time! They think they can do what they want in this country." Rashar started off across the road.

"Where are you going Rashar?"

"I am going to talk with him."

Tony threw up his hands. "Just leave it Rashar!!"

"I'll be one minute," he shouted back.

Tony shook his head and carried on towards the coffee-house.

Inside the fish and chip shop a small queue was waiting to get served. The Bengali owner was busy frying fish whilst his wife served across the counter. Suddenly she looked up and saw Rashar staring across at her.

"Look!!" she said suddenly in a broken English accent, "—we don't want any trouble."

Rashar turned and looked at the waiting customers. He did not need to say a word. One by one, they quickly left the premises.

"If you don't leave I will call the police!!" her husband shouted at him nervously.

Rashar started to inspect the shop. "This is very nice. The menu looks very expensive." Without warning, Rashar suddenly tore down the box menu over the counter. The women suddenly let out a scream.

Outside in the street a small crowd had gathered. A few seconds later and a loud crash of breaking glass echoed. Tony turned round to see that the Pakistani chip shop owner had just been thrown through the front window of his shop.

"Oh shit!!" he cursed aloud and ran towards the fish shop.

The street outside was covered in blood and glass. The proprietor's wife in white bloodstained catering overalls came rushing out of the shop screaming for help in Bengali. What crowds gathered around did nothing and came only to look. Soon another crash resounded, this time the cash register came crashing through the chip shop door window, its contents of money spilling onto the road in front of the shop.

The watching children scrambled to gather up the coins and notes, then ran off as they grabbed a handful each. By now they were all out of the coffee-houses and staring at the commotion across the road. Still, not one of those watching moved to help. Rashar came out of the broken chip shop door carrying a chair which he smashed into what little glass remained in the door and then threw it at the Pakistani on the ground. He started to lay into the man on ground with his feet.

Tony was suddenly on Rashar, and pulling him back. "For fuck sake Rashar!!" he shouted at him. "That's enough!!"

Rashar casually shrugged off Tony's grip and walked across the road. Tony stood staring down at the hysterical Asian woman cradling the bloody head of her unconscious husband. He turned round to see Rashar waiting for him across the road. "Well, are you coming or what?!" Rashar shouted at him.

Tony shook his head with anger. "You are a fuckin' psychopath Rashar, ya know that!!" he snapped at him.

Rashar laughed. "You think now he will come back tomorrow or the next day? I know these people Ahmed. They understand my language. That bastard is trying to take bread from my table. I treat him well. If he did this back in his own country they would put a bullet in his head."

"And you people wonder why your countries are nothing but fuckin' corrupt dustbins."

"One day Ahmed, you will push me too far. I don't have time for this. You must learn Ahmed," Rashar said to him. "It is business and in business, you have to do these things." Without further discussion, Rashar walked away.

Tony was suddenly aware of the silent eyes on him. He looked down almost in shame and followed Rashar into the coffee-house.

Down the road, in the silver Golf GTI, Angela and Bradley had watched the events with some concern.

"Bloody 'ell that big bloke's a bloody animal," said Angela aloud. "Shall I call the police or what?"

"No, it's none of our business; leave them to it. It's just Pakkis falling out over some shite," said Bradley without emotion. "I don't want to be stuck in the bloody cop shop all afternoon or we'll lose them."

§§§

The Old Sheik greeted Rashar with an enthusiastic hug in the traditional way.

"*Salem alicome achee*- peace be with you my brother. I see you have spoken with our Bengali brother. I did warn him. But what can I do? This country has no respect for the wisdom of the old."

Rashar kissed the Old Sheik's hand and then put it to his cheek. It was not a Godfather thing, but and an Arabic mark of respect for the age and wisdom of the Old Sheik. "How are you Sheik? Is your family well?"

"God is good to me, I have no complaints, and *Inshallah* He will continue to smile upon my house."

The Old Sheik turned to the face he had not seen for a long time. "Ahhh and look Allah smiles upon us more and sends us Ahmed." He held out his arms to Tony and they embraced as long lost friends. Tony, too, then kissed the Sheik's hand in the same way.

"How are you my old and good friend?" asked Tony.

"I am getting old Ahmed, and life gets no easier. These are troubled days for all of us. You must both come through and take food with me before we speak of business."

The Sheik snapped his fingers at others that worked in the coffee-house.

"Bring food for our guests." He led Rashar and Tony into to a sitting room at the back of the coffee-house. It was decorated in traditional Yemeni style and a great portrait of Saddam Hussein in battle fatigues took pride of place over an old fireplace. They took off their shoes and sat on a lush Persian carpet around a low coffee table. A great communal plate of rice and chicken was brought in and laid before them in the centre of the table. The Sheik bade them to eat and poured cold tea into small glasses. Tony and Rashar washed their hands on a table bowl nearby and began to eat.

"Everything is ready as always. The till rolls were finished this morning," said the Sheik.

Rashar smiled and took out a large envelope from inside his jacket and gave it to the Sheik. As Rashar and Tony tucked into the food with their fingers, the Sheik proceeded to count the notes inside the envelope with all the skill and speed of a Las Vegas card-shark. In seconds, he was finished. He smiled with satisfaction and suddenly looked curiously at Tony. "Do you have a wife Ahmed?" the Old Sheik enquired.

Tony laughed and shook his head. "No, women are expensive."

"I must speak with Rashar for a few moments alone. I hope you will not think badly of an old man." Suddenly the Sheik was on his feet and excited. "You should meet my daughter. She cooks, cleans, is very beautiful and does not answer back."

Sheik bade Rashar to follow him, and Tony was left alone in the room. He was curious about what they would speak of, but knew it could be nothing to do with the business at hand, since that was all open between them. It was Sheik Yunis's job to prepare a month's supply of phoney till for all thirty shops they were to visit, and each one would be given a date and time stamped till roll for every night of the previous month. They would be prepared in such away that the turnover figures would be as plausibly low as possible. It was a long job, and a job that could only be given to someone whom they could trust — Sheik

Yunis was such a man.

There were a lot of years in prison at stake if they got caught. In takeaway, life is a constant battle with the VAT office. What you paid them was always a matter of give and take, and in their own way they accepted you were usually fiddling them. But as long as the amount they were paid every three months was reasonable, they tended to leave you alone. Blatant fraud they came down on hard though, and if caught it was always a massive fine and a long prison sentence.

The Sheik led Rashar down to the cellar. The Sheik shook his head as if with a weight of troubles. "I must ask you a favour, my brother, and this thing I ask is most serious." The Old Sheik stared at Rashar in the damp semi-darkness.

"Ask my brother, and if it is within my power I shall do it for you," Rashar answered.

The Sheik smiled and nodded. "You are a good man. This thing I ask you understand, is a mark of my trust for you."

Rashar smiled. "Your trust is an honour to be bestowed."

"I need something to be removed. Of course," The Sheik went on, "...I will pay you well for this service."

§§§

Upstairs, Tony was suddenly joined in the room by a young Yemeni girl dressed in traditional clothing, and carrying a tray filled with more food. Her face was veiled but her large, black eyes were locked onto his face, her stare never moving from his. She almost glided around the table as if walking on air, and as she put down the food, neither had looked away. Suddenly, she sat down on the carpet across the table staring in silence. Tony smiled and the shine of a smile behind the silk veil brightened her eyes. She let down the veil from her face. Her beauty was stunning and the full glare of her white smile looked at him.

"*Salem*. I am Samina," she told him is crisp perfect English.

Tony smiled. "*Salem*. I am…"

"–Ahmed!" Samina interrupted. "Or perhaps you like Anthony better?" She laughed. "But I suppose that depends on which world you are in? Are you British or Arab today?"

"Is that important?" said Tony.

"Maybe," She answered with a mischievous little laugh.

"And perhaps I can ask the same question of you." He asked her the question in Arabic, "Are you British or Arabic?"

Samina suddenly giggled at him. "At school, I am British. My English friends call me Sam. At home I am Yemeni and I obey my father," adding suggestively, "…but only when my father is looking."

"So you are still at school. How old are you?"

Samina laughed. "You are not Arab. They do not ask such things. Age between a man and woman is only important to the British."

"You haven't answered my question?" said Tony.

"Is eighteen old enough for you Mr English?" she said mockingly. "Or perhaps you have an English wife?"

Tony smiled without answering.

She probed further. "Perhaps a girlfriend then?"

"Perhaps," Tony teased her.

"Then I would think she would be very beautiful perhaps?"

"Perhaps."

"You are not going to tell me anything are you?" she said giggling.

"And why would you want to know?"

"Maybe I am interested? Are you staying in Sheffield tonight? Maybe I could see you later on?"

"I don't think your father would be very pleased about that."

"Well, if you promise not to tell him, I promise I won't," she answered with a smile and began to slowly lean across the table towards him. "And besides what he cannot see won't hurt him, will it? I'll make you a proposition."

"And what's that?"

"No commitments or anything like that. Just a plain old English shag."

§§§

In the cellar, Rashar looked down at the blood-stained and battered body of the young man. "Is he dead?" he asked without emotion.

The Old Sheik spit on the body. "He was a thief and a liar, he stole many thousands from the people at my boarding house."

"Will he be missed?"

"He was illegal here— no papers, no family, no friends. Just chicken shit. He is of no consequence to anyone."

"You spoke of payment?"

The Old Sheik stroked his chin thoughtfully. "I thought perhaps five thousand."

"My brother, this thing you ask is not easy and not without risk," said Rashar. "I cannot keep this thing from Ahmed upstairs and he alone will want at least seven thousand."

"Forgive me. I think sometimes I am still in Yemen. Let us say twelve thousand and be agreed, but no more."

The two Arabs looked at each other and both knew the price was set in stone. Rashar smiled and they shook hands. "Now I have something else to show you," said the Old Sheik enthusiastically. He took Rashar over to a large chest in the corner of the cellar and opened it. Rashar's eyes opened wide with a sparkle. The chest was full of an assortment of shiny new hand-guns, several automatic rifles and some glistening Yemeni tribal knives. Sheik Yunis was not a terrorist or anything like that. Guns were just part of his Yemeni culture, a sign of power and standing. In parts of Yemen, to around without an AK47 hanging around your shoulder was almost to be considered partly dressed. Their possession, even in England, gave the Old Sheik a feeling of security.

Rashar reached into the chest and took out a folding stock AK47; it was an old friend he had not seen for many years. Where he came from in Iraq, like Yemen, is a gun culture. The carrying of an AK47 was merely part of your everyday clothing, a sign of power and status. He gently stroked the barrel as one might a favourite pet. He then snapped back the bolt and fired the trigger with a harsh metallic click. The sound brought a smile to his face.

"Beautiful, yes?" The Sheik laughed childishly. "I see you are man after my own heart," said the Sheik. "It is yours. A gift of my gratitude." The Old Sheik's voice then seemed to take on a note of warning. "Forgive me, my brother, if I am wrong. But I must ask this because it concerns me also."

Rashar was suddenly attentive. "Then ask and let us speak as trusted friends."

"I say this because you are like a son to me and it should not go further and so cause us both problems if I have not heard the truth. So I must have your word."

"*Wallah*, you have my word," said Rashar now intrigued.

"Are there problems in the company?" asked the Sheik.

Rashar shook his head. "No, not that I am aware of. Why do you ask such a thing?"

"Remember this. Amu Sultan is Iranian and Shia," said the Sheik with careful consideration. "In his blood and heart he owes neither you nor Ahmed loyalty."

Rashar grinned. "You tell me what I know already."

"And Ahmed?" asked the Sheik.

"Ahmed is English. He does not understand these things. If I spoke against Amu Sultan he would not trust my reasons and might betray me to Amu Sultan."

"Then Ahmed trusts Amu Sultan?" enquired the Sheik.

The question brought a half smile to Rashar's face in shadows of the cellar. "Ahmed trusts no one but himself. He is very clever in the ways of the English and the politics. He sees things others cannot."

"I have heard this about him," said the Sheik slowly. "Perhaps he could be useful?"

"Or dangerous," said Rashar.

"Perhaps this might be so," the Sheik said, "and you are no better judge because it is you who knows his mind and the intentions in his heart. Let us be wise men then and not fools and be cautious of Ahmed for the moment."

Rashar knew the Old Sheik was leading to some important point he was not quite sure how to put to Rashar. "What do you wish to speak of my old friend that causes you to go around in circles as if testing me?"

"Please forgive me, but age has given me the gift of caution, but I will speak plainly now and what I am going to say you should keep to yourself and if it be the truth, let Ahmed find it for himself. He will learn that way and turn to trust you."

"And what secret do you have to tell me my brother?" asked Rashar carefully.

"Just a rumour, no more. The future will declare it the truth or a lie. But you may make of it what you will and take some precaution for yourself just in case. If I am wrong there is no harm done."

"Then speak," said Rashar.

"I have a friend in Hull who has been approached to enquire his interest in the purchase of fifteen pizza shops. My friend asked if I might be interested to buy with him." The Sheik carefully paused.

"So what has this to do with me and Ahmed?" asked Rashar

"I made some enquiries through my solicitor who talked with my friend's solicitor and it would seem there are in all, thirty such shops for sale." The Sheik was looking at Rashar now. "My solicitor told me that all the shops being sold are in the name of Mohamed Farida."

Rashar suddenly smiled to himself as if in revelation. "That's why he sent Ahmed with me," he whispered aloud with an odd laugh. "He wanted us both out of the way." Something else that Amu Sultan had done was suddenly making sense. He had asked Rashar to lend him forty-five thousand pounds and had sworn him to secrecy. That would be nearly half of the amount that they would be collecting. If Rashar had worked this out right, then Amu Sultan would have borrowed the other half off Tony and sworn him to secrecy. It also meant that whatever Amu Sultan was planning would be over by the time that he and Tony got back to Hull. By then, surely Amu Sultan would be gone.

Rashar slowly nodded his head at the Sheik. "Thank you my brother," he said quietly.

"Do what you have to do," whispered the Sheik, "but be careful."

A curious grin spread across Rashar's face. "Perhaps for yourself Sheik, there is nothing more to do than buy."

The Old Sheik detected something more than just words in what Rashar said, a hint of advice perhaps? "Do we understand each other my son and perhaps we both have the same friend in Hull?" whispered the Sheik with a knowing smile. "Or is it my old foolishness that deceives my mind and tells me that a good friend stands in the shadows of this business."

Rashar answered him cryptically without a clear admission of anything. "I think I should speak no more than to say you are not deceiving yourself and it would be wise for the moment not speak the name the friend in Hull. Just to say that he has taken good advice to approach you."

The Sheik began to chuckle aloud. "It is a good move. You are more clever than I gave you credit for Rashar and I think we will do good business in the future."

"Then you will be keeping in contact with your friend?" asked Rashar.

"But of course," the Sheik answered quickly. "Do not worry. Your interests and mine are one. Just make sure the price is not a great one."

"Don't worry," said Rashar confidently. "The fish is already on the hook and cannot get off. By the time I have finished with this fish he will be glad just to be cut free."

§§§

Samina's lips were pressed hot and hard against Anthony's as they both rolled around on the carpet. By now she had wrestled her way on top of him and sat astride pressing her groin fiercely on his. If the Old Sheik came back and found them like this there would be hell to pay.

"So what do you say English?" she panted at Tony.

"You are crazy," Tony answered her. "If your father comes back now…"

She laughed, "—you would have to marry me, or he would kill you."

As the sound of footsteps and voices approached, Anthony quickly pushed Samina off him and tried to compose himself back at the table. Samina, too, was suddenly on her feet as footsteps came closer. Quickly and deftly she re-attached her veil to once again hide her face.

"Ahh, so I see my daughter has kept you company Ahmed. I hope you have not been too bored."

Samina was suddenly in the guise of a dutiful daughter again and started to leave the room. Smoothly gliding past Tony, she stopped to pick up an empty plate next to him. With a quick glance she looked at him and whispered through her veil, "Maybe see you later."

Pizza Wars

Tony felt her hand slide smoothly under the table. Gently, she squeezed him between the legs. A second later, she was gone.

"She is very beautiful Ahmed, is she not?" said the Old Sheik.

"Yes, she is." Anthony swallowed hard.

"She will make someone a good wife. She is a very good girl."

§§§

With an expression of indifference, solicitor Solomon Cohen looked over the silver-rimmed, half-moon spectacles that tipped the bridge of his nose. His client Amu Sultan sat opposite his spacious oak desk. A large pile of legal files surrounded Mr Cohen like a wall.

Solomon Cohen had been Amu Sultan's solicitor for over twenty years. Of course Farida knew he was Jewish and there where plenty of Asian and some Arab and Iranian lawyers around he could have used. Amu Sultan knew his own people well though, and trust them, he did not. It is a common misconception amongst many that Moslems hate Jews. In fact nothing could be more further from the truth in matters of business, where their discretion was guaranteed, their trust always unquestionable, their advice sound and impartial. And to Amu Sultan that was all that mattered.

"Well Mr Farida," Solomon started slowly, "of the forty-five properties you intend sell, twenty are leased and the others are freehold." He looked down at the documents and studied further. "Mmmm, I see the names on the leases and the freeholds is a one Mr Mohamed Farida?"

Amu Sultan gently smiled. "My brother, you understand. I merely run things for him in this country."

Solomon of course knew the real owner was Amu Sultan himself and his brother held the title deeds merely to protect assets from seizure in the event of financial troubles. Solomon had no problem with that since it was standard practice and totally legal.

"Now you have two partners within the company itself. A Mr Rashar Nuraman and a Mr Anthony Ahmed Debani?"

"Yes," Amu Sultan answered quickly, "but the company has no title over any of the leases or freeholds. Also, they are directors appointed by me under agreement, with no shares. This is not a limited company."

"Yes, I understand that Mr Farida. If you recall I drew up the partnership agreement between the three of you myself. And because it is not a limited company you are all proportionately personally responsible for the financial liabilities. Which from the figures in front of me are substantial, especially to the VAT office who are making a back claim against you all for three-and-a-half million pounds. Now, if you cannot find that sum they will simply bankrupt you all." Solomon looked long and hard at Amu Sultan. "I take it your partners are aware of that?"

Sometimes dodgy clients may know more about contract law than they would let on. In Amu Sultan's contract with Rashar and Tony, they were all simply directors and what Rashar and Tony did not know was that they were equally responsible for company debts including VAT and tax. There seemed to be an awkward pause before Amu Sultan eventually answered, with a subtle note of remonstration. "Mr Cohen, perhaps I have not made myself clear. I am here this morning only because my brother in Iran wishes to sell all his assets in the UK. My own personnel business problems or those of my partners are not of concern here. I hope we understand each other?"

The penny suddenly dropped with Solomon. Amu Sultan was bailing out and bailing out fast although as Solomon had pointed out, all three of them were held responsibility for the company's liabilities. Amu Sultan had no intention of hanging around long enough for the VAT office to come calling with their writs. The VAT office had already called him to be interviewed. At that time it had been made crystal clear to him that they knew everything, and had made it equally clear that they would get their pound of flesh one way or another.

Amu Sultan felt sure that somewhere along the line someone had been talking to the VAT office. They had just too much information on his secret empire for it to be merely a coincidental. They had names, dates, places, supplier's invoices, you name it. He also knew who had been doing the talking. His old enemy Husseini had been trying to move in on his takeaway turf for years. Well Amu Sultan had settled that account in way that Husseini would understand, and he would not be talking to anyone for a very long time, or doing much else for that matter. Something else had been nagging at the back of his mind though. Whilst Husseini might have been the one doing the talking to the VAT office, who had given him such a comprehensive knowledge of the workings of the company, and the documents that had been given to the Customs and Excise office?

Only two other people had access to such information. Whilst Amu Sultan did not trust Rashar, he knew he had little of the brains needed to put together such a plan. That left only one other person that could have betrayed him and could have put together such a subtle plan to get him out of the way—Ahmed.

He had misjudged Ahmed. Amu Farida knew the game. He was being squeezed out. Ahmed's plan, he felt sure, was to conquer him, take over his business and then use his silver tongue to negotiate with the VAT. It was clever and only Ahmed had such talents and confidence. But Amu Farida's ace card was that he had foiled Ahmed's plan and had a surprise up his sleeve. He would simply sell up and bolt for Iran. Proportionate liability would mean nothing to the VAT office; they would come after whoever they could get their hands on for the full amount owed and that would be Ahmed and Rashar.

Ahmed was a disappointment to him. Although he was of Arab blood, Farida thought he might have been different because he was English. It had been a bad error of judgement and one he was about to rectify. He would call on all the cunning and stealth he could muster to pay his betrayer back with interest. Whichever one of them it was did not matter now because Amu Sultan had put his plan of vengeance into play and it would deal with both Tony and Rashar. So they wanted to play games, well Amu Sultan would teach them a lesson they would not forget. Let them take the company, or what would be left of it. After Amu Sultan had finished there would be nothing to own but the debt.

The VAT office cared little who took the can for tax owed, just so long as someone did, and after them, others with less civilised manners would come calling. With no Amu Sultan around, that would leave Rashar and Anthony holding the baby and the three-and-a-half million pound VAT liability which Solomon was sure Farida had told them nothing about. Like any good solicitor, his client's ethics or morality was none of his legal concern. His first job, experience had taught him, was when dealing with men like Amu Sultan, make sure above all else that you got paid first. His second job was to take instructions from his client and carry them out.

Solomon once again inspected the papers in front of him.

"Well, there are a lot of assets to dispose of. There are two ways I can do it. I can try and sell them individually or as a complete lot. Individually would take a great deal of time and effort. It would be much quicker as a complete lot since there is already some interest." Solomon looked over to Amu Sultan for a decision.

"Then do whatever is quickest," Amu Sultan instructed him.

"I will get on to it straightaway," said Solomon smoothly. "I'll have some initial valuations done by this afternoon and let you have the figures."

§§§

Anthony was a bit curious as to why Rashar had asked him to take the car 'round the back. With the boot up he could see nothing of what was going on around the back of the car. Anthony felt a heavy thump and then heard the boot slammed shut. Rashar climbed into the passenger seat without much to say.

"What was that?" asked Anthony

"What?" answered Rashar innocently.

"What you just put in the boot?"

"Oh, just some meat the Sheik asked us to deliver."

"Meat!! He's not killing goat and passing it off as lamb again!" Anthony shouted at him. "What do you think this is, a fuckin' butcher's van? It'll stink the car out."

"Then you had better get a move on then," Rashar argued back.

"Where to?"

"Madjid's," said Rashar.

"That's in fuckin' Newcastle. We're going South?"

For an answer, Rashar threw him three neat bundles of twenty pound notes. "Here, this is for you. So, we just have to start in Newcastle. What's the big deal?"

"What's this?"

"Three grand," answered Rashar.

"I didn't ask how much. I meant what for?"

"Call it a present from the Sheik," answered Rashar.

"For what?" asked Anthony with rising curiosity.

"For doing this little job for the Sheik, that's your share."

Anthony's expression was suddenly suspicious. "Three grand for delivering some meat?" said Anthony incredulously. He gave a little laugh. "It's not a body is it?" he said joking.

Rashar's face was expressionless and he was not laughing. "Just drive Tony and we will get there quicker."

Shock registered on Anthony's face. "It's a body?!" It was not a question. "Are you serious about Madjid's?"

Rashar casually shook his head at such a fuss and started to rant at him in Arabic. "Sometimes you English are like women. How did you people ever conquer half the world?"

It was almost twilight as Tony's car pulled cautiously out of the alley-way from Sheik Yunis's shop. Inside the car across the street, the rolling snap of Bradley's camera as he rattled off more pictures.

"Mmmm, I wonder what's gone on there?" asked Angela curiously.

Tony had only travelled a few hundred yards. "Is that petrol in the can in the boot?" asked Rashar.

"Yeah, just for emergencies. Ya never know, do ya?"

"Just stop here a minute," Rashar told him.

Tony pulled up. "Now what?" he grumbled aloud.

Without answering, Rashar climbed out the car and went to the boot. From his mirror Tony watched Rashar take out the petrol can and start to walk back down the road towards the Pakistani chip shop. Suddenly Tony knew what Rashar was up to. He closed his eyes and cursed. "Oh fuck!!"

Bradley and Angela had also come to a halt down the road. They watched from their car, dumbstruck, as Rashar screwed off the top of the petrol can and threw it into the chip shop through the broken window. A second later flames and black smoke began to billow from inside the building. The few people that stood watching turned away as Rashar stared at them. There would be

51

no witnesses here.

"Did ya see that?!" said Angela in shock. "He's just set alight to the building!" She went for her mobile phone.

"What are you doing?" said Bradley quickly.

"What do you think? I'm calling the police."

Bradley snatched the phone from her hand.

"Ya just can't let him get away with it," she started to protest.

"Look love," Bradley expression was straight, "...there's something you need to understand. That's the way they do business. We're VAT, not the fuckin' police. They expect us to come after them for VAT money. It's all part of the game they play with us. When we pull 'em after squeezing them a bit they'll pay, because they know how the game works and they know the rules. If we get involved in their business disputes, they start to take things personally. And that's dangerous. Then they come looking for us. These are Arabs love, it's an eye for eye with them and I don't want my house sprayed with bullets or a petrol bomb through the window." Bradley gave her back the phone.

"So that's it?" said Angela incredulously. "We do nothing?"

For an answer Bradley nodded in the direction of the car up the road. "Just keep ya eye on them." It was not a request.

Rashar walked back to the car and climbed in. "You feel better now Rashar?" Tony asked sarcastically. Rashar did not even look at Tony. He put on his sunglasses and reclined his seat. "*Yellah*-Let's go."

Tony sighed and shook his head. "I need to get out of this fuckin' business," he said aloud.

Rashar's eyes were now closed. "And do what Ahmed? Work in some office nine-to-five for two hundred pound a week after tax." He gave a little laugh. "I don't think so."

"I was thinking maybe of going to University. I've got some money put aside."

Rashar suddenly opened his eyes. "University, mmm," he said thoughtfully, "...maybe I come with you?"

Tony rolled his eyes, almost smiling with amusement and drove down the road.

FOUR

It took almost the best part of three hours to get to Newcastle. It was eleven-thirty at night and dark as they approached the gates of a small factory on an industrial estate just outside of the city. Tony's car came to a halt on the road outside. The name on the gate illuminated in the car headlights: MADJID'S MINCE AND DONNER KEBAB MAKERS OF NEWCASTLE-UPON-TYNE. It also illuminated a large rowdy crowd of what looked liked protesters that blocked the main entrance to the factory. Tony and Rashar knew that all of Madjid's workers in the kebab factory were either asylum seekers - some without work permits - or simply just illegal immigrants. Like at most employers in industries associated with ethnic catering, they were used as cheap labour, very cheap labour. In some cases they were paid as little as ten pounds for a twelve-hour shift.

The pickets were huddled around an old oil drum that had been turned into a brazier to help keep them warm. Some of them were holding placards with logos like "Fair pay for a fair days work," and "Down with exploitation." On one placard was written the ultimate insult for a Moslem employer: MADJID IS HARAM. Haram means in English, "something unclean." They appeared to be led by what looked like an Englishman. He came straight over to Tony's car along with a group of fellow strikers and banged on the car door. Anthony slid down his window.

"Picket line here mate," he said to them in a Geordie accent. "What's your business?"

Before Tony could answer, Rashar replied, "Our business is

none of yours. And if you bang on the car like that again, I'll take your fuckin' head off!! Now get out of the way."

"And what's your fuckin' problem mate!!" the striker shouted back at Rashar.

Rashar's expression was suddenly set with rising anger. "At the moment you are my fuckin' problem and if you don't get out of the way…" Rashar went to reach for something in his bag. Tony knew enough about Rashar to know what was likely to come out. Anthony grabbed the bag in Rashar's hands and whispered in a low voice, "Just cool it Rashar. We don't want any trouble that will bring the coppers here," he reminded him flicking his eyes toward the boot of the car.

"Let me deal with this," Tony said quietly. Rashar's hands relaxed on the bag and Tony turned back to the English picket.

"Is the owner inside?" he asked him.

"Madjid ya mean man? Ay, the bastards inside all right."

"Well we have some business with him," said Tony.

"Well that's not my problem man. Nobody's getting through these gates while we're here. We're on strike mate and that's a picket line if ya didn't know it."

Tony noticed some other men next to the Englishman; they were speaking Arabic. Tony called them over in Arabic. "You two!! Come here!!" The two men looked surprised to hear their language.

"Never mind all that foreign babbling shit man. I'm in charge here!!" the English picket shouted at Tony.

Ignoring the Englishman, Tony called the two men again. Slowly, they came towards the car and looked into the window at Tony. "My friend here is getting angry. We have business inside and if you do not let us through I think he is going to spill some blood. Do you understand me?" stated Tony.

The two Arabs looked at Rashar sat next to Tony. A look of fear in their eyes was proof enough they recognised him. Many of the people who worked for Madjid would have at one time or another worked in a takeaway. One of the two men said something in Arabic to the others on the picket line and they began to back away from the car.

"What the fuck's wrong with you lot?" the English picket shouted at them. The two Arabs pulled the Englishman away from the car. "Let them pass," one of the Arabs said to him. "The man in the passenger seat is a very bad person. Someone will get hurt."

Tony's car passed through the gates without further hindrance.

The Englishman turned his anger on the others in the picket line."Why ya not fuckin' men!! Ya a bunch of pansies!! Do ya think ya win industrial disputes by shitting ya self man? Fuck you lot, ya not worth it!!" He pushed several of his fellow pickets aside and stormed off. "You fuckin' wogs have got no bottle!!

"Where are you going?" one of them shouted after him.

"Home man!! You lot are a fuckin' waste of time man!!"

Even though it was late into the evening, the lights in the factory office were on. The factory owner, Madjid Sallah, had been watching the confrontation from his office window. He could not help a sly smile of satisfaction as he shuffled his small fat figure out the office and towards the car as it pulled up outside. Tony and Rashar climbed out into the night chill as Madjid came to greet them with some enthusiasm. He wiped the beads of perspiration from his bald head with a handkerchief.

"*Salem alicome athwarn.* It is good to see you." The three men shook hands.

"You seem to have some problems?" said Anthony.

"These people are motherfuckers!" he shouted loudly, so that the crowd at the gate could hear him also. A jeer came from the people at the gate, much to Madjid's anger. "This is how they repay me for my generosity!" he shouted loudly again. "They have good jobs, with good wages and they spit in my face." Again the crowd outside jeered. "You are all bastards!!" Madjid shouted back at them.

"Just calm down my friend," said Tony. "Let's go inside and talk about this." Tony put a brotherly arm around Madjid and tried to lead him inside. Madjid was still shouting in the crowds' direction and promising vengeance. "You will see now," Madjid pointed to Rashar. "This man will sort you out!! He will sort you all out!!"

Rashar turned to look at the crowd at the gate. This time, no one jeered.

§§§

Madjid laughed and his voice calmed with smug satisfaction. He cursed at them in Arabic through his clenched teeth. "Yes, yes. You see. Cowards, all of them."

Then almost embarrassed by his outbursts in front of Rashar and Tony, Madjid regained his composure. "You must forgive me," he said suddenly. "I forget my manners with all this going on. Come inside my brothers and take some tea after your journey."

Anthony knew enough about Madjid to know that he was no more than a sweatshop owner. For all his gestures of magnanimity and honour, he was just another sleazy Arab businessman. And like all the rest he had come across, he was no more than a smiling assassin who would have no qualms about putting a knife in you once your back was turned and you were no longer useful. If there was one thing that Tony had learned about doing business with Arabs and Iranians, it was the meaning of the words of his father who spoke so harshly of his own people. "Never trust them in matters of business and beware especially of those who say 'You are like my brother,' because their knife is usually the sharpest."

The Arabs are only good for two things," Tony's father would go on, "...fluss and cuss, money and fanny." When his father spoke of "the Arabs" he did not mean the ordinary Arab, but the establishment Arabs—the wealthy and the corrupt self-appointed Arab rulers who lived off the fat of the land whilst those they ruled lived in poverty, ignorance, and thereby forced subservience. His father's words had served Tony well and the one time he neglected to heed them he had paid a severe price - almost forty thousand pounds - when an Iranian businessman had called him brother with a smile, shook his hand with warmth, and ripped him off. He never again neglected his father's words of wisdom.

Over these past few years he had learned a salutary lesson about human nature and greed. The sad truth was that there was virtually nothing that certain men would not do for money. Madjid Sallah was such a man, and the misery he could instill knew no bounds as money flowed into his pocket. Businessmen like Madjid were always ready to take full advantage of the overflowing reservoirs of cheap labour that had been streaming into the country in droves in search of a better life. Many of them would be illegal immigrants that had entered the country on the backs of lorries, perhaps after a trek that had taken them half-way across the world through desperate and dangerous lands filled with unscrupulous men who would fleece them of what few possessions they had.

It was hard for Anthony to understand what drove them to leave their family and homes for the shores of a strange country and an alien culture that was far from welcoming. They wanted a better life many had often told him, they wanted freedom to think, freedom from the grind of tyranny, freedom to find work and make money for perhaps an impoverished family back home. All the things they wanted were the things Tony took for granted.

With no protection under the law, they were prime targets for exploitation by the likes of men like Madjid. Using blackmail and intimidation the standard tools of Madjid's industrial relations he would work them for all they were worth. Complain and you might find yourself being knocked up in the middle of the night by the immigration service. They had escaped one tyranny only to be imprisoned in another. Tony had often asked himself why the Asian and Arab world had more than their fair share of such evil bastards like Madjid. Yet there was one truth Tony could not escape from, and that was, that one way or another his own wealth flowed from the misery of these wretched people. Whilst he might silently condemn men like Madjid, Rashar and Amu Sultan, they might have an excuse. They maybe knew no better, but Tony did know better and that made him worse than all the others put together, because that made him a hypocrite.

Outside the factory, some distance away from the gates, the two VAT officers were now confused as to why Rashar and Tony had not stuck to the usual collection route. They sat watching the gates in the creeping darkness, their impatience growing.

"This isn't on the bloody list. How long do we wait here?" asked Angela.

Bradley had slouched in his seat with his eyes closed, but was not asleep. "As long as it takes. This is home turf for you

Newcastle."

"I'm from Middlesbrough actually," she answered indignantly.

"In't that where they hung the Monkey saying it was a French spy or something?" Bradley chuckled to himself.

"That was Hartlepool," Angela sneered back.

Bradley sunk deeper into his seat and was now asleep. Angela looked down at him with glare. "Well at least someone's happy," she said aloud.

§§§

Madjid poured hot water from the kettle into three stained mugs containing Arabic coffee. Around the desk, Rashar and Tony made themselves comfortable. Rashar lit two cigarettes and passed one to Anthony. They spoke in English since Madjid's Arabic was of a Moroccan dialect and virtually incomprehensible to Rashar and Tony. Madjid was still sounding off about his problem with the strikers outside. He sat down in the chair across the desk.

"This is what happens when you are too generous with these people," said Madjid angrily. "I take them in when no one will help them, out of the goodness of my heart, because they are my own people. And this is how they repay me."

Tony and Rashar looked at each other in cynical silence.

"You are a good man Madjid," said Rashar indulging Madjid's Arab ego. "Allah will punish these people for their ingratitude."

Tony was almost trying not to laugh. "Yes, Allah will punish them I am sure," added Tony with a note of English sarcasm that was lost on Madjid.

"I only hope He punishes them before I go bankrupt," said Madjid, "...they have been out there now for a week. I have no kebab going out and no money coming in."

"What do they want?" asked Tony.

"What do they want!?" Madjid snapped back. "What greedy people like them always want! More money! They are even now asking for tea breaks. All this trouble is the fault of the Jews."

"The Jews?" asked Tony curiously. "What have they got to do with it?"

"They have opened a Kosher kebab factory almost on my

doorstep a mile away. They took some of my workers and spoiled them with more money and give them breaks to eat and breaks to drink tea. Now they ask for the same here. One Englishman who worked for me started all the trouble. That bastard you saw at the gate. I paid him the best money, more than my own people. I treat him like my own brother and he turned to stab me in the back. He started giving them ideas. Now they all want to fuck me."

"How much money do they want?" Tony enquired.

"I don't care what they want," demanded Madjid. "I will not be blackmailed."

Suddenly Madjid's voice dipped to a searching tone. "Perhaps you two could deal with the Jews for me. Go and talk with them, if you know what I mean. Rashar, you have a way of making people see good sense."

Rashar looked at Tony and allowed him to answer. "Look my friend," said Tony carefully. "We have no problems with the Jews and we don't want any problems with the Jews. We have always done good business with the Jews; they have done us no harm. You make a deal with the Jews, you shake their hand and the deal is done. You make business with the Arabs or Iranian, you shake their hand, and what happens?" Tony waited for an answer that did not come. "I tell you what happens, as soon as your back is turned the deal changes a thousand times. No my friend, our problem is not with the Jews. Like yours, our problems are always with our own."

"But I have always done good business with you. Have I ever robbed you Ahmed?" protested Madjid in rising voice.

"My friend you misunderstand me," interrupted Tony, "I was of course not speaking of yourself, but of many others."

Rashar suddenly had a thought. "Perhaps we might be able to help you Madjid. Did you know Ahmed here was once a big man with the British unions? He also has a silver tongue. Maybe he could speak with the men at the gate for you."

Madjid's eyes brightened. "You would speak to them for me?" asked Madjid with an enthusiastic smile. "Maybe make them see sense?"

Anthony was not quick to answer. "Perhaps."

"I would be most grateful for this service," Madjid smiled.

"Of course Ahmed will speak with them," said Rashar

returning Madjid's smile.

"It is that fuckin' Englishman who started all this trouble," cursed Madjid.

Tony turned and looked at Rashar. "I think Rashar can maybe deal with the Englishman, just so long as he does not get carried away. After all we are not gangsters, are we Rashar?"

Rashar curled his lip with contempt and ignored the remark. "Do you have his address?" Rashar asked Madjid.

Madjid shuffled through an office diary. "Yes. It's here." He handed him the open dairy and pointed to the name and address.

Rashar tore out the page and slipped it into his pocket. "I will go and speak with this Englishman for you. I am sure he can be persuaded to be reasonable," said Rashar.

Madjid's expression was one of relief. "That is all I want," said Madjid in a relaxed tone. "I am a reasonable man. I am just trying to do good business." A big smile was suddenly on his face. "You understand these things. Allah is good to give me such friends as you."

 Rashar was now smiling back at Madjid. "But we also need a small service from you my brother. Call it a payment for our services."

Madjid fell stone-faced. "Payment?" he repeated sourly. "But your company owes me for three months supply of donner kebab."

"Amu Sultan hasn't paid you?" Tony quizzed him curiously.

"You owe me almost thirty thousand pounds."

Tony looked at Rashar for an answer. "That's not like Amu Sultan. Are you sure Madjid?"

Madjid rumbled through a pile of invoices on his desk. "Then look for yourself."

Tony inspected the invoices. "Amu Sultan's getting absent minded I think," he said with a sudden smile that was strangely animated and that did not go unnoticed by Rashar. "I'll have a word with him when I get back."

"Money is not the payment we had mind," said Rashar.

"Then what? asked Madjid.

On the road outside the factory Angela Carrick gave her sleeping associate a sharp dig in the ribs as she watched two silhouettes emerge.

Bradley woke up with a start. "Where's the bleedin' fire?"

"I think they're coming out," she said looking through a pair of binoculars. She passed them to Bradley. "Here, look."

"Well there was no need for that," snapped Bradley complaining about the painful dig in the ribs. He snatched the binoculars off her and could see little in the dark except two figures lifting something out of the boot.

"Well?" said Angela waiting. "What are they up to?"

Bradley shook his head. "Dunno, they're taking something from the boot. Looks heavy whatever it is."

Tony and Rashar were struggling with the weight of the body that Rashar had so thoughtfully wrapped in a dirty, greasy carpet from Sheik Yunis's coffee-shop. Tony had the end with the feet sticking out.

"This bloody thing stinks, couldn't you have found something a bit cleaner to wrap the poor sod in." Tony shook his head and sighed. "How did I ever get involved in this business?"

They struggled down the yard and round the back of the factory carrying the bundle.

"This University thing you are thinking of doing?" enquired Rashar.

"Yeah," answered Tony.

"What exactly are you going to do?"

"Dunno really. I was thinking of Social Work. There's a national shortage of Social workers in this country."

Rashar stopped in his tracks and stared at Tony from the other end of the body. "Social work!" he repeated aloud. They were both panting from their struggle with the load.

"Yeah, ya guaranteed a job and the money's good, too."

Rashar just stared at Tony. "What ya looking at me like that for?"

Rashar shook his head. "Never mind. *Yellah*- Let's go." They struggled on in the dark. "Remind me," said Rashar, "to take his shoes off."

"His shoes? What a religious thing or Summat?" grunted Tony struggling.

"No, last time I forget and they blocked the mincer."

§§§

Jeff Bertram was pissed off. He had spent the best part of three weeks organising the pickets outside of Madjid's kebab factory. During that time he had effectively shut the factory down and felt sure that Madjid had been near to cracking and meeting their demands. Jeff was an old union hand and known in the region as a lefty, ready to take up any cause in the name of the revolution. Of course he was living in a revolutionary dream world and had virtually nothing to show for his years of struggle but a reputation as a trouble-maker that had made him almost unemployable.

He was forty-six years, and the sum total of his life was untidily piled into his grubby bed-sit flat where pride of place was displayed on the walls in the form of a Che Guevara poster. Here and there, a few old and tatty left-wing books were displayed so that anyone entering the flat would know he was a working class intellectual, a child of the revolution, not just a scruffy bum.

At a small junk shop table, Jeff sat angrily carving at the beans and toast that these days, had become a regular part of his diet. "Fucking wogs!!" he cursed aloud to himself in the empty flat. "No fuckin' guts! Should fuckin' send all the black bastards back!!" With his toast, he wiped the last of the beans from his plate and threw the dirty plate into the sink where it crashed noisily onto a pile of dirty pots. He took out a pouch of cheap smuggled tobacco, rolled himself a smoke and switched on a small portable television that had long since seen better days. Jeff stared at the screen but his thoughts where elsewhere. There were almost tears in his eyes. His delusions of political greatness once again dashed. He closed his eyes and shouted aloud in desperation, "Damn!! Damn!! Damn!!"

Instantly, his anonymous neighbours began knocking on the walls and shouting muffled abuse. "Ah, get fucked!!" Jeff shouted back and threw an empty beer bottle at the wall. Seconds later came a knock at the door. Jeff was up and on his feet; he was in the mood to hit somebody. He needed to hit somebody, anybody, and a neighbour would do. To Jeff's surprise it was not a

neighbour towering in the doorway, but Rashar. Taken aback for
second, Jeff swallowed hard. All he remembered next was
lightening flashes going through his head and being propelled
backwards at great speed.

Half dazed and now on the floor, he felt the bitter taste of salt
in his mouth. Rashar carelessly threw the table aside and sent the
television crashing to the floor. A sudden tightness gripped Jeff's
throat as he was thrown up in the air like a rag doll and then
pinned forcefully against the wall.

"I have a message for you Englishman. From Madjid." Rashar
hissed into his face. Jeff tried to answer but the words would not
come out. "You're sacked English," Rashar shook him.
"Understand!!" Jeff's dazed eyes stared back him. Rashar sneered
at him with an indifferent smile. He took away his hand from
Jeff's throat and let him fall to the floor. Rashar walked towards
the door, then stopped and turned to look at Jeff's broken and
bloodied figure. He looked around the flat and laughed. "Nice
place you got here."

A second later Jeff was alone, the front door wide open. There
was a strange echo in his head and strangled sounds coming
from the television. Then everything went black.

§§§

The weathered and worried Arab face of the man on the other of
the table stared at Tony as though he were his enemy. Tony felt
sure the man was in fear of him. "All we want, is what is fair,"
said the Arab in a careful voice. Tony was looking at him with a
strange smile. The word "fair" echoed in his mind. Now there was
a word that took Tony back to his own union days. He could hear
himself uttering the same word at powerful men, who many
years ago, sat in the same chair that he now occupied. How the
years had changed his fortunes.

He could almost see the faces of the men he had argued with
years ago. Their words he would never forget. "Fair!! What sort
of argument is that? Don't come here to negotiate and put "fair"
on the table. You give me a good reason to give you what you
want, but never argue that my terms are not fair. I am a
businessman; the word 'fair' is not in my dictionary."

In years to come, Tony learned the full value of that truth. "Fair" was the language of ordinary men, as was "justice." Neither existed in the hard world of business. The only way to move a businessman is to make it in his best interest to move.

"Why do you laugh at me?" asked the Arab with a sad, wounded voice.

Tony gently shook his head. "I am not laughing at you my friend. Your words bring back memories."

"Then is fairness and justice too much to ask?" the Arab asked him.

Insulted, Madjid jumped into the conversation. "What do you mean? I am a just man, an honourable man. I treat you all well. Even better than my own family. What more can you ask? Do you want my blood?" Tony was suddenly staring angrily at Madjid. "Madjid!! You ask me to deal with this. Why don't you just go and make us all a nice cup of tea."

Madjid could see from Tony's expression that it was not a request. Madjid was lost for words; he was unaccustomed to being spoken to like that in front of his lessers. Awkwardly, he lingered for a second and then hurried out of the office.

The Arab on the other side of table smiled. "He is very frightened of you."

"Well, he has no reason to be, except in his own mind. But forget him. I need to know what will get you and your men back to work?"

"Simple," said the Arab. "We want more money. We want breaks like the Jews give the men at the other factory."

"Then the answer is also simple my friend," Tony pointed to the door. "Walk through that door and go and work for the Jews. This is England; it is a free country. Go where you want, no one is stopping you."

The Arab paused. "There are no jobs left there now, for any of us, or we would."

"Then you have a problem then don't you?" said Tony.

"Do you know how much he pays us? He gives us ten pounds for working non-stop for twelve hours. The law of the English says we should get a minimum wage of £4.20 an hour. So Madjid is breaking the law."

"And who pays for your rent?" retorted Anthony. "Who pays

your rates? I suppose you also sign on the dole?"

The Arab was furious with Tony. "You sound just like him," he answered back angrily.

"No!" Tony snapped back. "I am not like him. I am just pointing out a few facts of life."

"Madjid is a thief," the Arab retorted,"he steals the lives of his own people and turns them into slaves. He exploits us and has no shame."

Tony shook his head and cynically laughed. "And in years to come when you perhaps have your own business in this country, you will do exactly as he. I have heard voices like yours a thousand times. And if Madjid is a thief, then you are no better than he. You steal money from the British when you sign on the dole."

The Arab was insulted."Then if I am a thief, I am only stealing from thieves." His voice lunged angrily at Tony across the table. "If I were to steal a million pounds from the English, it would be as nothing compared to the riches they have stolen from my country. Outside this gate only a few hours ago you spoke to me in Arabic and now you sit there with your white face and your blond hair and speak to me in your clean English voice and condemn me for what I am, for what the English have turned me into. It is because of their history in my land that I have to run from own country. It is only right that they pay."

It was an argument Tony had heard many times out of the mouths of asylum seekers. "You come to this country for refuge because your own government persecutes you and the first thing you do is criticise the people who give you shelter."

The Arab was almost amused. "The British give me nothing they do not owe me and what little they do give, they give grudgingly. I see the faces of the Englishmen every day and the way they look at me. I see the hatred in their faces because they think I am taking something from them. They have quickly forgotten what they stole from my people and all the Arab nations. They owe me."

Tony shook his head. "No, no my friend the faces of the people who look at you with so much hatred are the faces of ordinary people, and ordinary people have ordinary minds. To these ordinary people what they see in you is change, and change is hard for all ordinary people because it brings fear and insecurity for the future. Is it not the same with Arab or British? They owe you nothing because these people took nothing. These people are the sheep of the British nation, and all nations have their sheep. You should not confuse the sheep with the shepherd's. It is the shepherd's who stole from your country. The ordinary people just do as they are told, and like all ordinary men everywhere, their payment for their blood is a medal given to the orphan or widow. And as you say, it is their powerful masters who share out the spoils in secret in their palaces."

"To me, they are all the same," the Arab sneered.

"No! They are not all the same," Tony snapped back angrily. The Arab slowly smiled because he knew his words were hurting. "I see you consider my words an insult because it hurts the English blood in yours veins." He paused deliberately. "And what of the Arab blood that flows inside you? Do I insult that too? Who's side are you on?"

Tony seemed to look away and for one of the few times in his life he could not find the words to answer this man's question. "One day," said the Arab quietly, "you will have to make a choice."

Tony raised his head and looked back at the Arab. "I make my choice, I am on my side. Anthony Ahmed Debani's side. I am who I am. I owe no loyalty to anyone but myself. No one gave me anything, including the English, and the Arabs gave me even less. You come to this country and take. You think this country owes you something? Well it doesn't. It owes you fuck-all. You run from your country because of your government. There is a very famous English saying and you should listen to the words carefully. 'If there is something wrong with your government, then there is something wrong with your people.' Maybe you should go home and look in the mirror my friend and then maybe you will see the truth."

"You are a man who speaks with two languages in more ways than one," said the Arab. "You know nothing about me." The Arab was laughing at Tony. "Oh, I know what is inside your heart. You are a reject from the Englishman's world and now you have come into mine for refuge. You are an asylum seeker just like me, only yours in your head. You are a refugee in your own country. You do not know who you are. You name may be Ahmed but you know nothing about the Arabs."

The Arab was pushing all the right emotional buttons. Inside, Tony's anger was growing. He answered him back in Arabic. "Don't tell me about the Arabs my friend," Tony told him fiercely. "I will tell you about the Arabs. My father is Yemeni, a good man with a good heart. When my father came to this country many years ago he found himself alone in the middle of winter. He was freezing on a London railway station. He spoke no English and had no one to turn to. The only Embassy open in those days was the Saudi Embassy. An English taxi driver took pity on him and took him there without charging him. My father told me. Inside it was so warm compared to the cold outside. Such decorations and riches that adorned the walls and ceilings made my father think he was in a palace of a king. He had never seen the like before. He asked for something warm to drink and their help. Do you know what they did to him?"

Tony was glaring at the Arab and waiting for an answer that did not come. "They threw him out of the Embassy and back into the cold. That's the fuckin' Arabs, my friend. Outside, the English taxi driver was still there. Once again he helped my father and took him to a Somali lodging house in the east-end of London. Again without charge, they took him in. My father told me he would never forget the Englishman who helped him. And you want to know why he would never forget the kindness of this stranger?" Tony was staring hard at the Arab and again waiting. "The Englishman helped my father with his bags out of the taxi and took him to the door of the lodging house. My father shook his hand and thanked him. My father's last memory of the man who helped him was seeing a small golden Star of David hanging around his neck."

Tony got out of the chair so as to allay the tears of anger that grew in his eyes. He took out a cigarette and lit it, and waiting for emotion to leave his voice. "So do not tell me about the Arabs." Tony put his finger angrily to head. "In my head here, I have many such stories of the Arabs. So it is best to keep both the Arabs and the English out of this and speak to each other as equals and settle this matter. I am not your enemy."

The slam of a distant car door awoke Angela Carrick with a start. She rubbed the sleep from her eyes and looked at her watch. It was almost two in the morning. Next to her, Bradley was still asleep in the passenger seat. The car was now freezing cold, so she turned on the engine for warmth. Bradley then slowly emerged from his slumber. He tried to stretch out his aches and stiffness.

"What time is it?" he groaned.

"Just turned two," said Angela.

"What the bloody hell are they doing in there?" cursed Bradley. "I thought by now I'd at least have a comfortable hotel bed to sleep in."

"That big one has just come back."

"What do you mean just come back?" said Bradley with a rising voice. "Why didn't you wake me? We could have lost them."

"Well we didn't, did we? And besides that, I nodded off as well."

"This is turning into a fuckin' fiasco," said Bradley with growing frustration. "What the bloody hell are they doing in Newcastle and they haven't been to one takeaway yet. And we can't nick them until we catch them with their hands in a till."

"Have you thought that maybe they are not collecting?"

Bradley looked straight ahead of him at the factory gates and the group of pickets huddled around the brazier. "They have got to be collecting, otherwise why do they go Sheffield. We know that old raghead does the till rolls for 'em."

"So why do they come here?" asked Angela obviously.

"I don't fuckin' know do I," he snapped back her.

§§§

The clock on the office wall approached 2.45 in the morning. Madjid was staring at the clock and growing impatient. Opposite him, Rashar was half asleep with his feet up on Madjid's desk.

"It is getting late," said Madjid. "They have been talking now for over two hours."

Rashar eyes remained closed. "That's a good sign. Ahmed has probably talked him to death."

Madjid did not see the funny side but he stretched a feeble grin. He knew better than not to at least smile when Rashar made a joke. Abruptly, the door from the other office opened. Tony and the Arab striker emerged from the room both looking pleased. The two men shook hands.

"Then you will speak to Madjid?" the Arab striker said in a whispered tone.

"Don't worry. I'll sort it out."

The Arab looked at Tony for a moment and knew that he saw the truth in his face. He smiled and walked away.

"Good news," Tony announced to Madjid. "They are all going home, and they'll be back at work tomorrow."

Madjid's face was a picture of happiness.

As the pickets at the gates began to disperse, Angela and Bradley sat watching from the car. "Well," said Bradley curiously. "Looks like the strike's over."

§§§

Madjid's happiness did not last long. "You must be crazy Ahmed!!" he shouted at Tony. "You must be crazy!!"

"I heard you the first time," Tony retorted.

"But I cannot afford that. Do you know what you are asking? Three pounds twenty an hour with three tea breaks a day? What do you think I am? Made of money?"

"That's still one pound an hour below the minimum wage," Tony countered.

Madjid turned on Rashar. "Is this what you call a silver tongue? Ahmed is trying to bankrupt me. Please, please Rashar talk to him," he pleaded. Tony looked at Rashar and shook his head. Inside Tony's anger was rising and about to explode.

"Listen to me Madjid," Tony reasoned. "You do well out of these people. You have a big house in the posh part of the Newcastle. Three big posh cars. Your children go to the best schools…"

"So that is it!" Madjid shouted. "You of all people begrudge the money I have worked hard for?"

"You are taking the piss out of these people Madjid." Tony turned to Rashar. "You know how much he pays them?" He

69

paused. "Ten pounds for a twelve hour shift, fuckin' ten pounds."

Madjid was seething and shot back at Tony mockingly, "This is business Ahmed. In business you have to do these things. And what about you!! You accuse me, when you are guilty of the same crime. Your takeaways are full of these people. You treat them no better than I. You, too, have a big posh car."

"Amu Sultan pays our people well, that is why they all come to him," Tony snapped back. "Most are gone within a year to a shop of their own and our name is good."

Madjid was furiously pointing his finger at Tony. "I am not paying for your conscience Ahmed. If you want to be a holy man then go to Mecca. I pay what these people are worth."

"You, Madjid, are a fuckin' sweatshop owner." All restraint was now gone from Tony's voice. "It is people like you that give us all a bad name. Your life is one big fuckin' fiddle like all Arabs who make their money fucking their own people."

"You are insulting me now!!" Madjid screamed. He turned to Rashar. "Look Rashar, he is insulting me now!! Insulting the Arabs." Rashar was unmoved.

Tony's rant was not yet over. "To all your English neighbours you are a respectable businessman. Now listen, you fuckin' fat Arab bastard. That's the fuckin' deal."

"No!!" Madjid snarled back. "That is not the deal!! This is my factory. I made it with my blood. I tell you the deal and tell you what I do." Madjid's was finger was pointing almost into Tony's face. "I get rid of all these bastards. You think I let them fuck me when I can buy ten asylum seekers for a pound. Why should I pay more than I have to?"

Tony drew in a breath and started his words carefully. "Listen to my words Madjid and be a wise man, not a fool," he said ominously. "Do you know how much the fine is for employing people who have no visa and are signing on the dole?" He paused a moment for Madjid to get the message. "Well I'll tell ya!!" continued Tony slowly gauging every word. "Five thousand pounds for each person in your factory and that's if you don't go to prison as well."

Madjid's forehead was covered with nervous beads of sweat and he was visibly shaking. "And who would do this bad thing?" he asked in a low voice.

"You should take care of your family Madjid," Tony whispered harshly. It was an Arab threat that Madjid understood and he swallowed hard as he stared back at Tony's unnerving expression.

Across the room Rashar smiled to himself. Only Tony had such skill—the ability to speak the masked poetry of an Arabic threat in the soft words of an Englishman.

"And you should listen to my words well, so we have no misunderstanding between us. If you do not do as I ask, my brother Rashar there will go and see one of his friends in immigration. By tomorrow they will be crawling all over you and you will have no factory to worry about. Heed my words Madjid. Know me and know that I will do this."

Madjid was dumb struck. His chin dropped and his eyes widened. He could not believe what he was hearing. He turned to Rashar looking for support, but there was none. "You would do this to me Rashar?"

Rashar winced and threw up his hands in a gesture of impotence. "What can I do? He is the boss." He might not have agreed with what Tony had just done but deep down he disliked Madjid as much as Tony but for different reasons. And besides, Tony was now in his debt.

"Don't look at Rashar for an answer Madjid," Tony warned.

Madjid looked at Tony forlornly. "You treat me hard and I have done nothing but good business for you and your company. Why do I deserve this?"

Madjid's appeal to Tony's better nature was futile. Madjid represented everything Tony hated about this business, and more, he represented everything he hated about the ways of the Arab. If Tony's expression could have killed, Madjid would have been stone dead. The hatred in his eyes was barely concealed as he stared down at this pathetic defeated figure slumped in his office chair searching for a mercy he had shown to none. To Tony, this poetry of justice was almost laughable . "You should not feel so bad Madjid. In business," he said slowly, staring at Madjid, "…you have to do these things."

Madjid sunk further into his office chair in defeat. "Then I have no choice?"

"None!!" Tony was resolute.

FIVE

It was almost four in the morning by the time they reached the Newcastle hotel. It was cold, dark and pouring with rain. Tony parked the car and snapped on the handbrake. For a second, he sat there staring into the wet darkness beyond the windscreen, something his mind.

"Are we going to sit here all night or what?" said Rashar.

Anthony sighed with a troubled breath. "I'm thinking."

"About what?"

"Madjid said we owed him money."

"So?"

Tony bit his lip. "That's not like Amu Sultan." He took out his mobile phone.

"Who you calling?" said Rashar.

"Abdulla."

Rashar pointed at his watch. "It's four in the morning."

"Don't worry about it. You know Abdulla, he never sleeps, he'll be loading his lorries and counting his money," said Tony.

§§§

The dirty old warehouse was a hive of activity. Amongst the endless rows of stock that held everything from toilet rolls to brown rice, a small convoy of fork lifts dodged in and out the aisles piling their loads onto a regiments of waiting lorries. Orchestrating the mayhem into some sort of organisation, owner Abdulla Corane, with clipboard in hand, blasted out orders like

72

an angry sergeant major. The ringing of the night telephone in the warehouse sent him scurrying to his Porto-cabin office in corner.

"Good morning Express Catering Supplies," he answered in perfect English which immediately broke into Arabic. "Ahmed, do you know what time it is?"

"Never mind the time I need a favour," said Tony.

"Well if it isn't going to cost me any money, then ask?" said Abdulla casually.

"It is important what I ask goes no further," said Tony

"I mind my own business, you know that Ahmed."

"Then can you check if we owe you any money?" said Tony.

"No need to check, I had to speak with Amu Sultan it about it only this morning." Abdullah's tone suddenly changed. "Why is there a problem? 'Cause if there is I need to know about it."

"There's no problem. Just tell me how much it is?" said Tony.

Abdulla brought up their account on his desk computer. "I hope you are not hiding anything from me Ahmed."

"Just fuckin' tell me how much it is, will you Abdulla?"

Rashar watched Tony's face growing more concerned as the seconds passed. Tony stared at Rashar. "You are sure about that? …No, no there's nothing to worry about, you'll get your money just make sure you keep this call to yourself….I said there's nothing to worry about. You know me Abdulla, you'll get your money. I swear it…Ok…Ma' Salem a…" Anthony folded his phone closed with a solemn face.

"Well?" said Rashar.

"Amu Sultan hasn't paid him for three months. He owes him forty-five and half thousand pounds. Abdulla talked to Amu Sultan this morning and promised to settle the account in a few days." Rashar did not seem surprised and that made Tony curious. "What's going on Rashar?"

"I know little more than you," Rashar confessed. "Sheik Yunis told me to be careful, for both of us to be careful. He heard a rumour, that is all I know. Perhaps it is true. Perhaps not."

"And what is this rumour?" asked Tony.

"That Amu Sultan is selling out," said Rashar slowly.

Tony shook and laughed without humour. "Now that makes sense. He runs up all the bills, flogs the lot and runs." Tony scoffed at his own stupidity.

"And you are not angry that I kept it from you?" asked Rashar.

Tony grinned. "You worried I would not believe you, and would think you were playing mind games to poison me against Amu Sultan."

"Sometimes I think you read thoughts Ahmed," said Rashar. "I would have told you sooner or later. It is better you find this out for yourself. This way I am not responsible and we both know the truth."

"The fuckin' bastard," Tony cursed out loud. "I knew something was going on. That's why he sent me with you to get me out of the way. It just didn't make sense. And it's not like Amu Sultan to turn away from a shop like the one in Gold Thorpe." Tony suddenly turned and looked at Rashar in the twilight darkness. "So how much did he borrow off you?" he asked Rashar, amused at both their foolishness.

"Same as you I expect," said Rashar lighting two cigarettes and passing one Tony.

"Forty-five thousand pounds," said Tony shaking his head. He pulled hard on the cigarette. "So he sells up, sneaks off and leaves us with all the fuckin' debt. But why now, I wonder. The business is doing well. There has to be something else we don't know about."

"Perhaps there is nothing else," whispered Rashar. "You are English Ahmed. You might speak Arabic, but your mentality is English."

"What does that have to do with anything?" Tony grunted cynically.

"You must understand there are things done in my world that are done differently in yours," said Rashar. "I think you get confused. And that is dangerous."

"Like what?" said Tony.

"Things that are not important to you," said Rashar. "Loyalties, beliefs. Who you are and what you are very important in mine."

Tony knew that Rashar was leading up to something and was belabouring the point.

"Just get to the fuckin' point Rashar," said Tony his impatience growing.

"Amu Sultan is Shia. I am Sunni and so is your father," said Rashar.

Tony shook his head and laughed at Rashar. "Don't give me that garbage Rashar. It's me you're talking to not some donkey trader in Iraq. So kick that one out the fuckin' window. Amu Sultan's a businessman, the only God he's got is called money. There has to be a business reason."

"What does it matter? He has betrayed us," said Rashar.

"No he hasn't betrayed us. Only a friend can do that and Amu Sultan was never a friend. I learned long ago that you cannot do business with friends.

Rashar suddenly had that childish grin on his face. "And are we not friends?"

Tony began to laugh. "We are many things Rashar, but friends?" he smiled back at Rashar. "I don't think so."

"But I have always liked you Ahmed," said Rashar. "You are strange, a great puzzle to me. I have watched the way you operate. I can learn a lot from you of the ways of the English. And we have also the blood of Arab brothers running in both our veins."

"Don't give me that Arabic brother crap Rashar," Tony answered with a cynical smile. "There is no friendship in business. People like us just feed off each other's usefulness until we are no use to each other. I hoped for a while it could be different with Amu Sultan."

"Then we have to take care of him before he fucks us," said Rashar.

"Oh yeah Rashar, and what did you have in mind?" asked Tony already knowing the answer. "Some swift Arab justice I suppose?"

"Then what would you have me do. Let him fuck us over and walk away?" It was not a question that required an answer. "That is not how it works in my world Ahmed," said Rashar defiantly.

"How it works in your world Rashar, isn't how it works in mine," Tony countered emphatically.

"Look you don't have to do anything," said Rashar. "I will take care of it."

"Listen to me Rashar," Tony's voice was serious. "I do not love money so much that I go around just blowing people away." Tony massaged his tired forehead. "Let's think about this. There has to be another way."

"There are some who say you have powerful friends Ahmed," pondered Rashar aloud, slowly leading up to another thought. "There are some who even say you have spoken with The Brotherhood."

"People say many foolish things in ignorance Rashar," Tony replied. "What they don't know, their imaginations make up for them. Sometimes that can be useful, because you are feared for what does not exist. At least that way you don't have to do many bad things to make people fear you. You just leave it to ferment in the minds of men, and the badness in their thoughts will do the rest."

"Is it not so then?" asked Rashar.

Tony smiled to himself. "You ask too many questions Rashar."

"I am only asking," Rashar softly protested. "Perhaps they could help us?"

"First Rashar, if I knew such people, I would not tell you." Tony told him flatly. "Secondly, The Brotherhood are real Moslems, they do not involve themselves in matters of business, only God. And thirdly why should they help me? I am a Christian, but like most in England, in name only."

Tony's revelation was something of a surprise to Rashar. "But I thought you were a Moslem?"

"Then you thought wrong Rashar," said Tony simply.

"But your father was a Moslem?" Rashar queried.

"Yes, and my mother was a Christian. And she had me Baptised in the Christian faith, and like all good and dutiful English mothers she also sent me to Sunday school to learn about the good Lord Jesus and the Christian God."

"You are Christian then?" said Rashar visibly disappointed.

"You shouldn't worry about it too much Rashar," said Tony with a light smile, "I have no use for such things anyhow."

"You are not a believer then?" Rashar asked with a hint of outrage.

If Tony had not been dog tired, such words from someone like Rashar would have been amusing and the source for a good argument. "Will you do me a favour Rashar?" asked Tony.

"Ask, my brother."

Tony rolled his eyes and groaned, "Let's drop this conversation please. I'm tired and this subject is depressing me more than I am already."

"I am only interested," said Rashar. "If you are not a Moslem then why do you go to the Mosque?"

"How do you know I go to the Mosque?" Have you been watching me?"

Rashar shrugged his shoulders. "No secret, Amu Sultan told me."

Tony liked to think of himself as an agnostic when it came to questions of God, a practical man who had little time for superstition or religion of any sort. In Tony's opinion, never had any empire, in the history of man, spilled more blood than the empire of the God— regardless of religion or creed. Though he would admit it to no one, he seemed to spend an awful lot of time talking to Him in the solitary moments of life. "If you must know," Tony said awkwardly, "...I go because I find it relaxing to sit and listen to the Imam's sermon. I feel safe there. It's almost a feeling like smoking Hash."

"Ahhhh, you see," said Rashar his voice rising, "...this is Allah's way of calling you back to the religion of your Father. So you see, you are a Moslem because it is in your soul."

With a cynical expression on his weary face, Tony stared for a long time at Rashar. "Is that it Rashar?" he paused, "Have you finished? Can we drop it now?"

Rashar shrugged his shoulders. "I am just saying, that is all."

"Rashar?" Tony was staring at him hard. "How many people did you kill when you were in Iraq?"

"What has that to do with anything?"

"How many?" Tony asked again.

Rashar pursed his bottom lip to hazard a guess. "A few, I don't know. Is it really that important to you?"

Tony shook his head in disbelief. "For someone who does not remember the number of people he has killed, you want to tell me about God?" he said sarcastically. "It's people like you that give religion a bad name Rashar."

Rashar did not have a clue what Tony was arguing. "I am just worried that *Shatan*-Satan, does not claim your soul Ahmed."

"Then don't!" snapped back Tony. "Because you're pissing me off."

Outside the rained poured down heavy. Tony's breathing was

suddenly labored.

"I think something else also bothers you my friend."

"Sometimes I just get sick of it all," Tony answered solemnly. "All this Arab and Iranian garbage. We talk and smile at each other like brothers, and then treat each other like shit when our backs are turned. Everyone we meet seems to be a smiling assassin ready to put a knife in your back for a few quid. God, how I hate living in this sea of lies. All the time, moving about in the shadows. Hiding from the tax man, the VAT man and every fucker else. In the world of the Englishman, life was so simple. Work five days a week, pay your taxes and get drunk on a Friday and Saturday so you can forget Monday. Maybe one day I will return to that world. There's no complications there."

"Working is no good to make money. We make good money," answered Rashar simply.

"But it's not all about money is it Rashar?"

"Then what else is there?"

Tony's was frustrated. "I don't know. What about self respect?"

"You cannot eat self respect," Rashar answered with a harshness that hinted of experience. "Believe me I know."

"It was something that asylum seeker said to me," said Tony trying to recall the words, "...he said I was a reject from the Englishman's world. He said I was just as much an asylum seeker as he was. Maybe he was right."

"You have a weakness Ahmed," said Rashar, "...you should not feel sorry for these people."

· Anthony shook his head. "You're wrong Rashar; I don't feel sorry for them. I fear them. They make me feel uncomfortable and they scare the hell out of me. Suddenly I am reminded of my own history, of my own bad memories from the past. They come here for refuge, but in a small dirty sack in their mind, they carry with them their histories of hatred and their petty tribal mentalities. I listen to the English and how they hate them and suddenly I am a stranger in my own country. I was born here and to the English who know my name I have become one of them. I can see in the eyes of the English a hatred I have not seen since my childhood."

" You know something Rashar?" Tony was staring at him. "If I see asylum seekers in the street I cross the road so the watching

English who are staring at them will not think I am one of them."

Rashar laughed. "But you look like an Englishman. You are white and blonde. No one would know there was Arab in your blood."

"And that's what makes it so stupid," Tony pointed to his chest. "But it is what I feel in here. I don't feel white." Tony shook his head, the confusion swirling inside. "You know something Rashar, when I was a kid with my English friends, I used to do the same if I saw my own father in the street, because I was embarrassed."

"Your problem, Ahmed, is that you think too much. You should forget the English," said Rashar. "They gave you nothing and you owe them nothing."

"Another thing he said was that one day I would have to make a choice about whose side I am on. The English or the Arab?"

"And will you make such a choice?" asked Rashar.

Tony seemed to think a few moments before answering. "I think I already have."

The two men looked at each other and the lingering question remained unasked.

"I know what is in your mind," said Rashar smiling. "You look for answers which are not there. The questions you ask in your heart, only Allah can answer I think. I think one day you will have to make a choice. The Englishman's world or the Arab world. You have a problem inside your head my friend."

"And what's that Rashar?" asked Tony quietly.

"You are haunted by Arabs."

Tony turned and stared at Rashar, surprised at this hidden side to him.

"You are tired. I am tired also," Rashar whispered. He smiled with a look of mischief in his face. "Let us forget things for a while. Perhaps I know what we both need my young English brother."

§§§

The rain had begun to ease and had dwindled to a cold drizzle. Across the hotel car park, Angela Carrick was almost asleep at the wheel. Next to her Bradley watched the silhouette of two figures go into the hotel reception.

"Thank fuck for that," he said yawning aloud. "I thought for a minute they were gonna sleep in the car." He nudged Angela next to him. "Come on, Sleeping Beauty, let's book in and get some flaming sleep."

§§§

But for the dim light from a single bedside lamp, the hotel room was in darkness. The two young nubile girls seemed to enter the room as though in slow motion and walking on air. Their faces fleeted by in a haze like ghosts and they came to the floor to sit in a circle next to Tony and Rashar. One of the girls touched Tony and suddenly her lips were pressed against his. He responded hard and demanding. Her pearly white smile seemed to stare at him and Tony felt her take the small glass from his hand. The colourless liquid in the glass was not alcohol but water. The rim was covered in cellophane and sealed with an elastic band. On one side a straw protruded and another small hole had been punched through the makeshift lid.

In Rashar's hand a cigarette lighter burned a needle until it glowed red hot. The burning needle was then pressed against a small cube of pure Iranian cooked opium. The smoking cube was then held over the glass. The young girl sucked hard on the straw and drew the smouldering vapours into the glass and then into her lungs with a hungry eagerness, breathing out with uncontrollable cries of near sexual ecstasy. The greedy hands of the other girl then snatched the glass, and each in the circle took turns with equal urgency. Each time he drew on the straw, Tony's thoughts drifted slowly away and floated dreamily into the air on clouds of aromatic vapour. Like magic, all the tiredness and fatigue that had filled his head and body was suddenly replaced with a great surge of energy and pleasure beyond the imagination of dreams, or God.

Time was standing still, as four naked bodies rolled around the hotel room floor, limbs entangled, tearing and writhing at each other like wild insatiable demons. Death itself could have walked into the room and whisked them away; fear nor care would not have been bothered them. They were in the grip of an indescribable pleasure, a pleasure held captive in the soul like a prisoner that could not escape, that didn't want to escape.

SIX

It was almost six p.m. and all day Bradley and Angela had been sitting around the hotel bar growing impatient waiting for Rashar and Tony to make an appearance.

"Sod this for a game of soldiers," Bradley cursed rising out of his chair.

"Where you going?" asked Angela.

"Find out what's going on. You make sure their car's still in the car park and the bastards haven't sneaked off."

§§§

The hotel room was silent and still now — it was also a mess. The ashtrays were full, an array of spirit bottles and glass tumblers – some empty and half empty – dotted the floor, along with bed linen and clothing that had been discarded into untidy heaps. Tony lay on the bed loosely covered by a sheet and comatose in sleep. Across the room on a large studio settee, Rashar, too, had surrendered to a deep, opium-induced sleep. The two girls had long since departed having been well paid for their services. The false energy and hypnotic dreams that Rashar and Tony had enjoyed earlier had now worn off, leaving in its place a fatigue ten times more draining. It would be many more hours before they would awake.

§§§

"Yes, Sir?" said the male hotel receptionist with a pleasant smile.

"Two men booked in last night. Can you tell me if they are still here?" asked Bradley. The receptionist was taken aback. "I'm sorry sir, but that type of information is confidential." Bradley produced his ID and pushed it under the receptionist's nose. He glanced at it. "I'm afraid that makes no difference Sir. I'm sorry, but unless you have some sort of warrant, I still cannot give out that type of information."

"Get me your manager," Bradley demanded angrily. "I'm not talking to the monkey, get me the organ grinder." The receptionist disappeared into the back office and some moments later came back accompanied by the hotel manager. He reiterated to Bradley what the receptionist had already told him. "I'm sorry Sir. But as you have already been told, unless you have a warrant, information relating to our guests is confidential."

"Another clever bastard, eh?" retorted Bradley.

"There is really no need for that type of language Sir," the manager protested.

Bradley smiled at him. "This is a private hotel isn't it?" he commented cleverly.

"I do not see what that has to do with anything Sir."

Bradley took his mobile phone out of his pocket. "Well," said Bradley. "All I have to do is ring one number on this phone and have a word with a few friends and Customs and Excise will be swarming all over this place. I'll make sure they go over your bar accounts with a fuckin' tooth comb." He paused to let his threat sink in. "Do you get my drift?"

The hotel manager swallowed hard and tried to smile. His attitude suddenly changed. "I'm sure that will not be necessary Sir." He quickly and obediently spun 'round the hotel register for Bradley to inspect.

Bradley smiled cleverly and looked at the register. He saw that Rashar and Tony had not yet checked out. He spun the register back around and handed the manager his card. "Thank you. Now my mobile number is on that card. I will be around here somewhere all day. As soon as these two gorillas check out of here I want to know. You got that?"

The hotel manager smiled subserviently and took the card.

"Nice hotel ya got here," said Bradley sarcastically.

§§§

The fine spray from the shower felt like a thousand hot needles against Tony's skin. He turned the temperature dial and suddenly the stream of water was ice cold and waking his dulled senses into consciousness. Again, he turned the dial to hot and then cold.

In the hotel room, Rashar sat patiently waiting and smoking. He had changed into a smart grey flannel suit and whiled away the few moments admiring himself in the dressing table mirror through his shades.

"Move your arse!!" he shouted at Tony. "We are losing time."

Bradley and Angela Carrick were still waiting in the hotel bar, by this time fed up of drinking the coffee. Bradley took a call on his mobile. It was the hotel manager. "Thanks." He abruptly snapped shut his phone and stood up. "Come on, they're checking out."

The Casablanca takeaway in the centre of Newcastle was buzzing with customers. Across the counter, one of a group of five foreign workers was shaving a giant donner kebab while another pushed pizzas into an automatic oven. At the other end another worker took them out, sliced them into six, boxed them and passed them on to yet another who packed them up neatly for the waiting customers.

Khalile Hassan, the Sudanese manager, busily took the orders, slammed the money into the till and moved deftly on to the next customer. "Yes please?"

"A donner Abdul," the drunken customer shouted at him. "And I don't want no fuckin' garlic shit on it either Abdul."

"My name is not Abdul. And don't speak to me like that!!" Khalile shouted back at him. "We don't serve shit here. If you don't use manners, go somewhere else." With that, Khalile turned and spoke in Arabic to one of the chefs working behind him. "It is only the bastard English who are stupid enough to speak to someone who is cooking their food. Make sure you give him a little extra something Hafez and lots of it." Khalile turned back to the English with an artificial smile. "Your food will only be one minute….Sir."

Behind him, Hafez the chef did just as he was told. And out of sight of the customer, he scrapped the back of his throat, brought as much phlegm as he could and then spit on the donner kebab. He then covered it with chilli sauce and handed it across the counter to the waiting English customer. With the kebab now safely in his hands, the drunken punter thought it safe to have another jibe at Khalile. "Good night Abdul, ya black bastard," he shouted at him. Laughing, he left the shop.

Khalile chuckled at the stupidity. "The joke is on you English bastard!!" he shouted aloud. The chefs all howled with laughter.

Of all the Company's shops, this was the best earner in the group and Khalile Hassan, Rashar knew, was one of the dodgiest managers. Tony and Rashar sat outside in the car, watching the shop. Rashar was smiling at Tony. "Well, be my guest. Let's see how you do," said Rashar chuckling.

"What are you going to do?" asked Tony.

"I'll wait here."

Back inside the takeaway, through the window Khalile had spotted Tony walking towards the shop. "Quick!! Quick!!" he shouted in Arabic to the cooks behind him. "Take over. If anyone asks for me, you don't know where I am." Quickly dispensing of his white catering overalls and cap, without another word he rushed towards the back of the shop and out the back door.

The Arabic chef at the till stared uneasily over the counter at Tony. "Yes Sir. What would you like?" he mumbled in broken English.

Tony spoke back to him in Arabic. "I've come to see Khalile. My name is Ahmed, I have some business with him. Tell him I'm here, will you? He knows who I am."

The chef shrugged his shoulders. "He hasn't been here all day."

Tony stared at the chef with a cynical smile. "Really, now there's a surprise. Where is he?"

Again the chef shrugged his shoulders, this time more awkwardly, and before he could struggle out another feeble excuse, a commotion came from the back of the shop. It was Rashar, he had Khalile by the scruff of the neck and was casually frog marching him back into the shop.

"Look who I bumped into," Rashar announced with a big smile on his face. "I hope you were not trying to avoid us Khalile."

Khalile threw his hands up in a gesture of honesty, "Of course not, my brothers. Why would I do a thing like that?" he said sheepishly.

Just across the street, Bradley's long lens camera was rolling off snap after snap through the takeaway window. "Just look at the smarmy bastards. Just a few more pick-ups like this and we'll pull the fuckers in."

Upstairs in the office takeaway, Khalile - counting aloud in Arabic - slapped one thousand pound bundle after another onto the desk in front of Rashar and Tony.

"One thousand, two thousand, three thousand…"

Khalile stopped counting at nine thousand and smiled. Rashar and Tony stared back unimpressed. Khalile pulled two more bundles out of his office drawer and slapped them onto the pile. Tony looked at Rashar for an answer. Rashar curled his lip and nodded; the amount was about right. Tony took a thousand pound bundle off the pile, peeled back a hundred pounds to add to it, and then passed that back to Khalile — his cut, off the top. The rest Tony scooped off the desk and into Rashar's open hold-all. Before Khalile had finished counting his cut, Rashar and Tony were gone.

Bradley rattled off more pictures as Rashar and Tony exited the takeaway.

Two hours up the motorway and into Scotland, the car headlights illuminated the motorway sign which read: Next Exit for Glasgow Central. Within ten minutes of leaving the motorway, Tony and Rashar pulled up outside the Bianco takeaway down Easter House Road. It was the same routine. The man who ran this takeaway was known for his honesty. He was an Iranian asylum seeker — an engineer by profession and fluent in four languages including Arabic. He was known by the name of Syead. Whether it was false or not mattered little, in this business few used their real names. The less people knew about you the better; it made it difficult for those with a grudge to report you to the authorities.

This time, Rashar and Tony went in together; the staff were busy serving customers. The cashier nodded that Syead was upstairs. They could hear arguing as they climbed the dark back stairs to Syead's office. Tony knocked and Syead bade them to enter. Syead was in the middle of a heated argument with the English driver who delivered the customer telephone orders. Syead had just counted the delivery money; it was forty pounds short.

"I am sick of this!!" Syead shouted at the driver. "This is the third night you are short."

"Well it must have fell out me pockets," the driver defended.

"Check all your pockets now," Syead demanded.

The driver stood up, and in a demonstration of his innocence pulled his pockets inside out to show that they were empty. Tony and Rashar stood quietly watching, they had heard the same argument a thousand times before.

"This is what I have to put with," he spoke in Arabic.

The driver started to leave.

"Just a minute," said Rashar standing in the driver's way. He kicked the legs from beneath him in one smooth movement and sent him crashing to the floor. Rashar then lifted him up by his ankles and in a matter of seconds had removed his shoes and socks. Squeezed inside one of the socks was sixty pounds in ten-pound notes. Rashar took out the money and threw it on Syead's desk.

"Is this what you're looking for?" asked Rashar.

Syead smiled and counted the money. "There's sixty pounds here. You have been overcharging the customers as well, you thieving bastard."

The driver was back on his feet with a red face. "Some of that's me tips," the driver said sheepishly.

Syead threw a ten-pound note at him. "Don't bother coming back tomorrow; you're sacked."

If the driver was tempted to say anything, a glaring look from Rashar stopped him cold, and after scooping up his socks and shoes, he picked up the note and bolted quickly out of the office.

"You are four days early my friends," said Syead.

"We had some other business up here," said Rashar, "I hope it is not inconvenient."

"No, I have your money ready," Syead answered. "Please, please sit down. Will you take food?"

"You must forgive us," said Tony. "We are behind and in a hurry."

Syead lifted the carpet next to the desk, and from beneath a loose floorboard took out several bundles of twenty pound notes. In front of Rashar and Tony, he counted the bundles to a total of nine thousand pounds. Rashar handed Syead back the nine hundred pounds, and a parcel containing the forged till rolls for the next month's trading. Their business concluded, the three men shook hands and were gone.

Bradley's camera reeled off more pictures of the men as they left.

Some fifteen minutes later, Tony's car thundered down an empty, dark motorway heading south towards Sunderland— their next stop. Here, they collected eight thousand pounds; next, to Stockton— seven thousand pounds, Hartlepool; South Shields and so it went, driving through the night. By early the next evening they were again back in Yorkshire having collected from twenty takeaways and covering well over five hundred miles in just two days. With only ten takeaways left, they were two days ahead of the usual schedule, the total cash in the hold-all now standing at over sixty-five thousand pounds. Before calling it a day they decided to make one last pick up to the Arabian Nights takeaway in the Chappel Town district of Leeds. Mustafa the Algerian manager counted the one thousand pound bundles totaling well over the usual amount of fifteen thousand pounds. It had been a good month. Tony looked at Rashar, they both smiled. After giving Mustafa his ten percent cut they were gone.

The Push Inn down Kirkstall Road was packed. International football was on and England was playing Turkey with the match being shown on Sky Sports live in the next room. By the sound of the drunken customers, England was not having the match all its own way. Totally disinterested in football, Rashar and Tony ordered their drinks and took a seat in the back lounge away from the crowds and the noise.

"How much so far?" asked Tony.

Rashar studied the running total from a small note book he kept. "It's good," he said aloud. "Very good."

"So how much?"

Rashar smiled. "Almost eighty thousand and we still have ten collections to make."

"That is good," said Tony. "We have almost got our money back, and if the rest are as good, we should make something on the top."

From the table Tony had a clear view of the road outside. He paid no mind to the car that pulled up across the road containing a girl and a man. That was until the girl climbed out of the car and seemed to be searching the pub car park.

"Well?" said Bradley impatiently. "Can you see their car?"

"I could've sworn they pulled in here," said Angela.

"After all this, don't say we've bleedin' lost them," cursed Bradley.

Angela's voice was suddenly relieved. "No, no. I can see the car. They must be in the pub."

As he sat drinking in the pub, Tony's stare locked onto the girl across the road. There was something familiar about her. He was racking his brains trying to recall where he had seen her before, but no matter how hard he tried, he could not remember. His train of thought was abruptly broken when three drunken football fans came into the lounge for a half-time drink. Rashar looked at Tony and then out the pub window. He smiled lecherously when he saw what had taken Tony's attention.

Angela found herself looking right into the faces of Tony and Rashar as they stared at her from the pub window. Instinctively, she quickly climbed into the car and sped away.

"What's the rush?" Bradley asked.

"They're in the pub; they were staring at me from the pub window."

Bradley laughed. "Well, so what. With all that leg showing I don't blame them."

"That blond one saw me in Hull," said Angela.

§§§

Rashar downed half his pint in two savouring gulps. "Your thoughts are in your pants," he said in Arabic.

Tony thoughtfully shook his head. "I know her from somewhere but I cannot remember where."

"I think if you spent the night with her you would not forget it," said Rashar.

"No, I didn't mean that," said Tony still deep in thought.

At the other end of the bar, the three drunken football fans were suddenly aware of Tony and Rashar speaking in a foreign language. They looked at each other and started to sneer and laugh at them. One of the drunks leaned over on his bar stool and shouted across the lounge at Tony and Rashar. "Eh you two!! Are you fuckin' Turks or what?"

Tony blankly looked up at the staring drunk. "No!!" he answered flatly and then turned away.

The drunk persisted. "Are you fuckin' Arabs then?" he shouted at them laughing.

"Why don't you just mind your own business," said Tony straight faced. "And we'll mind ours."

"Only asking, not very friendly are ya Abdul?"

His two drunken companions started to laugh with him. Rashar was almost out of his chair.

"Leave it Rashar!!" said Tony gripping Rashar's shoulder. "We have other business."

By this time the bar manager realised that things could get out of hand.

"Look, just keep it down," he said to the drunks. "I don't want no trouble in here."

"I'm only asking them a question. It's a free country," the drunk protested.

"Not if your bothering my customers it's not," said the bar manager.

Again the drunk shouted again at Tony and Rashar. "If ya not Arabs, then I bet you two are fuckin' Israelis ain't ya?"

Tony could see Rashar starting to smoulder and knew what was in his mind. He leaned over and whispered to Rashar in Arabic. "Forget it Rashar. We don't need it."

The drunk shouted more abuse at them. "The way you fuckin' Israelis treat them Jews is a fuckin' disgrace."

If the comment had not been so stupidly ironic, it would have been amusing.

Suddenly nothing could hold Rashar back, like a bullet he was out of his chair and across the lounge. Tony jumped up to stand between them.

"Whatever you hate the most," Rashar shouted into the drunk man's face, "...that is what I am! What are you going to do about it?"

The two other drunks at the bar backed away and left their friend to his fate.

Rashar said again, "What are you going to do about it?"

Tony was trying to drag Rashar away. "Leave it Rashar!! It's not worth it!!"

"You open your fuckin' mouth again and you will be eating hospital food for your supper!" Rashar bellowed in concession. He shrugged off Tony's grip. "Alright, alright. Relax. This piece of shit isn't worth the time."

"Come on, let's go," urged Tony.

Outside, Rashar was apologetic. "I don't know what came over me. Why I let that piss-head wind me up I don't know. As usual Ahmed, you were right."

"That's good Rashar," said Tony, "because it means you're learning. What's worth it and what's not. Trouble like that we don't need."

Rashar smiled. "I should listen to you more Ahmed." He headed back into the pub.

"Where you going?" said Tony.

"I just need to take a leak. You go to the car."

Tony looked at Rashar with a dubious expression.

"Don't worry," Rashar tried to reassure him. "I just want a piss."

In the bar, the three drunks were laughing in drunken bravado at what had just gone on. "I tell ya' if the black bastard had started, I would have smashed his head in," said the one who had started

the argument. "Who the fuck do they think they are? Fuckin'
wogs."

The bar manager listening was not impressed. "When you lot
have finished your drinks I want you out," he told them straight.
"And don't come in here again. I've got my licence to think of."

"Ah, what ya frightened of?" the drunk shouted back.
"Upsetting a few bloody wogs? Should send all the fuckers back."

Suddenly, the bar manager stood bolt upright, staring wide-
eyed across the bar. The drunk was still rambling on. "If I had my
way, I'd kick all the black bastards out."

A few moments later, the drunk noticed the bar manager's
stare, and saw that his two friends had suddenly backed away
from the bar. "What up with ya'?" The drunk followed the bar
manager's eyes to find Rashar standing right behind him with a
slight grin on his face. In a low, calculating voice he said slowly,
"Then why don't you try throwing me out now you fuckin' ugly
English bastard!!"

Tony pulled up to the entrance of the car park entrance to wait for
Rashar. A few minutes later Rashar emerged and climbed into the
car. Tony didn't say anything; he didn't have to.

Turning south towards the city centre, Tony followed the signs
that pointed them to the M1 motorway and London. Tony could
only guess what had gone on in the pub. He was angry. With all
the troubles they had already, Rashar was taking risks that were
totally unnecessary. They were risks that could needlessly bring
them to the attention of the police and right now that was the last
thing they needed. For a few minutes they did not speak.

"There's blood on your jacket Rashar?" said Anthony in a
hostile tone.

"You don't have to worry," said Rashar casually. "It's not mine.
I sort out that fuckin' racist bastard."

Tony was seething. "Why do I waste my fuckin' time with you
Rashar. For the sake of belting some piece of shit drunk in a pub,
you risk getting us both arrested. We have important business to
sort out and you just can't raise your game."

"You can ignore people like that if you want. I say nothing,"
Rashar countered. "But don't tell me what to do. He insult me, so
I fuckin' teach the racist a lesson."

"You just don't get it, do ya' Rashar. The fuckin' penny just won't drop will it. When you walk down a street what do you do when you see a piece of dog shit? Do you deliberately put your foot in it?" Tony answered for him, his voice rising. "No, you don't. That bloke in the pub is just like a piece of dog shit. The world is full of them mate, and the trick is just to treat them like dog shit— to walk around it, avoid it. Otherwise it just sticks to your shoe and drags you down. You fuckin' bang on and on about racists?"

Tony was pointing at Rashar as he drove. "You make me fuckin' laugh Rashar, ya know that? I've lived in this country all my life, remember I was born here. Day after day I lived with it. They fuckin' even threw bricks at our windows when I was kid. They used to shout at my mother in the street and say she was a prostitute, just because she married a coloured man. Don't tell me about racism mate. I've lived it. And ya know when I started getting ahead mate? When I stopped wasting my time fighting with every fucker who called me a black bastard or a wog. I started to use my brain instead of my fists. People like that are a waste of fuckin' time. I sometimes bump into some of the people from when I was a kid. I see them all the time. These are the same people who tried to fuck us over because my Dad was an Arab. They were shit then and they are still shit now. The last one I saw was sweeping the fuckin' roads. I was the one laughing then. They look at my car, look at my clothes and I don't even waste my time to speak to them. I can see the jealously in their eyes." Tony smiled with satisfaction. "That's my fuckin' vengeance; not wasting my time fighting with them like you. You have to get above that Rashar."

Tony shook his head and sighed. "Why I fuckin' bother Rashar, I don't know."

"Then don't!!" Rashar snapped back furiously. Tony seemed to be speaking to him like he was child, and Rashar did not like it one bit. "Sometimes you go on like a woman. Maybe you can ignore racist bastard but I cannot."

"You keep fuckin' going on about racists," Tony blasted him. "A drunk in a pub makes a stupid remark and you stove his head in. That's not racism mate. I tell ya what racism is. You slag this country, but what about your own, if a Shiite Moslem goes into the wrong part of town, you don't just call him names, do ya Rashar. Ya blow his fuckin' head off with an A47. Now that's what I call racism."

Rashar was staring at Tony hard. He looked about to explode. He started Slowly, restraining his anger, each breath calculating and controlled he replied, "You have made your point Ahmed. Now just shut your mouth and find a hotel. I am tired."

"Then start fuckin' listening Rashar!!" Tony shouted at him. "And stop fuckin' about. We've got important business to sort out before Amu Sultan fucks us over and all you want to do is waste our time knocking ten balls of shit out of a drunken arsehole. For fuck sake Rashar, get your priorities right."

Rashar wanted to punch Tony's lights out. Nobody had ever talked to him like before and stayed on their feet for more than seconds afterward. But no matter how much he hated to admit it, he knew Tony was right; and for the moment, Rashar needed Tony's talents. There was also something else that he would never quite admit to himself. Deep down, he felt there was another side to Tony. Part of him was an unknown quantity and although it was a part he could not see, Rashar felt a certain fear. It was something he could not put his finger on, but his instincts told him to be cautious. "Alright! Alright!" Rashar shouted back. "Next time, I walk away like you say."

"Then you agree I am right?" Tony was determined to rub Rashar's nose in it for all it was worth in order to make his point. He waited for an answer.

Rashar smiled through his anger, knowing that Tony would not shut up until he had heard what he wanted. Dragging out the words, Rashar gave him what he wanted to hear. "You are right Ahmed," he answered with artificial calm. "Now does that satisfy you? Are you happy now?"

Tony smiled victoriously. "Good."

"So now can we find a hotel?" said Rashar through clenched teeth.

Tony eyes were in the rear mirror. "I think also we might have another problem."

"What problem?" said Rashar.

"That women outside the pub. Don't look now, but their car has been following us for the past few miles."

Pizza Wars

Rashar pulled down his sun visor and used the mirror to look behind him. He could see the car. "Are you sure?"

"I also remember where I have seen her before. She was in Hull when I picked you up in town."

Rashar put up the sun visor and broke into Arabic. That was always a sign that his guard was now up and his instincts on alert. "What do you think? We're carrying a lot of money. Robbers maybe?"

"No, I don't think so. She doesn't look dressed for that," said Tony thoughtfully.

"Then what?"

Tony's voice was heavy. "I don't know."

SEVEN

Amu Sultan visited his solicitors early that morning. He was in a
rush to settle all business affairs, and with good reason. Tony and
Rashar were out the way but matters with the VAT and tax office
had started to move faster. His experience told him that he
probably had no more than a few days, if that, before the
company assets would be siezed and the bank accounts frozen.
Whilst freezing the bank accounts would not affect him– he had
emptied his some weeks earlier– he felt sure that the VAT office
would extend the powers of the warrants to cover not only his
personal and company account bank accounts, but Rashar's and
Tony's as well.

It might take Rashar some time to work out how the VAT office
had discovered his bank account, but he knew Tony well enough
to know that it would take him all of about fifteen seconds.
Rashar he could handle, he was a man with only one string to his
bow and that was violence. Amu Sultan had enough money in his
pocket to buy fifty men like him who could make problems like
Rashar disappear for good. Tony though, was a different ball
game. Not only clever, Amu Sultan felt he could be dangerous,
and with money still in his pocket, very dangerous. So Amu
Sultan would ensure that the one thing Tony had no access to,
was money. In his mind it was not a malicious thing, just good
business sense. 'It is business. You have to do these things,' Amu
Sultan would often say to himself.

Of the two men, it was Tony he feared most. His tricks seemed
to come out of the darkness and hit you when you least expected.

He had watched Tony operate on too many occasions to underestimate his capability and reach. With little money in their pockets and a string of nasty debt collectors, not to mention the messy business of the VAT and tax office, both of them would be far too busy to seek him out for vengeance.

Anyway, by then Amu Sultan planned to be in Iran and well out of their reach. What Amu Sultan was sure of, was that what Tony had started–in his attempt to manipulate him out of the business–he would finish. Tony would only have himself to blame for starting the game and Amu Sultan was sure that it would only be a matter of time before Rashar turned on Tony, as he knew Arabs always did.

In the beginning of their business relationship, Amu Sultan had taken Tony under his wing. They had a mutual interest in helping each other. Both had something the other wanted. Tony needed money and a job, Amu Sultan needed someone he could trust, for a short time at least, until his expansion plans for his then small business were more securely rooted and making good money. Amu Sultan knew he could learn from him and that Tony's knowledge could be useful. He thought that Tony might have been different, but time had shown what was truly in Tony's blood could not be changed and it had got the better of him.

In those early days Amu Sultan tried not regard him as an Arab, and he had never treated him like one. If he had, maybe it might not have come to this. In his dealings with Tony, Amu Sultan had broken all of his own business rules for dealing with Arabs or his own people: Never give them too much money so they always have to rely on you, and never show all your cards. He had relied on Tony's skills too much, and in the process had let his guard down. And he had always paid him good wages, he knew now, too good.

Amu Sultan had given Tony respect because he regarded him as English, with an English mentality. Tony had the knowledge and experience of the working ways of the English political world, and a strange sixth sense of how to apply what he knew to get results with minimum cost and problems. Tony was indeed a special creature and now that he had found ambition, he had to be feared. It was time for all of them to go their separate ways. This was how it always was in their world of business and how it would always be. The young and strong sweep away the old and weak. As it is in with the laws of the wild, so it is with business.

It was a world of cross and double cross, of artificial smiles and brotherly talk all skillfully crafted to deceive the gullible into letting their guard down in a moment of trust. Only then would the carefully hidden knives of the smiling assassin come out of its sheath and be plunged deep into the back. This is what it had come to. After all Amu Sultan had done for Tony, this had been his payment. He had betrayed him and shown the true colours of his Arab blood. Amu Sultan should have known better, maybe he was getting old and a bit too long in the tooth for all these games. A few years ago, he would have spotted what was going on much earlier. But no matter, he had got there in end and the last smile of this game would be on his face.

Experience was always good to have, and in the years they had been doing business, what Amu Sultan had learned from Tony was worth more than money. Amu Sultan had always been a practical man, well versed in the weaknesses of human kind and the true nature of its being. Perhaps he might have been disappointed in Tony, but he was not surprised. It was another learning experience, and for Farida every learning experience in his business career was a valuable life tool never to be forgotten. He wished he could stick around just to see the look on Tony's face when he realised that his little game had been rumbled and that the tables had been turned. Turned against him with the very same political games and tricks that Amu Sultan had learned from him.

"I think we have finally arrived at a price Mr Farida?" announced Solomon Cohen with a reserved professional smile. "The buyer has agreed your price of 3.75 million, and I received your power of attorney from your brother's solicitor in Tehran yesterday afternoon. So barring any last minute hitches, we should exchange contracts and finalise the sale by this time tomorrow."

If Amu Sultan was happy at how quickly matters had been brought to this stage, he did not show it. Show that you are pleased with a solicitor's work and the price usually went up. "I do have one final instruction," said Amu Sultan with a note of reticence.

"And that is?" asked Solomon without curiosity.

"Perhaps you might think it strange but I have my reasons for this request," said Amu Sultan awkwardly.

As any good solicitor, Solomon knew what was coming next, but as a matter of legal courtesy he had to ask. He looked over his spectacles with a formal expression of interest. "And what would that be Mr Farida?"

"I would like the money in cash. I hope it will be of no trouble to you," Amu Sultan answered with a look of animated embarrassment.

"Not in the least Mr Farida," said Solomon easily. "If that is your instruction, I'm sure I can arrange it. I will need to give our bankers direct notice that they should have such an amount ready. Once the monies have been transferred into our account I will have it delivered to this office. I am sure you understand with it being such a substantial amount there will be the cost of security and of course a counting fee at both the bank and our office, when the money arrives."

Amu Sultan smiled and got up to leave. "Then I will leave matters in your most capable hands."

"Just one other matter Mr Farida," added Solomon. "Should we purchase a suitcase, or will you bring your own?"

"If it would be no trouble," replied Amu Sultan politely, "…and please, feel free to add it onto your final account which you may deduct directly from the money delivered."

§§§

It was five o'clock in the afternoon, and as workers made their way home, the traffic in the town centre of Grantham had ground to halt. Bradley and Angela were once again parked at the roadside, their attention focused on The Moroccan Palace takeaway. After following Tony and Rashar from Leeds they were now in the fifth town and eighth takeaway of the day. According to Angela's calculations, that left only one remaining collection and that was Luton.

"Bastard!!" Bradley shouted angrily down his mobile phone. "Are you sure about that?" He shook his head and sighed with a frustrated growl. Without the courtesy of a goodbye he snapped his phone shut.

"Problems?" said Angela.

"Would ya fuckin' believe it? Every one of the properties is in another name. The judge in Hull won't give an order to put cautions on the titles at the land registry until we find out if the name is real or just another name shuffle. Bloody marvellous."

"What about the bank accounts? asked Angela.

"Got the lot. Bank and credit card accounts all frozen. They said the judge wasn't too happy about sticking an ex-parte injunction on the bank accounts fronted by the family members, but he's done it."

"Well that's something, I suppose." Angela tried to sound optimistic.

"They might be bugger all in them yet," said Bradley, "...and even if there is, the big money's in the freeholds. Without them we'll be lucky to get a few thousand quid. That's not much of a hole in three million pounds VAT."

"They must be carrying nearly a hundred thousand pounds now," said Angela.

Bradley's face suddenly brightened with the thought. "Yeah, well, we'll have that off them when we make the nick in Luton."

Inside the Moroccan Palace takeaway, Tony and Rashar watched impatiently as Marsoud Jalile, the Iraqi manager, counted wads of money onto his scruffy office desk. They were both tired after a long day on the road and their tempers were wearing extremely thin. They had struggled and tussled to squeeze their money out of almost all of the last seven takeaway managers. At the last two pick ups, Tony had simply left the room, as a deluge of ranting excuses poured forth. He left Rashar to talk with them in a language more readily understood than civility and good manners. Two days ago Rashar's methods had been questionable, but by now Tony was too tired and pissed off to care. He had other thoughts dogging him and he was eager to get back to Hull to find out exactly what was going on.

A few moments alone with Rashar and the money had appeared like magic, but not before blood had been splattered across the office walls. It was all so pointless because the outcome was always inevitable. Yet why some of the takeaway managers chose to play this seemingly endless game was a mystery to Tony. Maybe Rashar was right, it was in the blood.

Motionless, Tony sat staring across the desk at Marsoud as, with the monotony of bad Arab poet reciting from a text he had repeated a thousand times, he rattled off all the usual excuses for not having the money.

"I tell you what can I do my brothers?" Marsoud was almost singing to them. "It has been a bad month and I am surrounded by thieves. Nearly all month the till has been down nearly a hundred pounds a night."

It was almost like bargaining with a Baghdad market trader, Marsoud went on and on and on. "Only yesterday both delivery drivers were attacked and robbed of their money. Six hundred pounds they lost. The poor men, what can I do, I shut the shop and had to take them to the hospital. But, thanks be to Allah they are alright. Amu Sultan is my good friend. He is like a brother to me, I know he will understand. He is a good man and *Inshallah* will have a long and happy life for his good heart."

Tony sighed, thankful that the opening grovelling pitch had not been as long as the previous two. Marsoud did not know yet, but if he thought his feeble attempt to fob them off would work he was about to be sadly and painfully mistaken. Tony massaged his forehead with growing fatigue, as Marsoud's counting stopped at four thousand pounds. For this takeaway the cash pick-up was almost seven thousand pounds short of the usual amount. What was wrong with these people? Tony asked himself silently. Why did it always have to be like this?

Inside his weary body he could feel tension beginning to tighten its grip. Tony let out a long disgruntled breath and looked at Rashar. He shook his head with a "here we go again" expression.

"I think I must speak alone with my Arab brother Marsoud Ahmed," said Rashar in quiet English. He was smiling at Marsoud but it was a smile that was without humour.

Marsoud's face suddenly dropped with anticipation and the knowledge of what was coming next. He nervously fumbled back into his desk drawers and rummaged through the junk and crumpled documents that were crammed inside them. "Perhaps

I might find another two thousand pounds," he quickly confessed. Tony and Rashar stared back at Marsoud unmoved by his sudden offer.

"No!" barked Tony oddly. "I think this time it is best if it is I who must speak alone with my Arab brother Marsoud."

Marsoud's expression brightened with what he thought might be a much softer option.

Rashar stared at Tony for a couple seconds and saw something in his face that he had never seen before. Rashar curled his lip, picked up the hold-all containing the money collected and got up to leave. "I'll just be outside if you need me," said Rashar a little bemused.

Tony voice was strangely emphatic. "I'll be two minutes," he said staring hard at Marsoud.

"Go and help yourself to some food downstairs," Marsoud happily announced to Rashar. "The chicken kebab is beautiful; I made it myself to a new recipe."

A second later, Rashar stood waiting on the landing outside. No sooner had the office door closed than a terrific rumpus came from inside. Rashar suspected what was happening but tried to resist the temptation of taking a peek. Curiosity got the better of him and he pulled back the door a couple of inches and spied through the gap. Rashar chuckled to himself. Inside, Tony had Marsoud's head by the hair and was slamming it into the desk with all his might. Rashar quickly shut the door and left Tony to it. Now who was learning from who? Rashar asked himself with a satisfied grin. A few more bangs and crashes followed and the office door opened. Tony stepped out with twelve, one thousand note bundles in his hands. He pushed the money at Rashar without a word and proceeded down the stairs as if nothing had happened.

Rashar could not resist another look into the office. The desk was upturned with papers and files strewn all over. On the office floor the carpet had been stripped back to reveal a missing floorboard. On the floor by the window, Marsoud lay clutching his bleeding nose. Rashar was laughed to himself again and then hurried down the stairs after Tony. "I think you make a good Social Worker Ahmed," he shouted sarcastically.

Back on the motorway Tony was driving down the M1 like a mad man. The motorway sign pointed to Luton, it was the last collection and Tony was in a hurry.

Rashar sat there watching him in silence. Tony had not said a word since getting in the car. Rashar looked at the speedometer; it read a hundred and twenty and rising.

"Slow down you are going to kill us both," said Rashar although there was no urgency in his voice. "Stop at the next garage. I need some cigarettes and you need petrol."

At the next petrol station, Tony pulled in. A few minutes later Bradley and Angela pulled in at a different pump. Tony finished filling up and leaned into the window of the car. "We've got company," he said to Rashar.

Rashar looked across the garage forecourt at Angela filling her tank and the man sat in the passenger seat.

"I think maybe we have a little talk with them when we get to Luton. Find out who they are and what they want," said Rashar thoughtfully.

Tony went to pay for the petrol.

§§§

Having filled up, Angela pulled her car up for a tyre check. There was nothing wrong with the tyre pressure she just wanted to let their quarry get back on the motorway first. Bradley was smiling as he watched Tony go into the station to pay.

"This should be interesting," he said aloud.

§§§

Inside the station kiosk Tony asked the female cashier for sixty cigarettes and handed her his bank debit card for payment. The cashier swiped the card through the machine only for it to reject the transaction. The cashier looked embarrassed.

"Something wrong?" asked Tony.

"Sorry Sir, but the machine's rejecting your transaction," she said awkwardly.

Tony thought no more about it and gave her his credit card.

103

The machine gave the same response. "Must be some mistake," said Tony. "No matter, I'll get you some cash. One minute." He was trying not to look at the other car parked across the forecourt, but he could see from the corner of his eye the girl going through what clearly was the pretence of putting air in her tyres. A sudden thought then struck him like a bolt of lightening.

"Oh fuckin' shit," Tony said aloud.

"What's wrong with you?" asked Rashar.

"Have you got a bankers card?" he asked him quickly.

"Why?"

"Mine doesn't work."

Rashar gripped the hold-all. "So take some cash," said Rashar obviously.

"Never mind that!" Tony argued back. "There's a cash machine in the petrol station. Go and draw some money out."

"What for? Just take some cash," Rashar repeated.

"Call it an experiment," said Tony

Rashar reluctantly climbed out of the car, cantankerously grumbling under his breath in Arabic. "What's your problem? I sometimes think you are going paranoid, perhaps you need to see a doctor or something."

"Stop moaning and just do it," Tony snapped back. "I have a bad feeling I know who our two 'friends' are."

Rashar and Tony stood at the cash machine inside the station. It did not even return Rashar's card on the first request. He tried again with his credit card only to get the same results.

By this time the cashier was looking at them with an accusing face. "Can you gentlemen pay or not?" she shouted across the kiosk. The eyes of the people waiting to pay were watching them now.

"What's going on?" Rashar shouted at the cash machine. "That bloody thing has eaten my cards."

"Just give her the cash and let's go," said Tony quickly.

Before Rashar had even got out his wallet to pay the cashier Tony was in a strange hurry to get back to the car. Rashar could not help but notice Tony's sudden and dramatic change of mood. "What's with you?"

"Will ya' pay the woman and hurry up!!" Tony demanded in a

harsh whisper.

Rashar gave the cashier a bundle of notes and stood waiting for his change.

"Never mind that! Keep the change." Tony was pulling Rashar out the door by the arm and almost frog marching him back to the car.

"What's the sudden rush?" asked Rashar.

"Just get in the car and I'll tell ya," said Tony.

Rashar had not even closed the car door when Tony revved up the car and screeched off onto the motorway. Rashar was thrown back into his seat. "What's wrong with you?"

"Our two friends following us," said Tony putting his foot down. "I think they're either VAT or the Tax Office. And I bet you a thousand quid that our bank accounts are frozen."

Rashar was sceptical and almost sure that Tony was panicking. "But how would they know?"

Tony looked straight at Rashar. "Well who do you fuckin' think soft lad!" he shouted at him.

"Amu Sultan?"

"Exactly. Amu Sultan!" repeated Tony. He threw Rashar his mobile phone. "Here check, if your account's frozen they will have to tell you."

Two minutes later and Rashar was off the phone. "Bastard!!" he said aloud.

"Well?" said Tony.

"High Court in Leeds has frozen my accounts." Now it was Rashar's turn to panic. "What do we do? If they stop us now they get all this money, then we have fuck-all."

Rashar started to look behind him trying to spot the following car. "Get your foot down Ahmed! Loose them! I tell you, *Wallah*, I fuckin' kill Amu Sultan for this."

"Just calm down Rashar," said Tony. "If they've frozen your accounts, they've frozen mine. Half the money in that bag is all I've got as well and there is no way they are getting their hands on it."

"You had better pull off the motorway," said Rashar.

"Why do we need to do that?" asked Tony looking at him.

"If we are going to get arrested," Rashar started to confess slowly, then there is something in the boot we need to get rid of quickly."

Tony was suddenly glaring at him with gritted teeth. "Like what?"

Rashar sort of smiled. "Just a present from Sheik Yunis."

Still locked onto their target four cars behind, Angela Carrick could clearly see them up ahead. Bradley was on his mobile phone putting the final touches on the arrests that had been pre-planned for Luton. He came off the phone with a satisfied face. "Everything's ready down there. As soon as they make the final collection we'll be waiting for them outside."

"What are they up to?" said Angela looking ahead.

In front of them, Tony had suddenly put on his hazard lights and was pulling onto the hard shoulder. What she did not notice was that they had pulled off the motorway about fifty yards short of a slip road.

"What do I do?" Angela quickly asked Bradley.

"Must have a puncture or something," said Bradley. "Just go straight past them and pull onto the hard shoulder a few hundred yards up the road where they can't see us. We'll just have to wait and see."

The moment that Angela had passed the motorway slip road, Tony's car screeched back onto the motorway and down the slip road. Angela looked into her mirror with a desperate expression. "They've just taken the slip road," she shouted aloud.

"Bastard!!" Bradley cursed through his teeth. "Back up!! Back up!!"

Angela looked at the cars pouring down the motorway behind and knew that any attempt to reverse would be suicide, but Bradley was still screaming his instruction. Screeching her tyres in reverse, she did not get far before a police patrol car pulled onto the hard shoulder and put an abrupt halt to their plans.

Bradley closed his eyes and cursed. "Oh shit!! That's all we need."

"They knew we where following them," said Angela. "What do we do now?"

Bradley's voice was deflated. "Well we won't get what's in the bag, that's for sure. Just carry on to Luton and we'll wait there.

Who knows we might be in luck. They might just have the cheek enough to turn up."

"And if they don't?" asked Angela.

Bradley shrugged his shoulders. "We just nick them when they get back to Hull."

At that moment, an unhappy looking motorway police officer began tapping on the car window. Angela wound down her window. "Yes officer?"

§§§

Tony and Rashar had been off the motorway for almost an hour. It was getting dark now and they were on one of those endless narrow country lanes lined with forestry on both sides. Neither of them had a clue where they where, they were just driving. Up ahead Rashar spotted a sign pointing to dirt track road.

"Down here, go down here!" Rashar demanded.

Tony did as instructed. Half a mile down the track Tony suddenly slammed on the brakes, bringing the car to an abrupt halt. He got out of the car without looking at Rashar. But for what little light came from the headlights they were in complete darkness. Tony pulled open the boot and a small light clicked on. Drawing back the spare wheel cover, there it was staring at him. Sheik Yunis's so-called present. A shiny, new, folding stock Kalashnikov AK47 assault rifle and next to it three fully loaded magazine clips. And it was in his car. For a few seconds, Tony could do nothing but stare into the boot. He could see the silent silhouette of Rashar stood just to the side of him. Rashar knew he was angry; he was about to find out how angry.

"What can I say?" Rashar started awkwardly, almost trying to lighten his voice with a smile.

Tony picked up the rifle by the muzzle. "I take it this is yours?" he asked softly, almost too softly. Then before Rashar knew it, Tony held the rifle muzzle in both hands, and using it like a club launched it into Rashar's stomach. The ferocity of the blow sent Rashar reeling arse over tit onto the dirt track road. Rashar rolled over on the ground moaning in agony. Tony was standing over him still clutching the rifle.

"Alright!! Alright!" Rashar conceded through his moans. "I

shouldn't have put it in the car. But was there any need for that?" Rashar slowly climbed to his feet. He was aware that Tony was still glaring at him in the black silence. "Okay, so I'm sorry," said Rashar. "What else do you want me to do?"

Without warning, Tony had suddenly slapped in a magazine clip and was pointing the rifle at Rashar. He froze and tried to diffuse the situation with one of his friendly smiles. "Be careful with that thing," said Rashar nervously, "...you don't know what you are doing."

For an answer, Tony snapped back the bolt with the ease of a child handling a catapult. "How do you know I don't know what I'm doing?" said Tony fiercely.

"Please Ahmed," Rashar was pleading at him, "...be careful. Just put the thing down before it goes off."

Tony started to laugh. "What's up Rashar, scared?"

"When someone points a gun at you, wouldn't you be scared?" Rashar answered.

Tony pulled the trigger without warning. Muzzle flashes lit up the darkness and the noise rattled like thunder echoing for miles across the serene peace of the English countryside. Rashar instinctively fell to the ground and covered his head with his hands. In shock for a moment, he thought he was a dead man, as a running line of bullets raked into the ground missing him by inches. No more than a second later the forest was again in silence.

Rashar lay still on the ground for a time, fearful. Slowly at first, he took his hands away from his face. Tony was still at the back of the car, his silhouette illuminated by the glow from the light of the open boot, the gun still pointing at him. The two men stared at each in the dark silence. Rashar could hardly believe what had just happened. Very carefully, and without taking his eyes off Tony, Rashar gathered himself together and climbed back on his feet. His nostrils burned as the acrid smelling blue clouds of cordite and gunpowder lingered in the air. Rashar knew there was a message for him here, it was an Arab message and he knew he had pushed Tony too far. He also knew that Tony, the man who never used violence, had a darker side to him. From now on, it would be wise to be more cautious.

"You fuckin' crazy Yemeni bastard!!" he screamed at the top of his voice. "You could have killed me."

"Don't shout at me Rashar, this thing is still pointing at you," said Tony his voice trembling with fury. "This gun is pointing at a very precious part of your anatomy."

Rashar's eyes opened wide with horror.

"My old man once told me that Arabs like you have only two things on their mind. One is money and the other is in your pants where you keep your fuckin' brains Rashar." Tony drew in a long breath, trying to calm down his anger. "And the way I feel right now Rashar, I could real easy blow your fuckin' cock off and just walk away. So if I were you Rashar, I'd talk really nicely and quietly if you don't want to loose your three piece sweet," he said adding with a sour note, "...*achee Arabia* – my Arab brother."

"Your English jokes are not very funny Ahmed," said Rashar trying now to act cool, "...and for an Arab like me in very bad taste."

"You should now know me better then Rashar," Tony warned him, "...and be more careful in the future that you do not cross the lines."

"Ahmed, Ahmed I'm sorry," Rashar pleaded. "What more can I say? I made mistake."

"Don't take the piss with me Rashar, I'm warning you now, you've pushed your luck for days. You should be careful Rashar," said Tony his voice hardening. "You let appearances deceive you. You see Rashar, you should use your brain more with me because you really don't know anything about me. You think I am weak, but you should understand that most of the time I just cannot be fuckin' bothered. You should not get confused with me, don't mistake good manners for weakness."

Tony was looking at Rashar with an irrational expression that was unnerving him. "This is a nice rifle Rashar, the AK47 handles real well. Sheik Yunis has taste. Folding stock, Yemeni hand-made copy I assume, and with East German Bakelite magazine. Now you don't see that very often, and fully loaded with a standard thirty-one rounds of steel core .223 ammunition."

The two men stared at each other in the dark silence. Rashar got the message.

"You surprise me Ahmed," said Rashar nervously. Tony still had the gun pointing at him with his finger inside the trigger guard. "So what do we do now?"

"Rashar, don't take me for a fool," Tony said. "There are lots of things you don't know about me. I'm not just a nice guy. I have done bad things too Rashar." He paused for impact. "But only when pushed. *"Anta tefham!!* – You understand?"

"What can I say Ahmed? I made a mistake I'm sorry." Rashar was back on his feet now and threw up his hands at his own stupidity.

"Next time you want to get ten years in prison Rashar," said Tony. "Leave me out of it. Okay?"

"Okay," Rashar quickly agreed. "Now will you please stop pointing that thing at me before it goes off again."

To Rashar's utter relief, Tony snapped out the magazine and threw it into the night black forest in one direction throwing the rifle and two other magazines in another direction. "Now will you stop fuckin' around Rashar and maybe, just maybe we might get this sorted mess out." He slammed the boot shut and threw the car keys at Rashar.

"Here, you drive, I've got some phone calls to make," said Tony as he climbed in the passenger side.

After a couple of seconds, Rashar regained his composure. He shook his head and blew out a long breath, thankful he was still alive. For just a moment, he thought he had pushed Tony so far that he had flipped. In the future he would be a lot warier with Tony, not least because he knew how to handle the rifle. That surprised him, as did his placement of the warning shots. Rashar could not help but wonder how and where he had learned. He lit a cigarette, wiped away the nervous beads of sweat that glistened on his forehead and climbed into the driver's side. He stared at Tony in the darkness.

"*Wallah,*-by God, I am sorry," Rashar whispered.

Tony took the cigarette from Rashar's mouth and pulled a hard satisfying breath into his lungs. "Forget it, we all have to learn," said Tony quietly. "Just sometimes you are a hard pupil my friend."

Rashar half laughed and started the car. "So where to?"

For an answer Tony took out his mobile phone. He was ringing Amu Sultan's mobile, but the number went on answering service. He then dialled Amu Sultan's home number, that too went to an electronic voice answering machine. With a troubled expression, he slowly folded his phone.

"Amu Sultan's not answering his mobile or home phone," he told Rashar.

"The bastard," said Rashar. "*Wallah* – I swear by God - He has checked out."

"Maybe," said Tony cautiously, "We'll see. In the meantime, head for Luton."

"That's the last collection," Rashar started to argue, "If like you say these people are VAT and if they are going to arrest us anywhere, it will be there. I don't want to argue with you Ahmed but that sounds a little stupid to me."

"That takeaway has fourteen grand waiting for us," said Tony resolutely. "Half of that money is mine and I want it. We don't have to go to the takeaway for the money. We'll get them to deliver the money to us at Abbas's place the Cork and Bell Pub. We'll split the money. You take my car back to Hull. Then find out where Amu Sultan is. But whatever you do, don't let him know you're back. Just ring me."

"What will you do with your half? It's a lot of money to be carrying around," said Rashar. "You obviously don't trust me with it."

Tony smiled. "Then I'll keep all the money with me in Luton, while you go back to Hull."

After a moments thought, Rashar was smiling too. He trusted Tony about as much as Tony trusted him. "You are right I think, maybe your first plan is better after all."

"I thought you might," said Tony.

"Then what do you have in mind?" asked Rashar with anticipation.

"Let's get the money first," said Tony thoughtfully. "Then maybe I go talk with our two friends."

"About what?"

"If they are tax or VAT, then maybe we can make a deal," said Tony.

Rashar laughed at the cheek. "You are crazy Ahmed. What type of deal?"

"A business deal," Tony answered simply. "These people will want their money, more than they want us."

Pizza Wars

"You are crazy Ahmed," Rashar repeated. "We've been fiddling them for years. We must owe them millions. And I don't know about you, but I don't have that type of cash."

Tony looked at Rashar with confidence. "Let me worry about that."

EIGHT

With Tony it was always the little things that rang the alarm bells in his head. This whole thing had the smell of a set-up about it. Someone, and he was not quite sure who, was playing a game. It was a game he had seen being played out many times in the pizza business. It was not played with any great imagination or skill and the crude tools deployed were mainly always the threat of the tax office, the VAT office, and occasionally plain old blackmail.

The players of the game did not just restrict themselves to these two government agencies. Others included: the Dole Office, the Housing Benefit office, Trading Standards, Health and Safety, The local planning office, Immigration Services, Special Branch, and at one time someone from the R.S.P.C.A. looking into claims that live goats were being kept on the premises to be slaughtered and minced into donner kebab. Amu Sultan during his many years in the takeaway business had been reported and visited by them all.

Those who used these tools knew that a great deal of trouble and disruption could be caused if the right information was given to these agencies, especially revenue agencies like the hated VAT office. Amu Sultan had become accustomed to men in suits knocking on his doors and would describe it as part of the rich tapestry of life in the takeaway business. Most of the time it could be put down to a disgruntled customer who had been thrown out of one of the shops. The visiting agencies were more than aware that allegations usually had business motives behind them, but the name of the game was trouble — to cause as much as possible.

Of all the government agencies that could come banging on the door, the most feared knock in the takeaway business was Customs and Excise, known widely as the VAT man. It was not unknown for them to secretly sit outside a shop for weeks, in some innocently disguised decorator's van, and count the customers going in and out to see if it matched declared VAT returns.

If that was not enough, it became an even worse nightmare if they chose to do the same thing sitting inside the shop, with clipboard and pen in hand. They became like a permanent unwanted fixture on the other side of the counter. It was like being haunted by a vindictive spirit that could not be exercised. At least when they were watching outside the figures could be fiddled with on the delivery side.

Once you had the VAT doing counting inside the shop, they would monitor the telephone calls as well. The only way round this was to intermittently disconnect the phone to bring delivery orders down otherwise the estimated VAT bill would be crippling if not bankrupting. And if they caught the shop being tricky, the VAT estimate would immediately be inflated out of spite.

It was one part of Tony's many jobs within the partnership to deal with the difficult government people who came banging on the door. It was like watching an artist at work Amu Sultan would say. Tony had this innate ability to conjure up, seemingly out of nowhere, some political or psychological device to make these government demons disappear. The racial harassment card was always a nice easy one to play and was one of Tony's favourites. It rarely failed and usually had the government men in suits beating a hasty retreat before they had even got their foot in the door. Government officials do not like getting sucked into any sort of political situations that might compromise their well-paid jobs and pensioned positions.

Whilst games could be played with most government suits, it was the Customs and Excise that posed the real problems, especially if they got their teeth into your secret till rolls. Tony and Amu Sultan had worked out that the prefered way of dealing with them was not to deal with them all. Instead, they devised a plan to send them to sleep and to ensure that the one takeaway VAT registered in Amu Sultan's name paid more than enough VAT to keep them happy. You still had to be careful because you have to understand the mind set of the VAT. They were accustomed to fighting for their money from businesses like the ethnic takeaway industry, any sudden changes to the spots of the Leopard and they might get paranoid that other things were going on. Tony pointed out to Amu Sultan that the VAT might get suspicious if they were the one takeaway in Yorkshire not fiddling their VAT. Behaviour like that usually led the authorities into thoughts that if they are not fiddling the VAT the takeaway must be doing something else equally if not more dodgy like laundering drugs money, another nefarious activity of some takeaway owners.

In many ways you could not win, because as an Arab or Iranian you were stereotyped anyway, but it all went with the territory and you just had to be more clever than your enemies and ensure you planned ahead for all eventualities. That way you could anticipate the problems and have a solution ready and waiting for whatever was thrown at you. Like the VAT for instance, getting suspicious merely because you paid everything on time.

It is sometimes better not to disappoint those who have a low opinion of you anyway, so the solution to that one was easy, don't disappoint them. So Tony didn't. Every now and then he would wake up the VAT office and a few others and simply invite them to raid by giving them an anonymous tip-off that Amu Sultan's takeaway was fiddling them. Whilst this might seem drastic, there was method to the madness, especially were the VAT office was concerned. They would storm in, work the place over, and find absolutely bugger-all but well kept books balanced right down to last penny. It had worked so well last time that after the VAT office raided and had done their sums, they actually had to give Amu Sultan a VAT rebate of seven thousand pounds due to overpayment.

A scheme like this had the added advantage of totally devaluing any future anonymous tip-offs against Amu Sultan. It also made it very difficult to raid the takeaway again even if there was proof; they risked finding nothing again and risked claims of racial harassment and intimidation. The company had worked well like this for years, protected by an illusionary ring of politics and scam. It had helped the company grow well beyond what was declared on the books.

It was a source of great satisfaction that the most serious problem in recent years had been caused by a civil dispute and not a government agency. It was a dispute between one of the company's takeaways near York and a local fish and chip shop nearby. For years, the two businesses had got on famously, until the old English couple who owned the fish and chip shop decided to retire and sell. They sold to another English couple who went by the name of Harrison. They were only a few years younger than the previous owners and they had an interest in several other fish and chip outlets dotted around the region.

At first glance, they looked innocent enough, typical of the type that ran an English fish and chips. Both in their late fifties and both overweight from too many years of dipping into the chip frying basket, they looked no different from other respectable English couples you might see in businesses across the country. Add the fact that their customers and markets were different, there was little potential for problems between them.

Although the chip shop made some money, it was nothing compared to the earnings of the Company's pizza takeaway. It was later discovered that the new fish shop owners had purchased the premises with the intention of shutting down the takeaway in order to maximise their profits. It did not take long for Amu Sultan to work out that something was going on, as the usual men in suits started one by one banging on the door with this and that allegation.

Events took a turn for the worst with a particularly nasty incident involving the takeaway manager. As he was buying a packet of cigarettes from the local super market, in walked a man built like a brick shit house. He laid into the manager with a vengeance, and knocked him out stone cold in the middle of the super market. If that wasn't enough, the man then started shouting to all and sundry that the manager was a paedophile and accused him of molesting his young daughter in the takeaway. It was all a load of bullshit of course but people being people, they believe these things. In the world of the ordinary man and the silly bastard, there is no smoke without fire.

By this time Amu Sultan had had enough, it had now gone too far and was threatening to get out of control. At this rate, it would not be long before the police became involved and that usually led to other complications. Do what you need to do Amu Sultan told Tony, but get rid of the problem.

Information being power, Tony's first task was to set about finding out as much as he could about Mr and Mrs Harrison — to dig the dirt on them and play a few of his own tricks. This was Tony's domain and he treated his work with same enthusiasm as a great classical artist might create his own masterpiece. The difference of course being that the painting is an illusion created in oils for the world of reality, Tony painted his illusion in the oils of reality, not for the world but for the very few.

Experience told Tony that the local planning office was the place to start. A file full of complaints against them written by the Harrisons c/o the fish and chip shop, was enough to confirm that they were the culprits. By day two Tony already had a plan in his mind to get rid of the couple. Amu Sultan almost had a heart attack from laughter as he listened to what Tony had in store for them.

One thing was clear from the start; these people were professionals and were probably to the fish shop business what Amu Sultan was to takeaway. It would have been surprising if they had not had a track record of this sort of thing; they were dodgy people. Dodgy people always had skeletons in the closet and no matter where they were, Tony would find them.

One phone call to a relative who worked at Social Security in Hull and — bingo! Poor old Mr Harrison apparently had been on invalidity benefit for the past twenty years for chronic back pain and arthritis. He had been separated from his wife for more than twenty-one years, the story went on, and lived alone. This was not totally surprising since many a business has been set up with the unsuspecting help of a subsidy from the Social Security and Housing benefit office.

The fact that Mr Harrison had been taking the piss by claiming Social Security for the last twenty years did seem a little bit over the top; and by claiming to be living alone, Mr Harrison was enjoying the maximum Social Security benefit, with rent and rates paid, and a mobility allowance towards the cost of buying a car. Tony was sure that Mr Harrison's landlord would probably turn out to be his wife using her maiden name on the title deeds. Tony's investigations revealed that whatever car had been purchased with the mobility allowance had been traded in almost immediately after purchase for a transit van. They even had the cheek to park the van on double yellow lines in the town centre with a disability badge displayed on the windscreen.

Tony also noticed that every Thursday and Friday Mr Harrison was conspicuously absent from the fish and chip shop. It turned out that those two days were his golf days and he spent the time belting balls at a nearby sixteen-hole bunkered golf course that stretched for miles. Tony was sure there would be more fiddles to find, but he already had enough for his purposes.

The next step was the easiest, from the local registries Tony legally purchased the Harrison's' marriage and birth certificates and the title details to all the properties he knew they owned. He was somewhat surprised to find most of the title deeds were in his wife's name, an indication that Mr Harrison must have trusted her. Therein would lay their downfall.

What is not commonly known, is that in England it is possible for two people to get divorced without them even knowing about it. This was to be the essence of Tony's plan. It was a simple matter for Tony to get the application forms for the divorce and simply fill in both party's statements on their behalf. Just so long as the grounds for divorce were kept mutual and simple, such as the irretrievable breakdown of marriage, there would be little to be queried. Any post from the divorce courts was sent to an address set up by Tony.

Next, he waited the few months for the first court decree to be sent back. Once the court documents came through the post, the second and final part of Tony's plan was put into action. Making sure that Mr Harrison was out of the way enjoying a good day's golf, Tony acquired the well paid services of a buxom young girl from Hull and a small baby which she borrowed from her sister.

With legal documents in her hand and carrying the small child, the young girl stormed into the Harrison's chip shop in the full throws of a busy dinner hour. Tony wanted to pay the Harrisons back, in kind, for the supermarket incident. He sat watching outside in the car as the young girl shouted across the chip counter about her long affair with Mr Harrison and how the baby in her arms was their love child. For the grand finale, the girl threw the divorce papers at Mrs Harrison just to show her that her husband planned to divorce her so they could marry. She then stormed out of the shop with crocodile tears pouring down her face. It was a performance second-to-none and she deserved an Oscar for it.

The watching eyes of the fish shop queue stared in silence at Mrs Harrison, as she read the divorce papers thrown at her by the young girl. No more than ten minutes later Tony spotted Mr Harrison parking his car and then making his way to the fish shop, whistling merrily as he went; it must have been a good day on the golf course.

Tony could not help himself; he wanted to see this close up. Hopping out of his car, he quickly went to buy some chips before the arrival of an oblivious Mr Harrison. Tony could see Mrs Harrison's face was set as she paced on the other side of counter waiting for her beloved. He had hardly got through the door when the first HP sauce bottle, skillfully thrown by his wife, hit him on the head without smashing. The second, although missing Mr Harrison, did smash — into the shop wall, splattering glass and sauce all over the fish shop walls and floor. What followed next was a one way slagging match as Mrs Harrison, now on the other side of counter, told her husband what she was going to do with him. Tony stood there watching the furore quietly eating his chips and enjoying every minute of it. Especially when Mrs Harrison floored her husband with a stiff right hand to the chin followed by smooth crafty kick to the ball bag as he hit the floor.

"And what are you staring at?!!" Mrs Harrison screamed at Tony.

"Nothing love," he answered innocently. "Have you got any vinegar?"

As she pulled on her coat and stormed out the fish shop, Mrs Harrison stopped outside to make one last affectionate gesture toward her husband, by hurling a nearby litter bin straight through the main window. That was the last Tony saw of her.

Pizza Wars

Nonchalantly eating his chips, Tony stood over the bewildered Mr Harrison as he lay groaning on the fish shop floor clutching his ball bag in agony, covered in red sauce.

"What the hell was all that about?" Mr Harrison groaned aloud.

Tony shook his head with disapproval. "You want to get up off that cold floor Mr Harrison," said Tony with a subtle hint of smug satisfaction. "It won't do your arthritis much good."

Mr Harrison was suddenly looking up at Tony towering over him holding his bag of chips. "Who the fuck are you?"

By the next day the fish shop was closed and a week later it was up for sale. Amu Sultan bought it at a knock down price and rented it out. Tony never did get round to reporting Mr Harrison for fiddling the Social Security and by the time he remembered he couldn't be bothered. He did what was necessary, the Harrisons were gone and that was all that mattered. It was a pointless exercise and a waste of ammunition to empty the gun for the sake of it, and who knows they might have been back sometime in the future, the ammunition might come in handy.

Takeaway is a bad business Amu Sultan used to say. About that Tony could not have agreed more, it was a shit business full of shit people. For any business, dealing direct with the public can be hard at any time. In the takeaway business you have two more of the worst aspects of human nature to tolerate, drink and racism. It can be a potentially explosive mixture and requires to be managed with great skill to avoid unwanted problems. Now just as Tony had been quietly contemplating jumping ship, this business with Amu Sultan had come out of the blue. Just another couple of months and he would have been out. This was how it had always been, one thing after another, only this time Tony's intuition told him that what was going on now was something different. He had a feeling that this time it was a big game with high stakes. To have a personal bank account frozen meant that whichever agency meant serious business and must have provided a judge with a powerful and plausible argument to do so.

Tony knew the Arab and Iranian mentality well enough to know that to work out the logic of what was going on, he had to take what he was being led to believe and reverse it. They think they are the masters of business sub defuse and deception, Tony thought to himself, but they are inept, obvious, ham fisted, and predictable. Slowly but surely, he was becaming aware of the emerging game in which he was being used as a pawn. Tony had a feeling he knew who the players were and why they had started the game.

NINE

In Luton town centre the usual throng of drunks and general rowdies spilled out of clubs and late night bars and onto the street after another heavy session giving promise of the approaching weekend. The police were out in force in their now familiar illuminated yellow jackets that had come to symbolise the violence that stalked the city streets. Dotted here and there, a small battalion of riot vans waited in reserve for the struggling human cargo that would be thrown into the back and transported to the local nick to sober up. It was nothing extraordinary, just what had come to be the never ending routine in these new times of violence, drink and more drink, until you either fell over or became violent.

It was the busiest time of the night for Bianco's Pizzeria located slap-bang in the middle of town in between night clubs and taxi ranks. The place was full and despite those now bringing their consumed purchases back up and splattering it all over the pavement, no one appeared deterred to try the same.

Across the street Bradley and Angela sat in the car watching the spectacle being played out in front of them. Bradley shook his head and sighed as if grieving a past life of errors. "Just look at them," he complained with contempt that bordered on hatred. "I sometimes wonder what the fuck this country is coming to. You didn't see that in my day, girls with skirts up to their arses, men pissing in the street. There's just no standards anymore. The country's just one big fuckin' brothel."

Angela Carrick was just not in the mood for discussing the wrongs of the world put right. She was tired, fed up and knew by now that Tony and Rashar had guessed the game and had decided not to play. She looked at her watch. It was almost half past two in the morning and three undercover Customs and Excise units, together with a couple of unmarked local police cars, had been covering the back and the front of the takeaway for almost three hours. Bradley knew what she was thinking and picked up his radio.

"All units. Anything?"

One by one each watching unit reported in with the same monotonous message, "Nothing this end,"..."Nothing this end..."

Bradley groaned out loud and looked at Angela. "Alright," he finally conceded,"...let's call it a day. Looks like we won't get our hands on that hold-all after all. We'll just have to snatch the bastards in Hull."

§§§

The drunken racial abuse was coming thick and fast across the counter as the never ending customer demands were shouted at Jalal Al Hashemi the Syrian manger manning the till for the rush hour. The takeaway chefs were running around like headless chickens and babbling their anger at customers, in a tongue they could not understand.

"Hey Abdul!!" yet another customer shouted at him, like a million before. "Do you speak English Abdul?"

Jalal had done the job for long enough to know that you took their money as quickly as possible, spit on their food while they were not looking and bade them a smiling, 'very good night you English bastard.' But just sometimes he could not resist a clever reply. "Yes, I speak English," he snapped back at him, "...and Arabic, French and German. How many languages do you speak?"

Why Jalal allowed himself to be tempted into responding he did not know because it always led to a scene in the shop that disrupted the service and slowed getting rid of them.

"Fuckin' clever you are ya black bastard!!" came the usual

slurred reply.

Jalal was in his stride now and ready to launch the wooden chair leg he kept hidden near the counter at the customer's head. "Look, I have people waiting," he shouted back him. "If you don't want food, just fuck off or I call the police."

Behind him, the telephone was ringing off the hook. "Take the call," Jalal snapped angrily at a loafing English delivery driver and then turned back to the raging customer. But before another word of abuse could leave the customer's lips an eagle police officer outside was pushing his way to the front with two burly colleagues. The man was dragged outside, arrested, and thrown in a riot van. The officer was a regular customer after hours and Jalal had kept on the right side of all the local police by giving them a big discount on food. It was a wise move and kept them on his side. Jalal gave the Officer a thumbs up and turned to another customer. Before he could take the order, the delivery driver was holding the phone at him.

"It's for you," the driver told Jalal.

"Can't you see I'm busy," retorted Jalal. "Tell them to call back."

"It's someone called Ahmed," the driver persisted.

"Take over," Jalal instructed one of the chefs and went to answer the phone.

"*Salem alicome achee* – welcome my brother," said Jalal with a genuine smile. "It is a large amount of money, almost twenty-six thousand this month," said Jalal into the phone. "I cannot entrust a delivery driver with that.....Look, if it is that important I will bring it myself. Where are you? ......Yes, I know it. The Cork and Bell is Ghazzani the Iranian's place....I'll finish up here. Give me an hour, Okay?....*Ma salem*." Jalal replaced the receiver.

The Cork and Bell pub was not any ordinary Public House. For a start, the Landlord was an Iranian called Hosni Ghazzani, and he and Tony had been friends since the first time that Tony had done the collecting for Amu Farida. Of his fifty years, Honsi had been in England thirty-five of them. Although still a fluent Farsi and Arabic speaker, Honsi had been in England so long he was more English than Iranian and had a better Luton accent than the locals who regarded him as one of their own.

From Indians, Pakistanis, Arabs, Iranians and Afro

Caribbeans, they came for miles. After hours when most of the usual customers had gone home, it became a magnet for all those in the ethnic community who kept late hours. It was what is commonly known in the Englishman's parlance as a 'lock in', but only for the chosen few.

When the place was full it had more nationalities drinking the night away than the United Nations. They came for a late drink, a game of pool, to chill out, and some to have a flutter in one of the many card games that took place at a few of the tables. No serious gambling, just a bit of fun to while away a few relaxing hours. Others sat around in the smoke filled bar chatting over the day's and night's events in their own tongue, creating an atmosphere that was almost claustrophobic and alien in such an English setting.

In the background the roll-down satellite television screen was tuned in to the Arabic or Iranian entertainment channel, its singers or commentators competing to be heard over the chatter. You could always tell when the news was on, as angry voices began to rise in passionate response to graphic pictures being shown in the news report. In fact, you could even guess who was being shown on the screen if those watching were hissing and booing. That was always reserved for the ruling Saudi or Kuwaiti families, they were not the most popular people amongst Arab and Iranian expatriate customers.

Tony came off the phone and went back to his pint of beer at a nearby table were Rashar was engrossed in a game of Black Jack with several others. He liked to think of himself as a bit of a card shark but the truth was that most of those around the table let him win because he had such a bad temper if he lost.

Rashar played his cards with a big clever smile and proudly scooped the small pot of a few pounds to his side of the table and staked it into neat columns as though they were gambling chips. The others silently threw in their hands and congratulated him on what a fine player he was and decided to call it a night on the cards.

Rashar sat counting his ill-gotten gains with grin. "What about you Ahmed? Do you want a game?"

Tony swilled down his pint for an answer and got up to go to the bar. "No thanks Rashar, you're too good for me," he said with a note of sarcasm that went straight over Rashar's head. "You want another drink?"

"Same again," said Rashar. "What's Jalal say?"

"He's bringing the money himself," said Tony.

"As soon as we split it, then I go back to Hull?" asked Rashar rechecking the plans.

"Just find out where Amu Sultan is and no more," Tony said again.

"And what are you going to do here?" asked Rashar.

Tony voice was suddenly animated and artificial. "Amu Sultan has to be sorted out," he said deliberately and added cryptically, "I have to see some people."

Rashar was looking at Tony with a hard smile. "We understand each other then Ahmed?" said Rashar in a low whisper.

"You are right Rashar," said Tony. "He has betrayed our loyalty and our friendship."

Rashar agreed with a slow nod of the head. "You understand things now."

"I'll get the drinks," Tony answered and went to the bar.

Rashar was smiling to himself. The smile did not go unnoticed by Tony who had briefly glanced back.

"Same again?" asked Ghazzani. "You're friend Rashar is trouble," said Ghazzani in a low voice, "The customers don't like him coming in and neither do I."

"He's not my friend," said Tony, "And I don't like him either."

"Ahh, it's business then," said Ghazzani.

Tony nodded, then leaned over as Ghazzani was pulling his pint and whispered, "I need somebody trustworthy to do a job for me. Do you know anybody like that? I will pay him very well."

Ghazzani put Tony's drink onto the bar and took the money. "I know just the man," said Ghazzani.

Tony put his finger over his mouth in a gesture of silence. "I'll speak to you later," he said in a low voice and with that he lifted the drinks and went back to the table to join Rashar. He was almost in his seat when four Arab looking men entered the pub and instantly changed the atmosphere. The unwelcoming eyes of the pub were suddenly on them though the men did no more than go to the bar and order a drink. Tony could see an uncomfortable expression growing on Ghazzani's face behind the bar.

"Throw them out," an accented voice shouted at Ghazzani.

"What's going on?" Tony asked a nearby Arab called Marzin.

"Asylum seekers," answered Marzin. "They give us all a bad name."

Tony shook his head with an irony that was totally lost on those around the table. "They look like Arabs," said Tony.

"Who cares," answered Marzin with an indifferent shrug of the shoulders. "Arabs, Iranians — since these people came, life has become difficult for all of us."

Anger was suddenly in Tony's voice. "So what are you? Are you special or something?" he snapped at Marzin.

Marzin was taken aback. "What do you mean?" he asked defensively.

"Do you have a fuckin' invitation from the Queen to be in this country or something?"

Marzin stared at Tony with an open mouth and what was trying to come out escaped in the language of stutter and gibberish. "But…but…..errr……" He was looking at the others round the table for support that did not come. Most of them felt the same way Marzin did but shied away from taking Tony on, because they knew in their hearts that he was right.

Tony snarled with contempt at the men around the table who sat silently staring at him and then got up and headed towards the bar.

"What's wrong with your friend?" Marzin asked Rashar.

Rashar carried on playing cards and shrugged his shoulders. "I have to apologise for Ahmed," he explained quietly, "…he is English."

The men round the table all nodded to themselves with sudden understanding.

"Ahhh, English," went a collective groan; that explained everything.

After being refused service, the four men headed toward the door to leave. Tony called after them. "Where are you going?"

The men turned around and expecting trouble one of them put up his hands in a sign of surrender. "Look alright," he said to Tony with a heavy Arab accent, "…we are going. We don't want any trouble."

"Neither do I," Tony answered them in Arabic. "I just thought I might buy you all a drink."

Surprised for a few moments, the four men looked at each other.

"I don't think your friends want us here," said the Arab.

"Don't worry about them," Tony said with a grin. "They are just frightened of you."

A curious expression crossed the Arab's face. "But why?" he asked in a low voice.

"Who knows, maybe you remind them of themselves," said Tony cryptically.

"Your Arabic is good," said the Arab gesturing to Tony's blonde hair. "Are you Circassian?"

Tony shook his head and then spoke in English. "No, my mother is English she is the one who has the blond hair. My father is Yemeni."

The Arab then shook his hand and introduced himself. "I am Adnan." He then introduced the other three. They were asylum seekers from Southern Iraq.

Much to Ghazzani's dismay, Tony took them back to the bar and held out a twenty pound note as though pointing an accusing finger. Ghazzani shrunk with embarrassment and not a little shame.

"It's not me," he protested to Tony in low voice, "it's the customers, they just don't like them."

"Don't worry about it. I know that," said Tony, "In business you have to do these things."

Each of the men got their drink.

"I am going back to the table over there," said Tony to the four Arabs. "I have some business to finish. No one will bother you."

Around the tables the chattering of the men was suddenly quelled as they sat listening and watching the news. Tony gently picked up his drink at the table where Rashar was playing cards and slipped silently into his chair. The eyes of all in the pub were locked onto the screen as they took in more bad news and pictures coming in from the Middle-East.

"Madjid was right about you Ahmed," Rashar whispered under his breath as he watched the television.

"What do you mean?" Tony asked back.

Pizza Wars

"If you want to be a holy man, you should go to Mecca," said Rashar with a grin.

Tony raised his glass at him sarcastically and laughed, "Cheers."

Even though there were some who didn't understand one word of the Arabic news, the pictures on the screen spoke for themselves — gunfire, missiles, tanks, death and then the unidentified faces of widows, orphans and old men crying in their despair. Who really knew who haunted the screen with the torment of spirits forsaken by God? Maybe they were Jews, maybe they were Arabs — it didn't matter since each had suffered equally in this never-ending conflict. So the pictures went on, and on, and the angry defiant voice of news reporter went on, and on and on.

Each dramatic sentence spoken, the words seemed scraped from the bowels of the reporter's brain, as if the conflict had gone on so long that it was necessary to find innovative phrases to describe the same old ways to die. This was the slick new westernised look, a breed of Arab news reporting for the new millennium. It was both fascinating and confusing the masses across the impoverished Arab world. It was a window to another world, an eye that saw everything and magnified the disparity. The incredible riches of wealth and decadence spread before the hungry and repressed in a mocking bravado of indifference.

Tony could not help but look into the faces of those watching; one by one he was searching deep into their expressions as though trying to read their minds and the thoughts going through them. Some watched without emotion, some with tears, some with boiling anger, some with indifference and some not at all. Then suddenly the horror was gone, as sexy Arabic young things danced across the screen in a grotesque caricatured enactment of an American commercial. As if to add to this unintentional satire, a deep textured Arabic voice burst forth to extol the refreshing virtues of American Coca-Cola. So completed the glossy illusion of a poor man's CNN satellite news channel.

"The Arab leaders are a disgrace," cursed Shahab, an Arab taxi driver who was playing cards with Rashar.

"They are nothing but women," piped up Marzin.

From the bar, Ghazzani swiftly switched the channel to quickly change the subject; the sights and sounds of an Arab music channel immediately filled the pub. Politics and the news depressed him and he felt a political discussion coming on; that was always the best way to empty a pub.

"We all have problems," said Ghazzani aloud. "Until they sort it out for themselves there will never be peace."

"What is there to sort out?" Shahab answered him in English. "The land belongs to Palestinians. The Jews stole it in 1948 with tricks and games."

Ghazzani picked up his own drink from behind the bar and went to join them at the table.

"You make everything sound so simple," he said to Shahab as he sat down.

"I know what is right and what is wrong," Shahab answered him. "Those questions are simple ones."

Rashar suddenly started to laugh as he played his cards.

"And what is so funny?" Ghazzani quizzed him.

"My friend Ahmed here is the great politician," he answered with a smile, "you should ask him such a question. He knows these things."

"So what do you say Ahmed?" Marzin asked him.

Tony held up his hands with a silent smile which suggested that he did not want to get drawn into the argument. "I say," he said gulping down the shallow remains of his pint and slamming down his empty glass, "...it's your round Rashar!"

They all laughed and Ghazzani called to one of his bar staff for another round of drinks. "On the house," he announced with a smile.

"Come on Ahmed," Rashar persisted, "you are avoiding the subject. Tell us what you think."

Tony knew what Rashar was trying to do. Rashar already knew his views and knew they would go down like a lead balloon in a room full of native Arabs. And Tony was almost, but not quite, drunk. "I don't want to bore our good friends here with politics."

"Not at all," said Marzin, "I would be interested to hear your views."

More drinks were brought to the table. "Come on Ahmed," said Rashar trying to goad him, "...don't be shy." Then he said sarcastically to all at the table, "Ahmed here is very clever with the politics. Everyone in Hull seeks his advice because he knows the ways of the English."

Tony laughed with a drunken smile. "Rashar is too generous. He flatters me."

"Come Ahmed," Shahab joined in, "…tell us what you think."

"What does it matter what I think," said Tony, "…it won't change anything."

"Because we are interested," Shahab answered. "Surely as an Arab you have a view about Palestine?"

"I am only half Arab," said Tony swallowing more beer. "Just like Ghazzani says, these things are complicated."

"What is complicated about stealing something that does not belong to you?" Marzin asked matter-of-factly. "That is wrong. What has happened to the Palestinians is a great injustice and the world ignores it. Why? Can you answer me that?"

Tony sighed. "You should understand my friend, that perhaps what you say might be true and it might not."

"It is true," Shahab snapped back. "History always speaks the truth."

"All the words you use," said Tony, "Truth, justice, right and wrong. All these words only exist in the world of ordinary people. It is politics that rules the world, and in that world all those words do not exist. There is only one driving force in politics, and that is what is in your interests. Truth, justice, right and wrong don't go into the equation."

"What Ahmed says is right," Ghazzani agreed.

"What is going on in Palestine is about change," said Tony. "The world changes all the time. History is littered with injustice to a thousand nations. If you wish to compare anything in history to what has happened to Palestinians, then look at the American Indian. They lost everything to the white European settler."

"How are the American Indians like the Palestinians?" asked Marzin intently.

"Because both the American Indian and the Palestinian are both natives," Tony argued back. "In the world of the future there is no room for natives anymore. The strong nations will always take what they have, because that is the nature of men."

Marzin glared at Tony. "But that is not right," he announced in a loud voice.

Tony shook his head with exasperation. "Then tell me," said Tony simply, "What you mean by 'right'?"

Marzin pointed vehemently at himself. "I know what is right Ahmed! It is you who are getting confused, because your mind is too complicated like all politicians. "Right, is something all good men know in their heart."

Tony smiled. "You are almost correct Marzin, but in politics 'right' is something measured in the head, not the heart. Man is designed to go forward and conquer. In the end that is what always defines what is right, even if in the minds of ordinary men it is wrong. Just like the Palestinians, the American Indians fought against the change that had been forced upon them. In the end they knew they could not win. A great Indian chief called Chief Joseph fought the American cavalry to a standstill, but still the white European kept coming. It was the wind of change.

Eventually the American Buffalo soldiers defeated Chief Joseph and he retreated into Canada. He then said some wise words to the Indian nation, he said 'Fighting the white man, is like fighting the wind, rain and the snow.' What Chief Joseph was talking about was change, the coming of change was as natural as the wind, rain and snow. He then spoke these words, and these were great words, 'I will fight no more forever.' That is what 'right' is Marzin, it is about recognising change."

"What are you saying?" asked Marzin.

"Just as when the white man came to America change was inevitable maybe," continued Tony, "…the return of the Jews brings the same inevitable change to the Arab world."

"Then maybe we don't want that change," said an emphatic Marzin.

Tony shook his and laughed with the irony. "And who do you speak for when you sit comfortably in the world of the English in preference to the land where you born? This change you have chosen for yourself you would deny to others? And yet they seek to have what you have Marzin. In their hundred of thousands the impoverished of the corrupt Arab world risk their lives to come to the West."

"It does not matter what you say," Shahab said in a rising voice. "All your clever words make no difference. Too much blood has been spilled in the Holy Land for peace. The Palestinians will not give up their fight like your Chief Joseph. The Palestinians and the American Indian are totally different peoples."

"So your war goes on then. Is that your answer?" said Tony flatly. "And all the ideas that can free the Arab world you keep locked in a box called Israel? That is the stupidity of the Arab leaders, they do the work of the Zionists for them and ensure that all Jews stay in the box and are forced to fight. The Zionists know their own people, and the box is not designed to keep the Arabs out, but the Jews in. The Arab leaders and the Zionists could not be better friends, they do well the work of each other. The Arab leaders don't want the Jews in their country, and the Zionists don't either. The Arab regimes fear the Jews not because of their military power, but because they bring new and fresh ideas that will make them redundant.

They fear change because they won't be able to treat their own people like shit anymore and live off the fat of the land. Men like Saddam Hussein speak easy words of liberating Palestine, and the ordinary Palestinian love him for that. Saddam Hussein has been the greatest ally of Israel. For years, he has distracted attention from the real problem. He, more than any, has played with the minds of the Palestinian people with empty words. Words are easy for politicians; they cost absolutely nothing. Never judge a man by great speeches. The greater the speech, the greater is the liar. Judge a man by his actions."

"Ahmed is right bout the American Indian," said Ghazzani thoughtfully. "I was brought up in the West and I never thought about it before, but you think about it. Where before have we heard of the Army protecting settlers? The history of America is being replayed in Palestine."

"Everything that has happened to the Palestinians," said Tony, "…can be paralleled to what happened to the American Indian. And it is not done without coincidence. Both the ordinary Jew and Palestinian in the street are no more than political pawns in a dark political game. Clever politicians will keep the natives talking with empty promises while, just like in the Americas, the settlements get bigger and consolidate."

"But the Americans are working for Palestinian state," said Shahab. "This they have promised."

"The word of a rich man given to a poor man is worthless," said Tony with a wry smile, "...even less so the word of a politician given to a native."

"What you say is the truth about the words of rich men and politicians. But what you say about Palestine, this is wrong. This will not happen in Palestine," said Marzin sceptically. "Unlike your Chief Joseph the Palestinians Arabs will not be defeated."

"I agree," said Tony. "But also the Israelis cannot and will not lose. Also you should not describe the Palestinians as Arabs. They are above that now. The Palestinians are no longer Arabs. They have shown their sword and have done alone what the hollow promises of the corrupt Arab leadership could not." Tony was looking them all.

"I don't understand what you mean," said Marzin.

"In six days Israel crushed three Arab armies in 1967. For the past three years the Palestinians standing alone have almost fought Israel to stalemate. Bomb for bomb, bullet for bullet. It is now time stop and for the people to talk as equals. The Palestinians have proved their metal to the whole world. If this madness is allowed to carry on, both sides will lose in a disaster the like of which history has never seen before. Israel was forged on the anvil of conflict and now Israel forges for itself its most dangerous enemy on that same anvil. Israel should beware the lessons of its own creation do not bring about its own destruction. For then we will all lose."

"So what is your answer then?" Rashar asked with a clever smile.

"History shows us that men like children, do not learn from past lessons of history. The conflict will carry on, and the West will play their games. Offering fool's gold to the natives just like they offered fools gold to the American natives," said Tony, "And now that the Palestinians have found death more attractive than life, when the weapon is given to them, and it will be, they will use it."

"You really believe that?" asked Ghazzani with a deep breath.

"Yes," said Tony emphatically. "If I told you what I really believed when I look at the conflict in Palestine, you would think me crazy. In the shadows there is a great game being played by evil men on both sides. It is a game not about Israeli, Arab,

Moslem and Jew, these are no more than tools evil men use to keep them divided. Until ordinary men start to open their minds and ask 'why?' they will always be the ones who have to pay the ultimate price."

The men round the table were now intrigued by Tony's words, captured by his understanding. Rashar was smiling to himself as he watched Tony work his magic on them in the same way he had on him.

"Then tell us what you see?" asked Shahab in a searching breath.

"There is something missing from the Israel that has yet to return," said Tony cryptically.

"And what is that?" asked Marzin.

Tony shook his head. "It is not for me to tell you. Some things you have to see for yourself to see through the charade."

Marzin was suddenly seething, "Ahh, you speak in riddles Ahmed."

"No," Rashar interrupted flatly, "…Ahmed understands the truth, in a way that other men do not."

"Politicians are clever," Tony answered, "because they hide the truth from their people, because they would not understand it and may fear it. The truth that I know is only for me; you would not understand it or why I believe it for the same reason that ordinary men are not told the truth."

"Then you will not tell us?" enquired Marzin.

Ghazzani tried to laugh. "I don't think I want know." It may have been a joke to lighten the moment, but Ghazzani knew about Tony and why people turned to him for advice. He did possess a gift for seeing the invisible.

"So the war will go on then, you think?" Shahab asked him.

"What else is there?" said Tony. "When desperate men find God, they become the most dangerous men in the world."

"But the West says that the Palestinians should have a state," said Marzin. "Are they lying?"

"No, they probably believe what they are saying," said Tony. "But the Israelis know one thing. That an independent Palestinian state is the first nail in the coffin of the State of Israel. The clever Israeli politicians know that Israel is like a fragile graft of skin. Such an artificial graft causes a dangerous wound that needs to heal. Disturb that wound and what the graft covers may be reclaimed by what lies beneath."

"Then America is lying to the Palestinians?"

"Whether you like it or not, America is a great nation," said Tony. "The world would be a more dangerous place without it. But America has its own agenda in all things. Let me ask you all a question." Tony paused and looked around the table. "There is one thing that America never neglects," Tony started to explain, "...come war, come recession, come whatever." Tony paused again and saw the confusion on their faces. "What do you think that is?" Tony waited for the answer he knew would not come. "Think about the question, understand what I am trying to tell you and don't feel insulted by what I am going to say. The Arab has to take out his Arab brain and try to understand the future in a western way. Then you will see things for what they are."

Shahab laughed. "You have a nice way of insulting us. So tell us the answer to this mysterious question."

Tony threw out his hands in an obvious gesture. "It's the space programme. America knows that is where man's destiny lies. In one hundred, two hundred or a thousand years are the Arabs and Jews, the Catholics and Protestants still going to be fighting each other over a religious belief or a piece of dusty land when men are walking on the stars?

America goes forward, always pushing the boundaries of technology, always challenging and asking questions. This conflict in the Holy Land not only divides the Arab world, but also hinders the economic development of the region. It disrupts development, and that works to the West's advantage, because there is one less competitor in the market. The rules of international economics are really no different to the economics of a takeaway. Stifle your competitor or kill it. And the West does this by the using the oldest game in the political book— divide and rule. For many years I worked in the world of the ordinary Englishman. This is how they rule them. When I saw the lie and told them, as ordinary men they did not understand what I was saying."

Ghazzani pursed his lips and gave a little laugh "It makes sense if you think about. We are all businessmen here, and we all do the same thing. No one wants competition."

Shahab's expression was thoughtful. "Mmm, that is interesting. You might be right. Maybe this is the West's hidden agenda. To keep us poor."

"The Moslem world is one of the richest in natural resources," said Honsi, "...but the corrupt governments squander it on Western toys for themselves."

A foxy smile spread across Tony's face. "The oil rich Arabs remind of the poor Englishman who wins the lottery. Suddenly he is surrounded by smiling men in slick suits all trying to take his riches and sell him things that he does not need. Just like the poor Englishman, he is flattered to be important, until the money is gone, and then so are the men in suits. That is how the West views the rich Arabs, just like the poor English lottery winner. Deep down a rich man will always despise a poor man who suddenly becomes rich without effort."

"And the Gulf Arabs have their lottery ticket in oil," said Honsi.

"Exactly," said Tony simply and then added with a smile to Ghazzani, "And let's not forget the Iranians. All of them, Arabs and Iranians have to wake up before it's too late and they get left behind. They all have to go west and follow them; that's where the future is. They can challenge America, not with guns or violence, but with commerce and competition, ideas and innovation. That is man's destiny. And as for all the Bin Ladens, Saddam Husseins, and Ariel Sharons in the world, they are little more than a distraction. They will always pull men in the opposite direction and take them backward. America will only go in one direction — forward. I am not saying America is perfect, but as a leader it is the best we've got. Some may say it is evil, but of all the nations which are evil, America is the least of all I think."

"America is selfish and greedy," snapped Marzin. "It does nothing but take from the weak."

"Of course it does," said Tony matter-of-factly. "But so do most men. And like most men, America will do what is in the interest of America. There are good and bad in all nations. But there are more good people than bad, otherwise civilisation would collapse and anarchy would reign."

"Then what of the fire that burns in the Holy Land?" asked

Shahab. "Where does America stand now?"

Tony lowered his head sighed. "Who knows, but I think if I were the Israelis I would worry that perhaps behind closed doors the Americans are adding up the cost of supporting Israel now that Bin Laden has reached them. America will not take many hits before the price of supporting Israel gets too costly. And that's why now the Americans talk about an Independent Palestinian state. The political status quo that has worked so well for The Americans since 1948 does not work anymore, and there is now a big price to pay. So they will try and change the structure, and if that means gambling with the security of the Israeli state, they will do it."

Marzin and Shahab shook their heads in disgust. "So after so many people are dead, America will sell out Israel to save its own neck."

"You surprise me my friends," said Tony with a cynical smile. "Don't you know what the currency of politics is? It is the blood of ordinary people. Ordinary people don't count in the political equations of clever men. The ordinary English have a word for it. They call themselves 'cannon fodder.' It is what serves your own vital interests. That is what counts."

Rashar suddenly joined the argument. "Then if what you say is true Ahmed and America changes it's policies towards the Arabs, you can put all this down to one man," he announced with a smile.

"And who would that be?" Ghazzani asked him.

"Osama Bin Laden, who else?" said Rashar.

Tony lowered his eyes with a soft smile. He would not have admitted it aloud, but Rashar was right. He was the most dangerous foe of all, because he understood his enemy. He understood what made the West tick – their symbolism, their media, their banking – and used all these things against them. He knew where to find the weaknesses of his enemy. History is full of men like Bin Laden. It is also full of their defeats and of the carnage and misery they eventually leave behind them. Until men learn that it is their injustice that produces such men, the world will struggle on from one disaster to another. But for now, the Arab people had someone who did not just talk, but delivered. And dead or alive, he was the hero of the repressed and impoverished all over the Islamic world.

It was not long before drink made its mark and the conversation descended into an incomprehensible language in both Arabic and English. As with all such male gatherings, it was not long before serious conversation gave way to jokes and the rise of laughter, as each struggled to tell the funniest jokes they could remember.

Shahab started giggling to himself. "Alright, alright," he said trying to quell his laughter, "...I've got one. How do you tell the difference between an Arab and an Iranian?"

"How?" Ghazzani asked.

"When you invite them into your house," started Shahab, "...the Iranian will leave his donkey outside." Again the belly laughs went round the table.

"I've got one," said Tony.

"General Tommy Franks is in Afghanistan leading the US marines into battle, but before the battle he gives his men a big stirring speech." Tony takes off in an American accent. 'Well boy's, he says to them, you see them mountains? Well we're gonna take them boys, and today we are gonna kick us some black Arab ass.' Anyway a big cheer went around the camp. Suddenly a Marine Sergeant shouts to General Franks. 'General! General! We've just spotted all three hundred Al Quada soldiers heading this way.'"

By this time, the whole pub was listening to Tony telling the joke.

"General Franks looks at his men with a fearless face and then shouts back to the Sergeant. 'Sergeant,' he shouts, 'fetch me my red cloak.' All the marines listening are suddenly struck with pride. One Marine asked another, 'What does he want a red cloak for?' The other Marine says, 'When he goes into battle it won't show the blood if he's wounded.' 'Wow, what a brave man,' the US marine says.

Suddenly the voice of the Sergeant is shouting again. 'General! General! Osama Bin Laden is with them.' General Franks suddenly gulps and shouts back to the Sergeant. 'Never mind my red cloak, just fetch me my brown trousers.'"

The tables erupted into hysteria for more than a few minutes and another tray of drinks were plonked in front of them. After that, it all seemed to go a little hazy.

TEN

Tony opened his eyes and looked at the electronic display on the bedside clock; it read 11.30 am. He knew he had had too much to drink when he swung out of the bed and felt his brain still on the pillow. For a few minutes he sat on the edge of the bed carefully nursing his face in his hands and trying to massage the pounding in his head. It was at that point he saw that someone had put him to bed fully dressed and with his shoes still on. A wafting smell of food was making his stomach growl with both nausea and hunger, and as he came round he realised that he was upstairs in the pub.

Outside the bedroom someone was gently knocking on the door. Tony asked them in. It was Ghazzani and he was carrying a red thermal pizza bag. He took one look at the state of Tony and laughed. "You really put some beer away last night."

Tony shook his head without a smile. "Tell me about it," he groaned.

Ghazzani threw the pizza bag onto the bed next to Tony. Jalal brought this last night, but you were too drunk to remember."

Tony looked at the bag, opened it and tipped out the contents. There were thirteen bundles of a thousand each.

"Rashar took some," said Ghazzani anticipating his question. "About half I think."

"Where is he now?" asked Tony.

Ghazzani rolled his eyes. "Downstairs in the bar eating me out of house and home."

Tony split off a bundle of notes from the pile of money and offered it to Ghazzani. "I think this should cover it."

"Put your money away Tony," said Ghazzani. "You're always welcome here, you know that. You helped me before with a favour and would take nothing. This is the way it is with friends. What kind of friend would I be if I took your money?" He gently smiled. "Now please, don't insult me, put your money away. But next time, try not to bring Rashar."

Tony laughed. "Okay, it's a deal."

"I'll go get you something to eat while you get a shower or something," said Ghazzani as he turned to leave.

"That friend of yours…?" Tony called after him.

Ghazzani turned in the door frame. "The one who can be trusted?"

"Yes, that one," said Tony.

"His name's Jazz. He's a taxi driver, Afro-Caribbean guy. He's downstairs now in the bar."

"And he's kosher?" asked Tony intently.

"Absolutely," said Ghazzani.

"Make sure that Rashar doesn't notice him," said Tony, "Point out Rashar to him and keep him out the way until Rashar's gone. That's important."

Ghazzani knew better than to ask what Tony was up to. That was his business and being curious or nosey only made people suspicious of your motives. Ghazzani turned to leave again but turned back with something else on his mind. "I wanted to ask you something," he said strangely.

"Then ask it my friend," Tony told him easily.

Ghazzani started in a low searching voice. "I watched those people listening to you last night…" he paused as if struggling to find another way to ask, "You have a way with words and people I have never seen."

Tony stared at him without interrupting and knew what he was going to ask.

"One thing you said struck me," continued Ghazzani. "You said there was something missing from Israel?" He paused again. "I just wondered what you meant?"

Tony tried badly to make light of the question in a feeble attempt to avoid answering it. "You shouldn't take any notice of me," answered Tony, "…it was just the drink talking."

Ghazzani lingered awkwardly for a second and knew his

question would not get an answer. He offered a weak smile and then left the room.

Tony joined Rashar in the living room and poured the contents of the hold-all onto the floor. The money from the Luton takeaway had already been split and what remained seemed to add up to well over a hundred thousand pounds. That would more than cover the amount that Amu Sultan had borrowed. Tony didn't bother to count it; he just divided out the bundles like a child dividing sweets. One for you and one for me until there was only one bundle left over.

"You take it," said Rashar in an uncharacteristic gesture of generosity designed to place Tony in his debt.

Owing men like Rashar was always risky; any form of repayment was sure to exceed one thousand pounds. But knowingly, and with an artificial smile, Tony took the money. He was sure now of all the invisible players in this illusion of smoke and mirrors and was already planning an end game of his own, he needed to gain Rashar's trust and confidence. Tony piled his share of the money into another hold-all and then threw Rashar his keys.

"Find Amu Sultan, but keep out of sight," said Tony.

"And what about you?" asked Rashar.

"Never mind me," Tony answered with feigned anger. "By the time I've finished with Amu Sultan, he'll regret the day he was born."

Rashar's smile was almost ecstatic, "Fix the bastard!!"

"Go now Rashar," Tony urged him, "I'll see you in two days."

Rashar grabbed his bag and the two men shook hands. Rashar gave a toothy smile and kissed Tony's hand. A second later, Rashar slammed the back door of the pub behind him. Tony stood motionless staring at the closed door. "Don't worry Rashar," he whispered aloud, "I will fix the bastard alright."

From the other side of the room Ghazzani entered the room through another door that led from the bar. "Rashar?" he asked aloud.

"He's gone," said Tony.

Behind Rashar anther man entered the room. It was the Afro-Caribbean taxi driver, Jazz. He was a muscular six-foot-two with short dreadlocks.

"Ghazzani tells me you're a man to be trusted?" Tony said at him. "I've got a job for you if you are interested, and the money is good."

A slow white smile broke across Jazz's face. "How good, man?" he asked in a crisp Caribbean accent.

"Two thousand for two days work plus expenses," Tony answered.

"That is good," said Jazz with the hint of proviso tinging his voice.

Tony wrote down an address on a piece of paper and gave it to Jazz. "That's the address of my brother's house in Hull." Tony threw him the hold-all full of money. "Take this bag there and give it to him. After that, you saw that guy who just left, I want you to follow him. Don't worry if you loose him. Just park yourself outside Hull Royal Infirmary and wait for him to show up. If he shows up follow him in and then tell me where goes."

Jazz curled his bottom lip. "Sounds like easy money man," he said with a doubt, "...maybe too easy." He lifted up the bag. "What's in the bag man?" he asked straight out. "If it's drugs you get yourself another mule man. I don't do that thing."

"Open it," Tony instructed him.

Jazz scratched his face suspiciously and stared at Tony.

"Open it," Tony said again.

Jazz unzipped and saw the money inside. He whistled aloud. "That's a lot of money man."

Tony anticipated the next question. "Don't worry, its takeaway money not drugs money. I have to see a couple of friends from the VAT and if I get it wrong I don't want them getting their hands on the it."

A big grin spread across Jazz's face and he started to laugh. "Well now, I ain't got no truck with robbing the tax man."

Without another word and Jazz was out the back door hot on Rashar's heels.

§§§

Sultan Farida was in shock, his facial muscles tensed with anger as he stared vacantly across Solomon Cohen's desk with raw hatred in his eyes.

"Mr Farida?" Solomon asked with quiet formality, "I need your decision."

A slow smile of surrender began to grow across Amu Sultan's tight perspiring face as he began to realise that he had been outfoxed.

"Two million you say?" he almost whispered.

"That's their offer," said Solomon softly. "It was as much a surprise as me as it was to you. As far as I was concerned we had an exchange of contracts to be signed today for the price we agreed: three-and-a-half million. On your way here I received a call and the offer was reduced to two million with the same conditions. The cash is already waiting at the bank to be delivered."

Amu Sultan sighed aloud. "And all I have to do is sign," he whispered aloud thoughtfully. "Do you think we can get them to move?"

"If you were not in a hurry," said Solomon, "I would say yes, but these people whoever they are, seem to let's say….erm….," Solomon pitched his next words diplomatically, "…know more than they should regarding your circumstances."

They had Amu Sultan by the balls, they knew and he knew it. His flight to Amsterdam was booked to leave that night, and from there he was to board an Iranian 747 Jumbo into Tehran. There was really no choice to make, it had been made for him. He had been skillfully manipulated into a corner with only two ways out. Sign the contract and walk with two million cash, or cut off his nose to spite his face and by tomorrow be sitting in a cell charged with fraud, watching the VAT office take the lot. Amu Sultan was a businessman and was not about to let his vanity and anger cloud his judgement in some grand gesture of defiance. A thoughtful smile spread across his face, he could always take his vengeance on Tony from the safety of Iran. That thought at least cheered him and slowly he took the pen that lay next to the contract and scribbled his name across the document.

Solomon sighed. As Amu Sultan's solicitor he felt as defeated as his client. He had not seen this coming but he consoled himself with the knowledge that Sultan had done little to help himself. He had been so engrossed in his little game that he had taken it to the wire and left absolutely no room to manoeuvre.

Amu Sultan pushed the signed documents back across the desk. After inspecting the signature Solomon put his own on the document and picked up the telephone.

"Hello Mr Rosenberg, my client Mr Farida has signed and I will fax the documents forthwith. We would expect delivery of the money within the hour and our business is complete......Indeed and good day to you Mr Rosenberg."

In a private side room off a hospital corridor on the top floor of the Hull Royal Infirmary, the solicitor Maxwell Rosenberg snapped shut his mobile phone and turned toward the hospital bed to speak with his client. The man had his head bandaged and he had numerous superficial cuts and bruises on his face. The injuries looked a lot worse than they actually were.

"Mr Farida has just signed the contract transferring all the properties to our holding company."

Including Reza Husseine who occupied the bed, there were five others in the room: The old Yemeni Sheik Yunis with his solicitor Jeffrey Kaufman and Rashar Nuraman, hot-foot from Luton with his solicitor Gerald Stein.

A great smile of victory stretched across Rashar's face and he began to laugh at his own cleverness. "We did it!!" He held out both his hands, one to Husseini and the other to Sheik Yunis, and they shook. "Welcome partners."

"Well done, my son," said Sheik Yunis, enthusiastically. "Allah smiles upon us all and we should be grateful."

"You have truly done well Rashar," said Husseini. "It is just a pity that I have to be in this hospital bed."

"I swear my brother, I did not know what Amu Sultan was planning," Rashar answered him with regret. "But in the end we have won and taken a five million pound business for two million. By now, Sultan will be planning his revenge on Ahmed, and all we will have to do from now on is count the money." Rashar then gritted his teeth. "Only I won't have to grovel anymore to that miserly Amu Sultan for his peanuts while he gets rich off me."

"And what of Ahmed," asked Husseini, "...are you sure he suspects nothing?"

Rashar grinned confidently. "At this very moment Ahmed is planning his vengeance on Amu Sultan. He does our job for us."

"We should still be careful of him," Hussieni said cautiously. "He is clever, perhaps we might offer him something, just to be on the safe side?"

"I have spoken with him," said Rashar starting to laugh, "he wishes to go back to being an Englishman. He plans to go to University," adding with amusement, "...to be a Social Worker."

Husseini was smiling now. "A social worker you say, he will be out of our world all together. A great pity, we could have used his talents." Husseini suddenly winced with pain at his aches and bruises as he tried delicately to move. "When this is over and I am out of this place I think I take a long holiday to Iran for a few months." His face twisted in anger and some pain. "That is if those morons at the Iranian Embassy ever get round to renewing my passport." He closed his eyes with a satisfying thought. "Maybe then I sort out Amu Sultan. You, Rashar, and the good Sheik here can take care of matters while I am away."

"Then you go on holiday and rest my brother," Rashar said with artificial concern. "I have some plans for the business."

Husseini was suddenly attentive. "What sort of plans?" he asked suspiciously.

"I am a man who does not stand still like Amu Sultan," said Rashar. "We should expand. I am always looking around. I have seen a fish shop in town called Gold Thorpe near Leeds. It is the only place for miles. My people have been watching it. It takes twenty-five grand a week."

Husseini eyes opened wide at the amount. "Twenty-five grand is good," he swooned. "And you can get it for a good price?"

"No, I have found good place for shop, very close to this one," said Rashar.

"Ahh, this is easy thing you do Rashar to find shop," said Husseini, "But shop is not good without planning permission."

Rashar's smile grew wider. "Planning permission is no problem," he answered, now promoting his cleverness. "It is all taken care of. I have the English councillor in my pocket, after I speak with him there will be no problem."

"So you do the politics now, that is good," answered Hussieni laughing, "I see Ahmed has been a good teacher."

The smile left Rashar face and was replaced with indignity. "I do not need Ahmed to teach me anything, it is me who teaches him. Why does everyone say he is clever, when it is me stood here, and my brains that fucked him and Amu Sultan. Now I ask, who is the clever one, me or Ahmed?"

Husseini was quick to correct himself. "Of course it is you Rashar," he answered deftly stroking Rashar's hurt ego. "You have shown great skill to both Sheik Yunis and myself."

Sheik Yunis suddenly interrupted and joined in this Rashar appreciation society. "You have shown Ahmed for what he is, a child," announced Sheik Yunis. "Now already you have been making plans to improve our business. I know I speak not only for myself, but also my brother Husseini here when I say, as partners who could ask for more."

Rashar started to smile. "Then I will have this shop for us in Gold Thorpe and when it is opened I will speak with owner of the other shop. With the help here of some of my Yemeni brother Sheik Yunis's friends, this man they call Peter Hardcastle will be gone."

"This will not be a problem," assured Sheik Yunis.

"After we speak," said Rashar, "I think things will be very good for us in this town."

The three men started to laugh.

"You are very clever Rashar," said Husseini still smiling, "Also very ambitious I think. This is good for the business." He then added more cautiously, "I hope you don't get too ambitious." There was more than hint of a warning in his voice.

§§§

On the motorway services just outside of Luton it was another miserable day. Outside the cafeteria it was pouring with rain and as if fate were adding insult to injury, the car had broken down and Tom Bradley and Angela Carrick had been towed off the motorway. As the rain pelted down against the windows, they sat silently drinking their instant coffee and mulling over their next move. At present, they did not have much to be happy about. The operation to snatch Rashar and Tony had turned into a farce and to make matters worse their boss had already been on the phone to tell them in no uncertain terms what he thought of them.

"I knew they spotted us in Leeds," said Angela suddenly.

"It doesn't really matter now does it?" Bradley snapped back. "It's academic; the fact is they've made complete bloody fools of us."

Angela tried to look on the bright side. "I don't see the problem really," said Angela, "like you said, we just pick them up in Hull."

"It's not as simple as that though is it?" Bradley argued back and listed his doubts. "We've lost the money in the hold-all, that was good evidence. They didn't make the last collection so we can't tie them into that takeaway. All we've got is a pile of bloody photographs and no evidence they were collecting anything."

"Oh come on," Angela answered obviously. "We know they were collecting the takings."

Bradley shook his head with exasperation. "We know that, yes. But the bloody Judge doesn't, does he? We've got court orders freezing all their business and personal accounts but Judge wasn't too happy about giving them. If they've got themselves a clever solicitor they can make mince of us. Don't be surprised if these bastards are waiting for us with their briefs when we get back to Hull."

"You worry too much," said Angela, "With the documents in Hull they're dead in the water. Conviction is a forgone conclusion. These people have been defrauding us for years."

"It just would have been nice to have the icing on the cake," retorted Bradley. "I don't like loose ends, and that fiasco in Luton won't go down well with Judge. That Ahmed's a real clever bastard. Ya never know what he's got up his sleeve. And that worries me."

Suddenly Angela Carrick's face lit up.

"What's up?" asked Bradley.

"That guy Ahmed," she answered still staring.

"What about him?"

She pointed in the direction of the cafeteria entrance. "He's just walked in and he's coming in our direction."

The next thing Bradley knew, Tony was sitting at their table in the seat next to him. Angela and Bradley were dumbstruck.

Tony smiled at them both in turn, and then announced

149

cheekily, "I take it your both from the Customs and Excise office?"

Angela and Bradley both looked at each without a word.

"I thought we might have a chat," said Tony, "So who's buying the coffee?"

Bradley looked him in the face then shook his head in amusement. "You're a real cheeky bastard you are," said Bradley with a contemptuous grin.

"Well, do I get that coffee or what?" Tony asked again.

Bradley nodded in Angela direction. "Get him a coffee."

Angela got up from her seat with a wry face and stared Tony out before leaving the table. Tony could not take his eyes off her as she walked towards the counter.

"Now she's one sexy girl," he said aloud. "Are you shagging her?"

Bradley was not amused. "I don't know what you find so funny. You know you're under arrest of course."

"Under arrest?" Tony queried, "What for?"

"Fraud, conspiracy to defraud," Bradley started to reel off. "They sound nice for starters but I'm sure we'll find a few more to add to that." Bradley looked Tony in the eye. "In fact, I know we will."

"I didn't catch your name?" said Tony.

"Tom Bradley."

Tony pointed in Angela's direction. "And the girl?"

"Angela Carrick."

It was time to begin the bluffing game. Tony knew what he wanted from Bradley and he knew how to get it. He needed answers to questions that he could not ask directly, but in a game of words he hoped to trick them into at least pointing a finger in the direction of those responsible for setting this whole thing up. He guessed that the Customs and Excise already had him dead in the water as far as defrauding the VAT office was concerned, otherwise they wouldn't have been able to mount an operation like this.

Only one document connected Tony to the VAT debt. That document was a secret Islamic Partnership Agreement signed by all three in the partnership: Tony, Amu Sultan and Rashar. Outside of the solicitor's vault the document had no value; it was merely a document of honour used within the community to disgrace anyone who violated its conditions. If that document was now in the hands of the Customs and Excise, as Tony suspected it was, only two people could have supplied it— either Amu Sultan or Rashar.

Since the conditions within the document gave Amu Sultan eighty percent of the company with Rashar and Tony holding ten percent each, it would have made no sense for Amu Sultan to have given them the document; his VAT liability was the greatest. Whoever had given the document to them had anticipated that Amu Sultan would have no option but to sell up and run like hell. Tony knew without a shadow of a doubt that the whole thing had been set up by Rashar, with Husseini's help, and Amu Sultan had taken his vengeance by having Husseini beaten up. He also felt sure that Rashar had probably seeded enough doubts in Amu Sultan's mind to make it look like Tony had set the whole thing up.

After a few minutes, Angela Carrick came back with Tony's coffee and slammed it without ceremony on his side of the table. Then she threw one those small containers of milk and two sachets of sugar at him. Her antics made Tony smile.

"Well, before we nick you," said Bradley harshly, "...what did you want a chat about?"

Tony started to put his milk and sugar into the coffee without haste and slowly stirred it in. "It was just a thought," he started carefully. I thought maybe we could make a deal?"

Bradley started to laugh, not with humour but contempt.

"We don't make deals," announced Angela Carrick. Bradley was oddly silent.

"Everybody makes deals," Tony answered cynically. He had already guessed that Bradley was the more senior of the two, and his hard-faced cynicism indicated that he had probably done this type of thing a hundred times before.

"Well, we don't," said Angela defiantly. "We'll be satisfied when you and your business associates are behind bars."

Tony was now looking at Tom Bradley who had as yet said nothing. "Is that right then Mr Bradley? Will you be satisfied with that?"

Bradley smiled because he knew exactly were the conversation was leading. "Well it's a start. By now I'm sure you know that all your bank accounts are frozen. So we'll get some money out of all you. Then there are your personal assets. You weren't a limited company so none of you have any protection."

Tony shook his head and laughed. "What are you going to take— the few grand in my personal account? My flat's rented and my car is leased. You can't touch any of it. So what assets are we talking about?"

"We've also frozen your brother's bank accounts," Bradley countered with smile equal to Tony's.

That was Bradley's first slip. Only two people knew that Tony's brother held money for him, and since his brother had also held money in bank accounts for Amu Sultan, only Rashar would have a reason to provide that fact.

"You can freeze my brother's accounts," said Tony confidently, "...but I know enough to know that you're not allowed to know how much is in them. For all you know, at this stage there might be next to nothing in them. And even if there is, you can be damn sure my brother will swear the money is his. You could take years getting your hands on any money in that account." Tony slowly smiled. "And if my brother proves the money is his, you get landed with one big compensation claim. You're taking a big risk Mr Bradley." Tony was to sowing the first seed of doubt in his mind, and gradually it was beginning to take root.

"Well even if we get nothing," Bradley answered with a hardening expression, "...we'll have the satisfaction of putting you behind bars."

"You've got nothing on me Mr Bradley," Tony said with deliberate arrogance. "Absolutely nothing. You know how it works, I get myself a clever solicitor and we could be at it for years."

Bradley was suddenly pointing his finger in Tony's direction and smiling. "Not with you we won't. You are as good as in prison."

It was now time to play the big bluff. "That document Husseini gave you means fuck-all. Are you sure it isn't a forgery?" he added with a subtle taunt.

Bradley was suddenly swallowing hard. "How did you know about the document?"

Tony shook his head with derision. "Dear oh dear, Mr Bradley, you didn't fall for that old chestnut did you?"

"He's lying!" Angela Carrick suddenly piped up.

Tony leaned across the table at them with a confident voice. "Am I? Are you sure?"

Angela and Bradley were struck into silence. It was something they had not considered. By now Tony knew he had them on the ropes and was not going to let them off easy. "The only way to prove that document is real is to ask either my solicitor, Sultan's or Rashar's and you know as well as I do what goes on between a solicitor and his client is totally privileged. Not even a judge would or could order that." Tony stared at them waiting for an answer; he knew they had none. "You are both fucked!" he said. "That document is worth fuck-all and I don't think even Rashar is stupid enough to let his solicitor authenticate it."

Bradley was suddenly attentive. "What makes you think Rashar gave it to us?"

Tony shook his head. "Rashar is daft, but not that daft," said Tony. "Rashar gave it to Husseini, and if my guess is right, it was Husseini who gave it to you." Tony paused and smiled at them both. "I think you've made a deal with Husseini to let Rashar off the hook for fuckin' over me and Amu Sultan."

Angela Carrick laughed with contempt at the suggestion. "That's ridiculous."

Tony looked at Bradley; there was no such denial forthcoming from him. "What do you say Mr Bradley?" taunted Tony. "Is it ridiculous?"

Bradley's answer was silence and Angela suddenly knew it was true. "Then you did make deal with Rashar!!"

"Of course he made a deal with him," said Tony. "You lot are just as bad as we are, just as long as you get your money."

Bradley was almost amused. "You have to do these things," he said casually.

"Now where have I heard that before?" said Tony

"You know how it works as well as I do," Bradley sneered at him. "I don't give a shit about your sordid little business disputes. I want what's owed to the department and if I have to get a bit of shit on my hands dealing with some of you, then so be it."

Bradley was glaring at Tony hard but he knew it was no more than bluff and bravado. "I know that partnership document is real," said Bradley with slow deliberation.

Tony rolled his eyes. "But you can't prove it's real, can you?" Tony leered at him. "That's the point. You have gone through all this trouble for nothing, and you've frozen my bank accounts for nothing. Now that's naughty." Tony rubbed it in. "The Judge is not going to like that one bit. You are in big trouble Bradley. Rashar hasn't just stuffed me and Amu Sultan, he's stuffed you as well. Even if your bosses were stupid enough to let this get to court, once my brief gets stuck into the deal, he's going to fuck you over good and proper. Even if you can prove the document is real, which is doubtful, any judge will know it has no legal value. It's an Islamic contract of honourable intention, it has value only within the community. Now you better make up mind; either arrest me or we make a deal that's get us both off the hook."

Bradley closed his eyes as the horror of it all dawned on him. "This is one big fuckin' mess from start to finish." He looked at Angela and took a big heavy breath. He wanted the ground to open up and swallow him. "They are going to throw the book at me for this one," he said aloud.

Angela stared at Tony without expression but was seething inside at his smugness. "You said something about a deal?" she asked in a staccato voice. Bradley was then also suddenly attentive.

With calculation, Tony took out a cigarette and lit it slowly. "Yes, I did, didn't I," he said carefully.

"What type of deal?" asked Bradley with gradually growing interest.

"As I said, something that gets us both off the hook," said Tony.

"And why are you on the hook?" asked Bradley curiously.

"Because at this very moment," Tony told them casually, "Amu Sultan is winging his way to Iran with a suitcase full of cash and has probably taken out a contract on me already."

Angela Carrick furrowed her brow, "Contract?" she asked naively, "What type of contract?"

Tony and Bradley looked at each other without a word. "And why should he do that?" Bradley asked.

"Because he thinks I set this whole thing up to take over the company," said Tony.

Bradley could not help but see the funny side. He laughed to himself. "And I thought we were in the shit," said Bradley, "So what did you have in mind?"

"A hypothetical question of course," Tony started, "How much do we owe you?"

"You mean you really don't know?" queried Bradley with surprise.

"I wouldn't be asking would I if I knew?" retorted Tony.

"Amu Sultan never told you we had interviewed him four times?" enquired Bradley.

"No," answered Tony with some irritation. "Just tell me how much we owe?"

"Three-and-a-half million pounds," Bradley said slowly.

For the first time it was Tony who seemed stuck for words. "Bloody hell, no wonder Amu Sultan pissed off so quickly," Tony rubbed his forehead with disbelief. "Three-and–a-half million quid?" he repeated aloud. "That's a lot of money."

"It's no more than you owe us," said Angela indignantly.

The amount would have to make Tony rethink what he had in mind. He sat for a moment raking through his thoughts. "Alright," he said after some thought. "This is the deal, you take it or leave it. I don't know if I can get you that much. I'll get you what I can."

"Just a minute," Bradley cut him short. "Why would you want to do that?" And what do you get in return?" he asked him more carefully.

"Simple," Tony answered. "I have to go and make the peace with Amu Sultan before he sends the bald headed traveller after me. After that I am out of this game for good with a clean slate and I get you lot off my back."

"And what about the three-and-a-half million back VAT?" asked Angela. "How do we get that?"

"Don't worry you'll get your money, or most of it," Tony answered confidently.

"How?" Bradley persisted.

"That's my business," Tony snapped back, "You'll just have to trust me."

Angela sneered back under her breath. "Trust you?" she laughed aloud.

Tony returned the gesture with a laugh of his own. "Well, you don't really have much choice do you?" he retorted.

"Now don't tell me your going to Iran to talk to Amu Sultan," said Bradley.

"No," said Tony, "Amu Sultan likes to take the scenic route you might say." He winked with a cheeky smile. "If I know Amu Sultan he'll be in Amsterdam for a few days. He likes the ladies if you know what I mean."

Bradley's expression was strangely awkward. "There might be a problem there," he said reticently.

"What do you mean, a problem?" asked Tony suspecting that Bradley was keeping something from him.

"We've got your passport," he confessed in a low voice, "Both of them."

Tony knew exactly what was coming next. "And just how did you do that?"

Bradley flicked his eyes with embarrassment. "We searched your flat."

In silence Tony stared at them. "I didn't hear that," said Tony, "because I'm going to get real angry. Now I have to go to London for a couple days to make arrangements. By the time I get back I want to find my passports where I left them and my front door back on its hinges." Something in his voice told both Bradley and Angela Carrick that it was not a request.

Tony stood up to leave. "I'll be flying out of Humberside Airport for Amsterdam in two days. I'll be stopping off to pick up my passport." A moment later he was walking out the door of the cafeteria.

In silence, both Bradley and Angela sat watching him disappear into the car park. They could not help the feeling they had just been stitched up and they had provided the needle and thread.

"Arrogant Arab bastard," Bradley swore aloud to himself. "I hope they blow each other's fuckin' brains out."

§§§

Tony climbed into his hire car. His mobile phone rang; it was Jazz calling from Hull. "Where are you now?" asked Tony.

"Parked outside the hospital like you said to," answered Jazz.

"And have you seen my 'friend'?" Tony enquired with interest.

"Better than that man," said Jazz. "I followed him inside."

"And?"

"He went to a ward on the tenth floor and into a side room," said Jazz. "I asked a passing nurse and she told me it was a private room."

"Now that's interesting," said Tony.

"There's more man," said Jazz his voice getting excited, "I went into the ward and walked past the side room. Apart from your friend, there were three other guys in suits around the bed."

Tony laughed aloud. "Solicitors," said Tony.

"Yeah, could be." Jazz agreed. "There was also some old guy dressed like Osama Bin Laden."

Now that was something Tony was not expecting. "About sixty-five to seventy, small with a long grey beard?"

"Yeah, that's him man," said Jazz. "Ya know him?"

"Yeah, I know him," said Tony sighing heavily. "You've done good Jazz. You might as well get back to Luton."

"But I'm enjoying this man," answered Jazz laughing.

"Have you delivered that package to my brother's house yet?" asked Tony.

"No, not yet."

"Well, you've earned yourself a bonus," said Tony, "Take out another thousand for yourself and drop the money off; I'll see you some time."

"Safe man," Jazz howled down the phone.

"Cheers."

Tony sat quietly thinking to himself for a few minutes. The involvement of Sheik Yunis had been a big surprise and an even bigger disappointment. What he had in mind for Rashar and Husseini would now have to include the Old Sheik. That complicated matters because Yunis was Yemeni in the traditional sense of the word and he would seek vengeance for whatever befell him with a Yemeni determination. Tony would have to be doubly careful that whatever he had planned did not point the finger of suspicion in his direction.

<u>ELEVEN</u>

An afternoon in the luxurious splendour and peaceful tranquillity of the tea room in the Grovenor House Hotel was a civilised way to spend time. At over four pounds for a cup of coffee, it ensured the financial pedigree of those with whom you rubbed shoulders. It was a discrete sort of place to do business. From the four corners of the globe, the anonymously wealthy came and went. Many of the nearby diplomatic world held endless court over a glass of the finest wine or a china cup filled with some exclusive beverage reserved only for the few.

At any time of day, the tea room was always well frequented with a rich cosmopolitan mixture of the cultured and influential from what seemed be all the races of the world. The incomprehensible sound of genial chatter in a labyrinth of different languages seemed to blend almost too perfectly with the gentle aroma of exotic smells that emanated in every direction. In a charcoal grey Armani suit and Gucci shoes, Tony did not look out of place as he sat in silent contemplation at his table by the window, the magnified heat of afternoon sunshine washing over his olive skin.

Behind the tint of his Versace shades, Tony gazed thoughtfully out at the never-ending throng of people and traffic that come day or night, was Park Lane. He was an alien in this world and although he did not look it, inside he felt like a pretender, an outsider who had no right to be seated next to the powerful, rich and without a doubt— greedy. On the few occasions that he had had reason to visit the hotel, it was the scene played out in front that had always fascinated him and that he could have watched for hours.

Endlessly limousines came and went, depositing their masters at the hotel steps to be fussed over by a chauffer and then a grovelling decadently uniformed concierge. And of all those he watched in this ritual of the wealthy, none fascinated him more than the oil-rich Arab. Their limousines queued up outside like ocean liners waiting to dock. In all their glory, and splendour of magnificent Arab robes and hands that dripped in gold and jewels, they and their family chattel climbed out to be toadied to like Hollywood starlets.

More often than not, a sycophantic native servant or servant of their own, would scurry behind them laden with up to a hundred shopping bags. Baring the name of Selfridges or Harrod's, the items contained were typically some fashionable playthings or items of clothing, the price of which could feed some poor Arab family or save hundreds of dying children.

Tony hated and despised them for what they were and what they had become. The wealth they threw around like so much confetti was not theirs waste on frivolous toys and pointless things, that by tomorrow, would become another unwanted fancy. These beings drained the life-blood of the whole Arab people. This was the real truth of Arab oil. It was not money this new native nouveau-riche flaunted so arrogantly, it was blood and hope; the blood and hope of millions of their own people frittered away frivolously on the whims of the self indulgent and greedy.

"*I remember,*" intruded the echo of a past voice suddenly circling in Tony's thoughts, "*...he was one of those rich Gulf Arabs. One of those who would call himself a 'Saudi businessman' one who's business risk pisses from a hole in the ground of the desert.*"

Then as the voice grew clearer the hazy features of the Arab who spoke the words to him many years ago appeared like a desert mirage.

"*He was generous to all who worked in the Hotel, all that was except the Arabs, who he treated with contempt because that is their way. And then on his final day we were all ordered to form in a line from the elevator to the front door of the hotel to bid him goodbye. Then dressed like a fine Prince he slowly walked along the lines of waiting hotel staff,*" *porters, cooks, cleaners, everyone. This native servant at his side clung to him like a toad and clutched in his hands a great bundle of money. To each person in the line a fifty-pound note was stripped from the hand of the native servant and given with a smile equally as generous, until finally, at the end of the line, he came to me. Suddenly I was invisible and he passed me by with even the smile removed from his face.*

"You mean he gave you nothing?" asked another voice in the mirage that was Tony's.

"Nothing."

"Why, I don't understand why?"

The face of the Arab mirage smiled. "*I am an Arab!*" the mirage shouted with bitter laughter.

"I see the Arabs still hold fascination for you Ahmed," intruded another mildly accented voice. This time it was not a mirage, but an old acquaintance that towered in front of him in a smart plain black suit that blended almost too neatly with a trimmed Islamic beard and a collarless shirt that symbolically left no place for a tie. Beside him a duo of what might have been twins, both of them muscular Iranian giants dressed in identical attire remained guardedly close. With hard expressionless faces, their cold staring eyes darted around the room. As one of them turned, his unbuttoned jacket pulled back for no more than a second, to reveal a holstered gun hanging beneath his left arm.

Tony slowly removed his shades and stood up to shake the hand held out to him. A slow smile went across his face. "How are you, Sir?" he asked softly.

The man smiled back with equal warmth and casually bade away the bodyguards who obediently retired to stand watch over their charge at a discrete distance. "I am well," answered the man with a manner that was almost humble but then rolled his eyes, "...but the day has been a difficult one, and how are you Ahmed?" He gestured for Tony to return to his seat then discretely indicated to his bodyguards to move away to a more comfortable distance. He then sat down sat down himself in the opposite chair.

"I am fine thank you Sir," said Tony returning to his chair.

The waiter was on the table in a second. "I see you have already ordered coffee Ahmed," said the man anticipating. "I hope you don't mind but I have a weakness English tea since my days at Hull University." The waiter scribbled the order and retreated.

The man shook his with defeat. "I have just come from your BBC radio," said the man, "the radio four programme I think you might call it."

"Yes, I know the one," said Tony smiling. "Did they give you a hard time?"

"No matter how I try to explain the politics of Iran," he answered in defeat, "...they do not want to know. They do not understand us; they do not want to understand us I think. They talk only of their own great freedoms and this mysterious thing they call democracy. When I pointed out to them that in our Parliament all racial and religious groups have their own MP, even the Jews, it was an enlightenment to them. But they did not wish to talk about that. Only the bad things they perceive about they are interested in."

"These are difficult days," Tony answered, "For the Western politicians their great demon Communism is dead. They are looking for a new enemy and Islam is the new great threat. So what you see and read is this process of demonization. Islam is convenient for them. The Western politician will always need a bogeyman because they fear a challenge to their world dominance. If they did not have an enemy they would simply create one."

Both men laughed. "I see you are still the politician Ahmed," said the man, "...and you are right sadly. I think there are bad days ahead of us all." He suddenly slapped the table with a broad smile. "Now, that is enough misery for one day. Let us forget this depressing subject and talk of happier things. How is Hull these days?" asked the man.

"As always," answered Tony, "time moves slow there."

The man smiled with a look of nostalgia. "Yes, I remember that time always moved slow in Hull," said the man, "though I did enjoy those days."

The waiter came and went quickly after leaving a gentile silver tray complete with ornate tea pot and two bone china cups and saucers. The man started to pour out the tea for himself since Tony's cup was still half full with coffee. His voice dipped to a lower tone and broke into Arabic.

"I hope you understand Tony," the man started to explain, "that I am here only to listen and speak as we have spoken to each other before when you last the visited me at the Embassy." He paused for a second and lingered with a stare. "I cannot help you with business. I hope you are aware of that? You should be also careful what you say. This place is like the Embassy there are bugs everywhere."

At that moment two very English looking men came into the tea room and sat down a short distance away. While their attire was smart, it was below par for the setting. They made an effort to hide their interest in what was going on at Tony's table. The Iranian was looking at Tony with an obvious smile as he watched Tony staring back at them. "I take it they are following you," said Tony.

The Iranian was still smiling. "The British government are very thoughtful and concerned about our security," he said sarcastically. "We have such an escort everywhere. I think now also they will be interested in you."

Unconcerned, Tony returned to the reason for his visit, though his voice was more guarded. "It is not for business reasons I came here and I do not need help. I think I have something to say that will be of interest to you. Indirectly it may be to my advantage, but also to yours."

"Then I am intrigued," said the man.

"One of your fellow countrymen is causing me a problem," Tony started, his eyes now and then cautiously flicking towards the watching Englishmen. "It is nothing I cannot handle, but I think he causes you a big problem too."

The man's interest was growing. "Go on," he told him in almost an inaudible whisper. "But be careful."

"This is what I know," said Tony, "then it will be for you to make your own judgement. The man I speak of came to this country five years ago on the back of lorry and claimed political asylum. He lives in Hull. Only a year later and his wife and three children were given visas to enter the country. Then after a few more months, his brother and parents are given visas. He is now a very rich man."

"And what are you saying?" asked the man with almost a whisper.

"Perhaps this man," said Tony, taking care with his words, "...worked somewhere sensitive in Iran. Perhaps he exchanges what he knows for favours from the English government. Sometimes it is so."

The man across the table stared back in thoughtful silence for a few moments and then started to smile. His voice grew louder and he was once again speaking English. "You disappoint me Ahmed," he told him heavily and then the smile was gone and replaced with a cultured disapproval. "Did I come here, that you might use me in a business dispute?"

Tony noticed that the two Englishmen were trying very badly not to show interest in this outburst. "No," answered Tony respectfully, "I did not come for that."

"You should know me better than that Ahmed," he snapped. Then with a wave of the hand he called over the waiter and requested the bill which a second later was placed on the table. The man took out his pen and furiously signed his name across the hotel bill. "You may have your coffee at my expense," he said sternly, "...but do not use me as a fool." He slid the bill across the table to Tony and without another word was on his feet and walking towards the front door.

Tony sighed to himself as through the window he watched him leave and get into a waiting limousine. He cursed in mime to himself that he had messed things up so badly, but for the life of him could not understand why. He then noticed that the two Englishmen had suddenly disappeared, leaving a table full of half consumed beverages. Then suddenly he became aware of the beverage bill on the table. What was written on it was not a signature but a note of a few words.

Careful of ears. General Mohamed Reza Husseini holidays in Iran soon. SAVAMA awaits him.

Keeping a straight face, Tony replaced his shades and looked back out of the window at the enduring hustle and bustle outside. So that was it, Husseini was a former General. Tony's guess had been right and more telling than that, the man who had just left the table already knew what was in Tony's mind. That much he had confirmed by writing the name that had not passed Tony's lips. Tony tried hard not to smile, then stealthily slid the note into his jacket pocket. If Husseini was planning one of his yearly visits home, he was in big shit if SAVAMA was waiting for him. SAVAMA was an acronym for the Iranian Intelligence and the name alone was enough to strike fear in the heart of any Iranian.

One down, and two to go. Not forgetting of course that he still had the task of finding Amu Sultan, who by now, would be somewhere in Amsterdam partaking in the pleasures of female Dutch flesh pots.

In the night darkness, a small jet airliner climbed out of Humberside Airport and above the moon silvered clouds. With the cabin lights low and the steady hypnotic drone of the engines humming through Tony's fatigued body, a haze of sleep gradually overtook him. In the echo of a dream he could hear the melodic preaching of the Imam drifting in and out as he sat with his back against the wall on the lush carpet beneath him. He had not come to pray but to rest and let the soft chanting Arabic voice bathe away his troubled thoughts. Now hidden in his other world, he wore the traditional Yemeni tied garb of a spangled purple Kafia headdress. The large room was dotted with others who had come for the same purpose. The teachings relayed from a microphone in the main prayer room downstairs and as always the old man next to him bothered him with inquisitive croaking whispers and questions that never changed.

"I never see you pray."

"I come to think," Tony whispered back.

"It is a place for thoughts of God," said the old man without judgement, "...but you declare yourself an unbeliever?"

"The words I hear soothe me like the sound of rain. I come for that and the poetry of wisdom," Tony answered him. "Would you deny this to me?"

"I do not deny you what is not mine to take," said the old man gently rebuking him. "It is you who denies the God of your father."

"The God you speak of causes me much confusion," said Tony.

"How so is this?"

Tony closed his eyes and sighed, "Such good and beautiful words, yet men soak them in blood."

"Is it not true," started the old man slowly, "that a carpenter may create a thing of great beauty with his tools and that the same tools that create beauty to behold, may be used to inflict great injury or death?"

"It is men then?" said Tony.

"God has given great words and wisdom as a gift to men," the old man answered, "Like the tools of the carpenter he must use them skillfully for the purpose they were gifted to him."

Tony paused to dwell on the old man's words. "And the truth?" he asked him suddenly.

The old leered at him with his whispers. "The truth can only be found in that which is good."

"And is to deny God," said Tony, "is this good or bad?"

The old man almost chuckled. "You do not deny God. I think you only have your differences with Him because of what men do. In this God is not responsible."

"Those who possess power have responsibility," said Tony. "Would you deny this?"

"In the world of men I do not deny this truth," the old man argued back quietly, "...but the domain of God and the heavens has no measure to the world of men. As with the carpenter, his tools can create as equally as destroy. This is the gift of choice that God has bestowed upon men. Without such a choice, how would we know evil if it deceived us in the masquerade of good?"

Tony smiled at him with the warmth of respect, "The answers you give, as all men like you, are always a clever riddle."

"And life is not?" the old man countered him.

"For some it is not," answered Tony heavily. "For many I think."

"There is a time when all men wonder," the old man said stoutly.

"Perhaps briefly," conceded Tony reluctantly, "...but when answers are denied, the questions are asked no more and men go about their deeds."

"You speak of the burden of ordinary men," said the old man, "...but is not good in our presence greater than the evil?"

Tony seemed to lower his head. "For a short time more I think. The screams grow louder."

The old man looked at him and smiled forlornly. "Then maybe the time of God approaches."

Suddenly the Imam's voice seemed to rise to a crescendo.

Tony's breath was long and heavy. "I hope so," he whispered at him. "*Inshallah* let it be soon."

The old man's features began to fade until in front of Tony's eyes the ghost powdered face of a pretty young air stewardess filled his vision and for a split second he thought it an apparition.

"I'm sorry Sir," the young girl smiled at him, "I hope I didn't startle you. We are just coming into land at Schiphol Airport. Would you fasten your safety belt please?"

Tony smiled back then rubbed the sleep from his eyes.

§§§

It was midnight in ward ten at Hull Royal Infirmary and the night staff had settled down to a tea break at the dimly lit desk in the ward corridor. Apart from the methodical tap of a porter's heels on lino and the subdued giggles of nurses gossiping, the ward was in silence. In an office up the corridor the muffle of a conversation could just be heard.

"Are you a relative of Mr Husseini?" the Sister asked down the phone.

A heavily accented voice came down the line. "Yes, I am his brother, I am calling from Iran."

"Well in that case," said the Sister, "I am pleased to say that Mr Husseini has made a good recovery and is comfortable. He has seen the Doctor tonight and should be discharged sometime tomorrow afternoon." The Sister smiled. "I am sure you will be able to ask him all of these questions yourself in a few days. He tells me he is looking forward to going home for a few weeks."

In the exit foyer at Schiphol Airport Tony was on his mobile phone. He was smiling too. "Yes, we are all looking forward to seeing him," he said, imitating a Farsi accent. "Thank you so much for speaking with me. My family are so grateful to your British hospitals. I will give my parents the good news. Goodnight."

"Goodnight." The Sister put down the phone and smiling at the manners of the caller, she joined the rest of her staff for some tea at the corridor desk.

"Who was that?" asked a nurse.

"Mr Husseini's brother asking how he was," answered the

Sister.

"It's a bit late to be calling at this hour," said the nurse.

"He was calling from Iran," answered the Sister, "I could hardly put the phone down on him could I? Anyway, he seemed happy enough."

Amu Sultan had always been a creature of habit. Just as Tony knew that on his twice-yearly trips home to Iran he always stopped off for a five-day break in Amsterdam, he also knew exactly where he would be staying. Amu Sultan enjoyed luxury and had the money to be able to afford it. He also liked many other things such as Napoleon Brandy, Russian Vodka, more than a few pints of Guinness, and last but not least, the company of more than one young woman at a time. For his age he had the sexual appetite and stamina of a young bull moose.

It was one o'clock in the morning. Outside the airport arrival hall in Schiphol Tony jumped into a waiting taxi.

"Where to?" asked the taxi driver.

"I need to do some shopping," said Tony.

"It is late, we shall have to go to the town centre," answered the taxi driver.

"Then we had better go," Tony instructed him. "I shouldn't be too long then you can drop me back here at the Amsterdam Hilton after I'm done."

In the back of the taxi Tony was again on his mobile. The voice of a female night receptionist at the Amsterdam Hilton Hotel answered.

"Good morning," said Tony. "Do you speak English?"

"Of course," answered the female voice with the tone of almost perfect English indignity.

"Could you connect me to Sultan Farida's room please?" Tony asked politely.

"One moment please," the female voice replied and a moment later the sound of an internal phone came down the line. Tony smiled to himself at the predictability of old habits.

A double executive room at the Amsterdam Hilton cost two hundred and twenty-two Euros a night, in sterling that is nearly one hundred and fifty-six pounds. For the money it was sheer luxury and Amu Sultan did not begrudge one penny of it. The expensive bottles of drink surrounded by an army of empty and half-full glasses, bore witness to the money he had already spent on two young blondes that had retreated drunk and giggling into the shower. Sultan was already naked, drunk and awaiting his prize under the duvet of the King size bed. He was not sober enough to pay attention to the time when bedside telephone rang. He answered it on drunken auto-pilot and forgetting himself, started speaking Farsi.

"Hello, who's that and what do you want?" he stammered down the phone.

"What do you mean, wrong number you arsehole," he shouted in drunken English and slammed the receiver down.

In the taxi Tony was laughing to himself and then again rang the hotel. Once more the female receptionist answered.

Tony started with animated anger, "I have just rung your Hotel," Tony argued down the phone, "And you have put me through to the wrong room. Mr Sultan Farida is in room six. This type of service is just unacceptable from the Hilton."

The unsteady voice of the receptionist came back nervous and apologetic. "I'm terribly sorry Sir, but I could have sworn I put you through room seventeen. I'll try it again."

"No." Tony interrupted resolutely. "It's too late now. I don't want to disturb Mr Farida, I'll call him in the morning."

"I'm terribly sorry…." But Tony had already hung up.

"Room seventeen," he said to himself with a smile.

Within half-an-hour they were in Central Amsterdam where the place was bustling with life and would be all night. The taxi driver took Tony to one of the many all night shopping centres. Tony climbed out of the cab and handed the taxi driver a clump of gilders he had not bothered to count.

"Wait here. I should not be long," he said hurriedly.

The taxi driver happily started to count notes with a big smile. "Don't worry about it," he answered more than content. "You take your time."

But for the street light creeping in through the curtains, the hotel room was in darkness. The urgent whispers and groans of the women in the bed carried throughout the silent room. The darkened silhouette of the duvet that covered them moved in rhythm to the squeals of delight beneath it, as Amu Sultan wrestled and grunted from one women to another in a seemingly endless lust that went on for more than an hour. Sounds of ecstasy rose to their inevitable crescendo in a frenzy of urgency— first with one girl who slumped back onto the bed exhausted and spent, and then with the second girl, until she too collapsed with fatigue beneath him. Still, Amu Farida kept going.

"Don't you ever stop?" panted the first girl pushing herself up to rest on the headboard of the bed. For an answer, Amu Sultan pressed his lips fiercely against hers. Unable to take anymore she pushed him away to carry on with her friend.

"You certainly get your money's worth," she giggled aloud. In the semi-darkness she groped for a cigarette. It was the flash of her lighter that illuminated the figure seated in the corner of the room. He was wearing a long black overcoat and black leather gloves. She screamed in horror, at the top of her voice. Still screaming, she switched on the bedside lamp.

"What is going on??!" Amu Sultan shouted, then found himself staring directly at Tony who was casually looking at him from the chair across the room. For just a split second, Amu Sultan thought he was dreaming. A second later and in almost a single movement, he climbed out of the bed and switched on the overhead light. He was not dreaming and Tony was still staring at him. Amu Sultan froze in shock, unaware that he was stark naked.

"Who are you?" one of the girls screamed lifting up the duvet to cover her breasts.

"Your time is up girls," announced Tony. "I have some business with your client here. So why don't you get dressed and fuck off."

The girls did not need asking twice and were out the bed in a single bounce. They grabbed their clothes and ran into the bathroom firmly locking the door behind them.

It had all happened so fast. And Amu Sultan still drunk, was still in shock. "You are bastard Ahmed," he shouted at him, "You are bastard."

Tony looked at Amu Sultan standing before him and shook his head with disapproval. "Oh Amu Sultan," he sighed heavily. "Amu Sultan, what the fuck am I going to do with you?" He stood up and threw him the bath robe that was on the back of the chair. "Put your cock away Sultan and put this on."

Amu Sultan hurriedly put on the bath robe and then went to the phone.

Tony rolled his eyes. "What are you doing now Amu?"

"I call the fuckin' police for you, you bastard," he shouted back.

Tony pulled a plastic bag out of his overcoat pocket that was packed with a white powder. "Hey, Amu Farida!!" he called after him.

Amu Sultan turned round and Tony threw the bag of white powder at him. Farida deftly caught it with one hand. He looked at the white powder in the bag and then back at Tony. "What the fuck is this?" he shouted at him.

"Cocaine, what do think it is."

Amu Sultan threw it on the bed like it was a red hot turd. "You are Yemeni *maloone*!! –a crazy Yemeni," Amu Sultan screamed at him.

"Just call the police Amu Sultan and let's get this over with," Tony said now calling his bluff.

Suddenly Amu Sultan was confused as to why Tony now wanted him to call the police. He worried that Tony had something up his sleeve, and of course, he did. Tony showed him his hands with a big smile; he was wearing gloves. "It's not my fingerprints all over that cocaine is it Amu Sultan?"

"You are bastard!!" he leered at him as he dropped the phone and grabbed the bag desperately trying to wipe it of his fingerprints.

"You can't be sure you'll get them all off," said Tony antagonising him further. Tony snatched the bag off him, tore it open, and sprinkled the contents around the room and on the bed.

It was at that precise moment that the two Dutch prostitutes emerged from the bathroom dressed and in a hurry to leave. Tony had to admit that Amu Sultan certainly had taste. They were stunningly beautiful, with slender teasing bodies squeezed into very expensive clothes; their services were certain to be equally as expensive. Their hurry to leave suddenly turned into panic when they spotted the split bag and white powder sprinkled around the room. They did not need to guess at what it was, and something told them that Arabs, Iranians and white powder was not a combination they cared to poke their noses into.

"Look, we don't want any trouble," one of them said nervously to Tony. "If your friend Mr Sharif just pays us what he owes, we are gone. You won't have a problem with us. We haven't seen anything."

"But this has nothing to do with me either," protested Amu Sultan. "It is that Yemeni bastard. I don't know this man," he said pointed at Tony.

Tony almost laughed and looked at Amu Sultan. "Mr Sharif, eh?" he said with a mischievous smile. "It wouldn't be Omar by any chance would it?" he said mocking Amu Sultan further.

"So you do know him," the other prostitute piped up. "Look, just pay us our money, and what you do is your business."

Tony had a wide grin all over his face. "Of course we know each other, don't we Omar?" he said looking at Amu Sultan. "Now come on Omar, it's getting late so just pay these good ladies for their services and they can be getting home."

The two prostitutes stood waiting as Amu Sultan reluctantly went into a bedside drawer for his wallet. Sliding out a wedge of gilders, he handed the money to one of the prostitutes. After counting it, she split it and gave the other half to her friend. To sweeten them further, Tony handed them a smaller wedge of gilders from his pocket. The two girls looked at each reluctantly.

"Call it a tip," said Tony. The girls eagerly took the money and in a matter of seconds were out the hotel room door.

Tony sat himself down at a nearby table. The smile had gone from his face and his voice was stern now. "Sit down Amu Sultan." It was not a request. "We need to talk."

Amu Sultan's face was set with rage and for an answer he snatched out a long bladed hunting knife from beneath his mattress. He stood glaring at Tony with an expression that meant business. "I am going to slit your fuckin' throat you English-Arab bastard," he growled at him.

Tony groaned and ran his fingers through his hair with growing frustration. "Just put the fuckin' knife down Amu, before someone gets hurt."

He slowly started to move in, with the knife held tightly in his hand. "You are right Ahmed," he said with a crazy smile, "Someone is going to get hurt. You! You thieving piece of camel shit."

While Amu Sultan might have seemed easy meat to those who did not know, Tony had seen him fight on too many occasions and knew what he was capable of, particularly armed with a knife. Tony had anticipated such an outburst and had come well prepared.

"You're making a big mistake Amu Sultan," Tony told him slowly.

"No, I don't make mistake," Amu Sultan answered him, "You do. I treat you like a son and you take your Arab knife and put it in my back. Now you come to rob me. You are bastard Ahmed." He started to laugh irrationally. "Now I have knife," he said waving it about like a wild-eyed mad man.

Tony did not look worried. Suddenly Amu Sultan stopped in his tracks and froze like a statue. He was staring down the barrel of a small silver automatic pistol pointing directly at his head.

"I won't ask again. Just put the fuckin' knife down and stick your arse on that chair. Or so help me, I'll blow your fuckin' head off."

Amu Sultan grit his teeth, the knife held tightly in his hand. "You think I am going to let you just take my money?" he said with contempt.

"I don't want your fuckin' money, you greedy Iranian bastard. Is that all you people think of, money? Don't you think if I had come here to steal your money I would have just come through the door with a few people and just taken it?"

"But you don't know where it is, do you Ahmed?" Amu Sultan replied. "That is why you came with the gun."

Tony shook his head with disbelief. "Being the money-loving bastard you are," said Tony, "I know you well enough to know exactly where your money is Amu Sultan. You and your money are never far apart."

"Where then?" Amu Sultan challenged him.

Tony rolled his eyes and simply pointed his finger at a door in the wardrobe—the one with the key missing from the lock. "It's in a suitcase in there," Tony answered confidently.

Amu Sultan's chin dropped and he stared at him without

another word. Tony knew he had guessed right.

"So you see Amu Sultan," said Tony slowly, "If I came here to rob you I would have just taken it."

There was no more argument. Amu Sultan almost fell into the chair, let the knife fall onto the table, and put his head into his hands. Tony looked across the table and let out one long sigh that seemed to sum up both their feelings. Then like a biblical revelation striking a holy prophet, the penny dropped in Amu Sultan's brain and he realised that not only had he been conned, but that it was Rashar who had set it all up and not Tony.

"This is big fuckin' mess," Amu Sultan said in low shameful whisper.

"Well that didn't take too long, did it Amu Sultan?" Tony snapped at him indignantly. "All you had to do was think about it. I thought that you knew me better than this. What did I ever do to you to make you think I would do such a thing?"

Amu Sultan's head was hung in foolishness and shame. Tony was shouting at him with anger that Amu Sultan had never witnessed before.

"Come On!! Tell me what I ever fuckin' did!!" Tony screamed at him again.

Amu Sultan fists clenched with the thoughts of what he wanted to do to Rashar. "What can I say?" he replied shamefully. "It was all so clever I thought it had to be you. Even though in the back my mind a whisper was telling me it was not."

Tony's anger subsided to hurt. "Then why didn't you listen to the whispers?"

"Things happened so fast." Amu Sultan answered. "The VAT, problems with tax man, court, this and that." Amu Sultan sort of laughed, "I compliment him, Rashar was clever. I never thought he had the brains for something like this."

After a long pause, Amu Sultan looked across the table at Tony staring thoughtfully back at him. "I'm sorry Ahmed," he said in a low whisper. "What more can I say?"

Tony slowly took out his cigarettes, put one in his mouth and threw one at Farida. He then aimed the gun, leaned towards Amu Sultan, and pulled the trigger. A small lighter flame came out the other end. Farida started laugh and lit his cigarette. "You are Yemeni *maloone* - crazy Yemeni. You and your crazy English jokes." He pulled hard and deep on the cigarette. "This is big fuckin' mess," he said again.

"You shouldn't feel so bad Amu Sultan," said Tony, "For a while he had me fooled too."

"We both make mistake I think."

Tony yawned with a tired groan. "We just forgot the logic of our own people for a while."

As if a passage from a holy book, Amu Sultan stared into his own mind and repeated the golden rule aloud. "Whatever they make you believe, the truth is the opposite." Amu Sultan shook his head with anger at his own stupidity. "How could I forget?"

"What is done is done," Tony sighed with a fateful resignation. "But we have to pay them back."

Amu Sultan was suddenly attentive. "What do mean by them?"

"Husseini and Sheik Yunis were both in on the set up," said Tony.

Amu Sultan did not look surprised. "Husseini I might have guessed. Sheik Yunis, this I did not know."

"You don't really seem surprised about Yunis."

Amu Sultan sighed. "Surprised no, disappointed, yes."

"And you surprise me Amu Sultan," said Tony. "You sound defeated."

"I am getting too old for all these games," Amu Sultan answered. "England has been good to me and I have made good money. The new takes over from the old. What do I care anymore, I am going home to Iran." He shrugged his shoulders without a care. "Fuck them all, let them have it and the thousand plagues that go with it."

Tony's anger was suddenly rising again. "And what about me Amu Sultan?" he said at him. "I cannot run away to Iran. I have to go back to England and face this mess."

"Come to Iran with me," said Amu Sultan with sudden enthusiasm. "I have money, you and I can do good business together, and I get you a beautiful Iranian wife who does not answer back like the English women."

Tony started to laugh. "It's a nice thought, but England is my home."

"Okay, okay, Mr Englishman," conceded Amu Sultan. "You

want to go back to England. I give you lot of money and we stay friends."

The word friend resounded in Tony's head and struck him into a strange silence. It was word that Tony had never heard Amu Sultan say to him in all the years he had known him.

"I don't want your money Amu Sultan," said Tony emphatically.

"Then what else is there?" announced Amu Sultan throwing up his hands.

"In the years I've known you," Tony began slowly, "...you have taught me a lot. Things I could have never learned in my world. Everything I have learned is in here," said Tony pointing to his forehead. "You taught me how every experience; even the bad ones were valuable. What I learned from you about business I could not have learned at the best University." Tony's voice was intense as he struggled with his words. "I am grateful for all the things you have done for me. But I learned from you that because of the way things worked, we could never be real friends in business..."

"—Did I ever say that you were not my friend?" Amu Sultan protested.

"Let me finish," said Tony, "...but in the end between us, there can only be friendship, because for me, that is all I wanted."

"I think I know what you are saying," Amu Sultan answered him, "...there are many things I do not tell you, and also the same is true for you. I do not tell these things, because like you there may be temptation in the future."

"That is because there is business that comes between this friendship," said Tony.

"But of course," said Amu Sultan, "...this is the simple rule of business, the two are a dangerous mix, because sometimes with trust comes foolishness."

"Then let us put all our business aside," Tony told him, "...and what we have to do now, we do as friends."

"Then what are you saying?" asked Amu Sultan.

"We need to take our vengeance," Tony began to explain slowly. "And for what I have in mind, it can only be done with the trust of your friendship and let business be put aside."

"I have made my plans Ahmed," said Amu Sultan stoutly.

"And returning to England is not part of them."

Tony sighed and averted his eyes. "Then our new friendship begins badly," said Tony, "...because you have no choice. I am not returning to England to creep about in shadows. I intend to settle all accounts and then the slate is wiped clean. I'm out of this business."

"Your words sound like a threat," said Amu Sultan.

"And you know me better than that," Tony answered. "I don't make threats. Tell me this, why should you go to Iran and leave this mess behind for me? Why should Rashar walk away a rich man at our expense without a consequence?" Tony paused and stared hard into Amu Sultan's eyes. "If you try go home, and leave me to this, then I have made arrangements for people to be waiting for you at the airport in Iran. You have a choice Amu Sultan, you either pay your taxes in England, or those waiting for you and suitcase, will make you pay them in Iran."

Amu Sultan chuckled to himself, he knew that Tony had the political contacts to make good on what he promised. For Amu Sultan it was checkmate. The two men sat looking at each other as a mutual smile emerged. "You are bastard Ahmed," conceded Amu Sultan, slightly amused.

"You shouldn't feel so bad," said Tony with irony, "...in business you have to do these things."

"Three-and-a-half million pounds is a lot of money to give VAT man," said Amu Sultan begrudgingly.

Tony began to shake his head, "Don't worry," he said, "...you won't have to give them anything. Rashar and Sheik Yunis will be doing that."

Amu Sultan was suddenly feeling better, and he had the feeling that whatever Tony had planned for them, it would be no more than they deserved.

"And what of Husseini in this matter?" asked Amu Sultan with growing interest.

"As we speak, he is being taken care of," Tony answered cryptically.

"How so?" asked Amu Sultan.

Tony's face stiffened with contempt at the mention of his name. "Do not concern yourself with this Amu Sultan," Tony answered him straight faced. "The only thing I will tell you is this, that whatever happens to Husseini, it will not be my hand on the dagger," said Tony. "What happens to Husseini he has brought on himself. Within a few days, I don't think we should ever hear from him again. Let those like him who dwell in the darkness be dealt with by men who speak a language he will understand."

It was all Amu Sultan needed to hear and knew it was all Tony would tell him.

"So what do you have in mind?" asked Amu Sultan quietly.

"There are only two fish left to fry. Let greed be the downfall of Rashar and Sheik Yunis," Tony started to explain, and spun his finger around in a slow circle. "We turn this trick around," he said gritting his teeth with almost spiteful pleasure. "And then..." he declared through his teeth, "...we fuck both of them."

As the gold-plated ornate clock on the hotel room wall swept its hours late into the morning, so the pieces of Tony's final game with Rashar and Sheik Yunis were put to Amu Sultan. Both of them would play the last few cards from a deck that Tony had stacked against the unwitting Yunis and Rashar. Then, like the men Tony knew they were— men who played games for high stakes and lost, they would be looking for someone to blame for a misfortune they thought they had inflicted on other. Only by the time their invisible opponent had played the final hand, both Rashar and Sheik Yunis would stare upon each other with suspicious eyes and vengeful intentions.

Amu Sultan was still listening intently to Tony as he shook his head in awe. What Tony had planned for these two thieves was truly the inspiration of the Devil.

"Sometimes I fear you Ahmed, because of what is in your mind," Amu Sultan said carefully. "I am glad you are my friend."

"Then you like it?" asked Tony.

Amu Sultan could not resist a smile. "Yes, I like. This is good I think," he said as the smile turned into a snigger of laughter. "Truly you are fuckin' bad bastard Ahmed. You have the mind of *Shatan* - Satan." Then both men where laughing out loud, the noise resounding around the silent hotel room. Amu Sultan offered his hand across the table to Tony. "We fuck them both," snarled Amu Sultan. The men shook hands and sealed their malicious intentions in a mutual alliance of self-interest and vengeance.

Pizza Wars

The anger in Tony's voice was confident. "We fuck them both," he growled back.

TWELVE

Councillor Bob Ronson did not like being called away from the Guildhall bar at the best of times. Let no one say that Councillor Ronson did not take his civic responsibilities seriously and even more seriously when the drinks and food were all graciously provided at the expense of the local rate-payers.

"Well, this had better be good Mavis," Ronson's bulbous red face bellowed at his prim little nubile secretary whose prowess with a word processor and shorthand had nothing on her prowess between the sheets at the local Motel fives miles down the road.

"He's in there," she said squawked back in her common high-pitched voice that made even Ronson cringe in the wrong company. Mavis pointed at the closed door of his private office.

"Who's in there?" Ronson demanded to know.

"Some Pakistani bloke," answered Mavis in a dizzy spin, "he just walked in and said he wanted to see you."

"Did he now?!" Ronson fumed. "Pakistani you say? Well we'll just have to see about this won't we?" And with that, he stormed into his office purposefully and slammed the door behind him with a crash.

"Just who the bloody hell are you?" Ronson demanded to know at the top of his voice.

The face of a smiling Rashar beamed back at him. "Good afternoon Councillor Ronson," Rashar took out a large brown envelope and threw it routinely onto the desk. "This is for you," he told Ronson confidently.

Ronson was totally confused and by now a little more cautious. Puzzled, he delicately pointed to the envelope. "For me?" he asked curiously.

Rashar's grin was bigger and cheekier. "For you my friend."

Ronson took a breath and asked a question he had the feeling he already knew the answer to. "And just what is it?"

"Why money of course," said Rashar obviously. "Your payment."

Not a man prone to look a gift-horse in the mouth, Ronson moved on to the next question. He coughed awkwardly. "I'm sorry I didn't catch your name."

"My name is Rashar Nuraman," said Rashar, "…friends, and I hope we will be friends Councillor, just call me Rashar."

"Well Mr Rashar," Ronson enquired with care. "…may I ask payment for what?"

"You are going to give me planning permission," Rashar started confidently, "…for a takeaway at the old shoe shop in the square."

Councillor Ronson was suddenly on his moral high horse and feigning his outrage for all his political worth. "How dare you!!" he shouted at Rashar. "How dare you come into my office an offer me a bribe? I don't know what country you from, but this is England."

"I am from Iraq," Rashar informed him.

"Well I don't care where you are from," said Ronson continuing his tirade, "…but you look here my brown-faced friend. You get the hell out of my office before I call the police, and take your money with you. This is a town of decent British folk and we don't want your insidious native ways here. We've had your sort before."

Of course what Ronson had neglected to tell Rashar was that for all his moral posturning, the real motive behind his outburst was that he already had a deal with Peter Hardcastle, and Hardcastle was a man not known for taking a double-cross lying down. In fact, that was usually the position his enemies found themselves in after meeting his fist.

Rashar slowly got to his feet and picked up the envelope. He did not look or sound disappointed. "Well, I thought we could do business," he said easily, "…but if those are your thoughts then what can I say Mr Burgess?" 'He took great pleasure in emphasising the name.

Ronson's chin almost hit the floor as the name left Rashar's lips. He stood in shock. Rashar stared at him, the smile back on his face. The charade was over and Ronson knew it. "You don't understand," said Ronson heavily. His voice lost its pretentious tones and the airs and graces had also gone. "You don't fuck about with a man like Hardcastle." He turned and looked at Rashar, the fear evident in his face. "He's a psychopath."

"You don't have to worry about this man," said Rashar.

"You don't know him," countered Ronson with a nervous laugh.

"If he causes problem, I have people to deal with him."

Ronson shook his head vehemently. "I'm not getting involved in anything like that."

"Don't worry, my people are professionals and will speak to him in his language," said Rashar. "There will be no trouble."

Ronson's breath was almost audible, Rashar could smell his fear, and knew he could only make one decision. He threw the envelope back onto the desk. Ronson stared at it and his breath began to relax. "How much is in there?" he asked Rashar with a steadying voice.

"How does four thousand sound?" Rashar answered.

Ronson smiled through his nerves. "Six sounds better."

Rashar gave a little laugh, took out another thousand from inside his jacket and threw it on top of the envelope. "Five."

"Hardcastle also pays me ten percent off the top monthly," said Ronson now in full negotiation mode.

"I give you two-and-a-half off the top a month," Rashar answered, "And once a year, if there is no problem another two-and-a-half." He paused and waited for an answer. "Take it, or leave it."

Ronson knew he had no choice and Rashar did not have to wait long. "I'll take it," Ronson reluctantly agreed. "Just make sure you keep Hardcastle away from me."

"Don't worry," Rashar said with a grin. "I take care of everything. I do my job, just make sure you do your job. Believe me, Hardcastle is as a child to me." His last words had the ring of a threat to Ronson, because that is exactly what it was. The two men stared at each other and Ronson swallowed hard. A second later, Rashar was gone.

At Tehran's Mehrabad International Airport, Terminal Four Arrivals were awash with Iranian expatriates from flight 1478 from Amsterdam. In green battle fatigues with AK47s hanging from their shoulders, Iranian Customs and Immigration were never the most polite in dealing with their own nationals returning home from the West. They were viewed with a mixture of suspicion and envy by guards who saw them as possible spies and traitors to The Revolution. It was an annual ritual of humiliation that the passengers quietly tolerated rather than risk being carted off to the local Customs post for a more intense inspection, after which most of their valuables would be confiscated or simply just stolen.

A short distance away from the immigration desk, four Iranians in long black overcoats and identical well-trimmed beards stood stone faced and motionless, ominously observing the incoming passengers. Passengers cleared through the customs desk seemed know instinctively not to venture a stare in their direction.

As a wheelchair bound man emerged through the automatic doors, one of the four men in black shouted an instruction in Farsi. No more than a second later, soldiers armed to the teeth seemingly appeared from nowhere, spreading panic among the waiting passengers. The rush of soldiers and the crunch of scrambling military boots sounded almost like gunfire as noise echoed around the terminal. A drone of dramatic gossip rose from the waiting passengers as they watched in awe. The soldiers surrounded the man in the wheelchair with a metallic chorus of snapping rifle bolts. Both the man pushing the wheelchair and his charge froze in fear as they stared down the barrells of at least thirty rifles. Pushing their way through the soldiers, the four men in black overcoats were suddenly glaring down at them. One of the men smiled without humour at the man in wheelchair and sarcastically he greeted him in Farsi.

"Welcome home General, we have prepared the best rooms for you," he with a spiteful grin, "...at Ovin Prison."

Just the name Ovin Prison struck fear in Husseini. "What have I done?" he pleaded pathetically.

With a swiping gesture of the hand the Iranian Secret Service officer snapped out an order. "Take him away."

The last the passengers saw of the man was him being pulled from his wheel chair and dragged without ceremony across the marble floor by a hoard of soldiers. A car waiting for him outside the airport. No more than a minute later, those who dared to look watched the car, followed by a small convoy of army jeeps, speed away into the Tehran night. They needed no further reminder of where they where and the talk soon fell silent as the watching eyes of the customs officers fell back on them. The methodical thud of the customs stamp began again.

§§§

Cheers Café was by no stretch of the imagination, the best place to eat in Hull. Situated in Hull's Hessle Road district, it had a reputation as notorious as its English proprietor, known locally, as Big Alan. Big Allen liked to think of himself as a bit of a ladies man and always had a constant supply of crass, buxom young things in tow working behind the counter to service not only the needs of shady regulars but Alan's after hour sexual activities.

For some reason the young girls seemed to find him irresistible, or so Allen claimed. He had a crude sort of charm that gave him an endearing quality that made him well liked and trusted locally. He liked to brag that he was thirty-five, especially to the ladies, but in actual fact looked even older than his actual fifty-two years. Standing five-foot-six in his stocking feet, and with a figure that would flatter an old beer barrel, it was more reasonable to assume that what the young females found most irresistible about Allen was the huge roll of notes that he would often pull from his pocket and flaunt. Few girls resisted and usually they found themselves in his bed, and for a few weeks showered with gifts, until Allen's need for fresh flesh took him onto the next conquest.

More than twenty years ago, Allen had been Amu Sultan's partner in his first business venture. It was in the restaurant business and it started and ended as a disaster, leaving Amu

Sultan with an empty bank account and a fifty thousand pound debt. Allen was not a businessman. He liked to be liked and had spent most of his time impressing the customers by giving them free food and drink, much to Farida's constant fury.

Eventually they went their separate ways, but despite their mutual bad experience they remained inseparable friends because Amu Sultan appreciated and valued Allen's most important asset. While he might not have been the best business brain in the world, he was an honest friend who accepted people for what they were. Colour, religion, or sexuality didn't matter and no favour was too great to ask of him.

The café was a meeting place for all the dodgy wheeler-dealers in the area. They came in with everything from car radios and counterfeit cigarettes, to tobacco smuggled from the ships docked nearby. You name it; they could get it for you at a fraction of the price— no questions asked. In Cheers café you kept your own counsel and looked after your own business, that way you remained healthy.

Allen almost threw the two plates of bacon and eggs on the table in front of Tony and Amu Sultan. Before Amu Sultan had time to get his wallet out Allen was already glaring at him as if insulted. "Put ya' fuckin' money away. It's on the house."

The two men tucked into the breakfast. Amu Sultan expression was without gratitude. "You never change," he chastised him. "You will never make money like this."

"You let me worry about that," he chuckled. "We're not all like you bleedin' Pakkis."

From anyone else such a remark from an Englishman would have been swiftly followed by an ambulance.

"I told you before fat bastard," Amu Sultan returned the gesture, "I am not a Pakki, I am Persian." His lecherous eyes could not resist looking over at the young girl taking the money at the till. "I see you still like the young tarts."

Allen's dirty laugh filled the café. "That's me, still like them young and tight."

Tony moved the conversation on to the matter in hand, and the favour he had telephoned Allen to do from Amsterdam. "Did you get the fax?" Tony asked Allen.

Allen took out several sheets of paper and slid them across the table to Tony. "You owe me a tenner," said Allen. "I had to pay over the phone with my credit card."

"Pay the man," Tony said to Amu Sultan and he started to study the documents as he ate.

"What do you want that shit for anyway?" queried Allen.

Tony was engrossed in the documents. "They're company documents," he answered still studying them. Then slowly he began to smile to himself as he ran his finger over a particular line. "Look here," he passed the document to Amu Sultan.

Farida, too, now smiled at what he read. "They have split the company into two million shares," he said aloud.

"And look who has one-and-a-half million," Tony pointed out with interest.

"Husseini," Amu Sultan whispered aloud.

"Yunis and Rashar must have only have put up a quarter-of-a-million each," said Tony.

Amu Sultan screwed up his face. "I don't understand why they have done it this way."

"Isn't it obvious?" said Tony. "You sold the business for two million cash. They've divided up the company for the amount they paid for it and each one holds shares equivalent to the amount of money they put up."

"But that is crazy," Amu Sultan said slowly.

Tony started to laugh. "Of course it's crazy," agreed Tony. "But Rashar and Sheik Yunis don't understand what they have done. They don't understand how the legal system works. The pair of soft bastards think they are in Yemen."

"Husseini has control then?" said Amu Sultan aloud.

"Exactly, he can do what he likes and they can't do a thing to stop him," said Tony. "He's going to fuck them both then," said Amu Sultan. "Once a thief always a thief," said Tony, "You know that."

Allen was suddenly up on his feet. "Don't mind me, but this conversation is getting a bit boring." With now only Tony, Amu Sultan and the young girl in the café, Allen shut the café door and put up the closed sign. "I'll drop the latch, you two let yourselves out when you're ready." He nodded with a grin in the direction of the cashier and winked. "I think we'll cash up early." The two of them disappeared upstairs carrying the cash drawer from the till and leaving Tony and Amu Sultan alone.

"And look," Tony again pointed the company documents. "...they have all mis-spelled their names. Now isn't that a surprise."

Amu Sultan read the names aloud, almost laughing as he did so. "Husseinali, Yunisini and Rashar Nuramanan," Amu Sultan shrugged his shoulders. "They are name shuffling, so what? Almost everybody does that if they are dodgy. If it goes broke they disappear and no one knows their real names."

Tony seemed to be speaking his thoughts aloud. "That makes things a lot easier for us." He thoughtfully bit the corner of lip. "I think it will work," he said softly.

"What will work?" Amu Sultan asked with rising curiosity.

Before Tony could answer, his mobile phone rang. Tony answered it and smiled as soon as he heard the Iranian accented voice. "Hello Sir, how are you?"

Across the table, Amu Sultan stopped eating his bacon and eggs as curiosity got the better of him.

"I am well thank you Ahmed," said the Ambassador. Apologetically he continued, "I hope you understand the motives for my theatrics when last we met."

"Of course, I know how difficult these things are," Tony answered cryptically.

"It leaves me only to say that I will be moving on soon, so I thought I would give you a call before I depart," the Ambassador told him. "My two years are up and I shall be returning to Iran. Tehran does not like us staying in office for too long, in case we get too friendly with the natives." He laughed. "I am sure you understand what I mean."

Tony laughed back politely. "Of course Sir."

"I thought you might like to know that on my return I might look in on your friend who has just returned home."

Tony was all smiles, "That would be very good of you Sir. Please give him my best regards."

The Ambassador laughed heartily. "I will indeed Ahmed. Look after yourself and perhaps *Inshallah* we might speak again in the future."

"*Inshallah* –God willing," Tony reciprocated.

"Good-bye Ahmed, and good luck."

"And the same to you Sir....and thanks." Tony closed his phone with a latent grin on his face. Amu Sultan sat looking at him, waiting for answers. They did not come.

"Well come on then, who was that?" asked Amu Sultan almost exploding with curiosity.

Tony furrowed his brow insignificantly. "Just a friend," he said flippantly.

Amu Sultan knew something was going on, and it was clear that Tony was not going to tell him anything. If he was angry or hurt he did not show it, because he knew, as well as anybody, the rules that Tony was playing by— they were his rules too. He tucked back into his full English breakfast without further enquiry.

While Tony had a degree of trust in Amu Sultan, it was not enough for him to know what the future held. And just like his father had told him so often, "Today's friends could be tomorrow's enemies." The simple fact was that Amu Sultan did not need to know, so why take the risk of telling him something that he could use against him in the future. After all, you cannot use what you do not know.

§§§

Peter Hardcastle did not know where it came from or what had hit him. One second he was having a laugh with one of his staff and the next minute he was staring into the faces of six Asian looking youths that had surrounded him.

His first thought was that they were after the takings in his briefcase and being an instinctive brawler, with his free hand he let go an almighty swipe at one of the youths sending him flying across the alley in the darkness. His success was short lived as the first crash of a baseball bat came down on his head and the concrete floor came rushing up to meet him.

Even as loss of consciousness threatened to overtake his senses, he tried to fight back, as more blows rained down on him from all directions until he was reduced to curling up like a hedgehog to protect himself. Though he was now defenceless, the bats gave way to the thud of feet mercilessly laying into every part of him until all senses of pain had surrendered. Vaguely, through the blood and haze, he could feel a mountain of lumps sprouting around his face and the tear of wounds oozing blood like water. It crossed his foggy thoughts that perhaps his history had finally caught up with him and that one of the many enemies he had trodden into the ground was finally serving up the same violence as revenge.

Aware now that the rain of blows had ceased and that he was still alive, the glare of a bright torch suddenly blinded what little vision remained in his eyes. A hand gripped him by the throat and he could just make out the sounds of a foreign voice growling into his face like a wild hungry beast.

Rashar's grip around Peter Hardcastle's neck was like a vice and he lifted his head and shoulders off the concrete. "Now listen to me Englishman!" he shouted into his face. "Your time is over in this town. Take your money and go." He shook Hardcastle's head like a puppet. "You understand me English?"

Peter Hardcastle could feel his heart pounding in his chest and knew now what it felt like to feel the fear he had so readily imposed on others.

"Look Englishman, look!!" Rashar taunted him with a mocking sneer and forced Hardcastle's limp head toward the direction of the chip shop as flames began to burst through the roof and windows. Punishing his weakness, Rashar suddenly started to laugh. Then gesturing his next orders to those stood around him, the pungent smell of petrol filled Hardcastle's nostrils as the he felt the cold liquid being poured over him. Hardcastle's senses returned with panic and he struggled and pleaded for the same mercy he had callously denied to many.

"No, no, please!" he began to cry like some wretched beaten child. "Anything, anything, please!!"

Rashar slowly smiled to himself and knew that he had won. It made no difference to Rashar whether this man lived or died. Rashar had taken from this man the next best thing to his life. He had taken his self-respect. And when such a warrior surrenders that, he is no longer a warrior and no longer a threat. Rashar had shown his sword to his enemy and he had chosen humiliation rather than the mere threat of death. Rashar knew in his heart that this man had things to live for and would not return for vengeance. The new sweeps away the old and the weaker is left defeated.

"I let you live this time English," he whispered into his face. "If I see you again," he said with an emphatic pause, "...do not doubt that I will kill you." He slammed Hardcastle back to the concrete and quietly walked away.

THIRTEEN

There are many ways of doing business. You can go by the book and employ clever accountants and solicitors to perform the immoral but legal fiddles for you, or you can simply just fiddle your way through all the laws and regulations yourself, leaving behind a trail of confusion and deception designed to confound anyone who might come after you. These are two options, there are many others. In the takeaway world the method usually employed is the second one.

Remember that in the world of the foreigner, names and identities can be manipulated to be meaningless, thereby allowing an escape route in times of emergency. By a mere slip of the pen, a foreign name can be misspelled, and in the Arab culture a person not only has a name but may also have a title that resembles a name. For instance a person called Mohamed Abdul may also be called by the name of his first born child with the prefix of Abu. Abu in Arabic means father. So a man with a first borne child which has the name Nasir may be addressed Abu Nasir which means very simply, Father of Nasir. All this can lead to a great deal of confusion for government agencies like the Inland Revenue and VAT office when it comes to finding who owns or runs a certain takeaway.

While all this makes it extremely difficult to establish identity, it also makes those using these methods extremely vulnerable to anyone who knows how to use the system against them. In the case of Husseini, now languishing in Ovin Prison, it had to be remembered that he was the majority shareholder in a company under the shuffled name of Husseinali. Since Husseinali was effectively out of the way and not likely to see the shores of Great Britain again, there was nothing to stop anyone from simply impersonating him, going to another solicitor and having the original documents transferred. As the majority share holder, they would be positioned to sell the whole business.

Solicitors are often cleverer than their clients would like to think, but on the whole, a good solicitor will never ask too many obvious questions. For one, the less they know the less likely they are to compromise themselves, and secondly, they do not want to lose a good fee-paying client whatever they might suspect. Husseini had been involved in so many business scams during his short time in the UK he had changed solicitors more times than a prostitute changes clients. Consequently, no long-term relationship had been built up with any one solicitor and it was rumoured and probably true, that he rarely settled the final accounts before he fled. Tony was banking on the fact that Husseini had not settled his account with his current solicitor, Mr Emanuel Rosenberg of the offices of Rosenburg, Bloom and Winestock.

Tony was sure what he had in mind would work like a charm. Amu Sultan was not so sure. The two of them walked down the old cobbled streets of The Land of Green Ginger in Hull, an area almost exclusively occupied by solicitors' offices of one sort or another.

"I must be crazy to let you talk me into this," said Amu Sultan nervously as his doubts over Tony's plan grew by the second.

"Stop worrying," Tony tried to assure him. "It'll work."

"I just hope you are right," said Amu Sultan looking for more assurance.

Tony stopped walking and tried to calm Amu Sultan's nerves. "Have I ever failed?" he asked Amu Sultan straight out. "And even if you get rumbled what can they do?" Tony smiled. "Fuckall. That's what they can do. Don't you understand Husseinali doesn't exist? And who's gonna complain, certainly not Husseini I can assure you of that."

Amu Sultan stared Tony straight in the face with more doubts, "You keep saying that, but how do I know that?"

Tony shook his head with growing exasperation. Unless Amu Sultan got a grip on himself, he was sure he would screw up the whole plan.

"Alright, alright," Tony conceded. "You want to know where Husseini is?" He paused and stood looking at Amu Sultan. "Then I'll tell you." He paused again.

"Well?" asked Amu Sultan.

"He's in Ovin Prison," Tony declared.

Amu Sultan's mouth opened like a gold fish. "Ovin Prison Tehran?" he asked with screech of disbelief. He giggled to himself. "What is he doing there, you dodgy bastard?"

Tony shrugged his shoulders. "*Wallah* - I swear, it was nothing to do with me. He did it all himself."

Amu Sultan was suddenly sniggering aloud. "You fuckin' clever bastard. How did you do that?"

Tony held out his hands in a gesture of innocence. "It was nothing to do with me."

Amu Sultan tried to mask his amusement with a serious face. "Of course, I believe you Ahmed."

"*Wallah* – I swear," said Tony.

"I said, I believe you," answered Amu Sultan making a very poor attempt to sound credible. "What's your problem?"

"Then you do believe me?" Tony asked slowly.

"I just said, didn't I?" answered a still smiling Amu Sultan. "Now let's go." And he started off down the street with a new-found enthusiasm in his step.

"What's the sudden hurry?" Tony called after him.

Amu Sultan turned round and chuckled. "If you can put Husseini in Ovin Prison," he answered with a great big smile, "...then this is a piece of cake. Now let's go." With that Amu Sultan carried on down the street audibly laughing to himself. Behind him, Tony shook his head and hurried to catch up.

§§§

The building work was going well, on schedule and on budget. Rashar and Sheik Yunis looked happy as they inspected the progress of the newest addition to their takeaway empire. Surrounded by the building dust and the noise of the busy workmen, Rashar took in a proud breath as he looked around the old shoe shop in Gold Thorpe Market Square.

"I think we make a lot of money," announced Rashar with a self-satisfying feeling of cleverness.

The Old Sheik smiled in agreement, "You are a man of many talents my son," said the Sheik in a tone that begged a question. "You have surprised with this endeavour and my faith in you grows as it should…"

Rashar was smiling in anticipation. "I know what is on your mind," Rashar answered him. "You wonder why I did not keep this one just between us."

The Old Sheik stared with a curious grin. "You read my thoughts well and it is a question I must ask."

"The answer is simple my brother," said Rashar. "Husseini takes us both for fools. You and I both know Husseini for the thief he is. Perhaps already he plans our fall."

"If you see these things," said the Sheik, "…then why do you do business with him?"

"My old friend," Rashar started to laugh, "was it really just I who saw this thing?" He stared for a moment at the Old Sheik and then the Sheik began to laugh with him. "You and I are both of the same blood," said Rashar, "I must apologise for saying nothing, but I knew our intentions between us were honourable and I also knew you to be a wise man, as you have just shown."

"Then you have plans for Husseini?" whispered the Old Sheik.

"I think we both have plans for Husseini my old friend."

Sheik Yunis shook his head and laughed. "I think perhaps you are right."

The two men walked outside and for no more than a second they gave a cursory glance across the road. They were less than fifty yards away from the black and charred shell of Peter Hardcastle's fish shop on the other side of the market square. Since the night of the fire there had been no sign of Hardcastle after he discharged himself from hospital. What enquiries the local police had made turned up nothing more than a strong suspicion about who was responsible, and suspicion was not proof.

Whilst they were concerned about the fire, they were more concerned that whatever had gone on was over. It was a business dispute of sorts, that much they knew— a conflict between thieves with the mentality of street dogs fighting over a bone. Sometimes in such cases, and with resources so scarce, the police took a philosophical view that justice has a curious way of serving itself and what goes round comes around. Hardcastle's day had come and gone. For the police, business disputes are like domestic disputes— more trouble than they are worth.

§§§

The bright young face of Isador Barnett tried not to show too much excitement as the smartly dressed foreign gentlemen took a seat opposite his desk. Isador was relatively new to the Land of Green Ginger and had opened his office no more than a month ago. This was his third new client and his business was growing by the day.

Isador smiled politely and carefully re-read the name pencilled in his appointment diary. "So Mr.....Husseinali, what can I do for you?"

Across the desk a big friendly smile broke across Amu Sultan's face. "I am having big problem with my solicitor and I am not happy with him. I come to you for help," he announced confidently and placed ten one thousand pound wads of twenty pound notes on the desk as an appetiser.

As the cash seemed to stare back him, Isador's smile broadened to match Amu Sultan's. "Well...erm... that's certainly what I am here for Mr Husseinali," he answered happily.

"I want to move all my business papers to you," said Amu Sultan. "There will be a matter of the account with other solicitor to settle and I hope you will take of this for me?"

"That is absolutely no problem Mr Husseinali," said Isador with pen enthusiastically poised. "And just who was your solicitor?"

Amu Sultan was now totally confident and in his stride. "Mr Rosenberg, of Rosenberg, Bloom and Winestock. He is very bad man."

Isador knew better than to be drawn into name-calling and responded with an animated smile. "I'll get onto that straight away."

"I am in big hurry to sell my business," continued Amu Sultan. "This is between us."

"—Of course," interjected Isador soundly.

"I already have buyer," Amu Sultan went on, "...and this, too, will be good business for you."

"Well I had better take the name of this buyer then," he said looking across at Amu Sultan.

"Now what is it his name now?" said Amu Sultan pretending to be raking his brain. "Oh yes, Sultan Farida."

"And Mr Sultan Farida's solicitor is?" asked Isador scribing as he talked.

§§§

Arnold Rosenberg knew exactly what type of man Husseini was from the day he stepped into his office. He was not the least bit surprised to get a phone call from Isador Barnett requesting the transfer of Husseini's files. It was a much played dusty old trick that men like Husseni used to either avoid paying their final account or get a substantial reduction in exchange for their files.

"The files are not a problem," Mr Rosenberg casually replied. "The problem is that I require my final account for work done for Mr Husseini, or whatever his name is, to be settled before you get anything. Then you can have the files with my blessing and relief I might add."

With the pile of money still on the desk staring at him, Isador Barnett could only come to the conclusion that Mr Rosenberg's comments were sour grapes.

"Well then, we don't have a problem," answered Isador with a smile as he played with the wads of cash on the desk. "I'll send someone over immediately."

"You won't get the files until I get our money."

"And how much is that?" asked Isador coyly.

Being some years older than Isador Barnett and with a lot more experience with men such as Husseini, Mr Rosenberg got the distinct impression that his former client was in some sort of a rush to do another dodgy deal. This probably being the reason he was changing solicitors. If that was the case, it presented a wonderful opportunity to lever the money owed out of his former client.

Shuffling through a number of files on his desk, Mr Rosenberg opened the one marked Husseini. Inside was an invoice which he read out over the phone. "Your client owes us £7525.25 including disbursements."

Isador replied with a thoughtful, "Hmm...," which Mr Rosenberg detected was his opening gambit to get the bill lowered.

"Of course," went on Mr Rosenberg, "...for speedy settlement I might be able to reduce the amount somewhat."

Isador started reluctantly, "Mmmmm, I thought perhaps four thousand pounds might be a figure we could agree on."

"I think five thousand pounds might be more agreeable," retorted Mr Rosenberg.

"I'll send the cash across now," answered Isador confidently. "I assume you will have the files ready to collect?"

Mr Rosenberg was pleasantly surprised. He had been ready to accept four thousand five hundred pounds, four thousand if push came to shove. "For cash Mr Barnett, the files will be ready and waiting."

"I'll send my secretary across now," said Isador smiling. "Goodbye Mr Rosenberg."

No sooner had he cleared his phone than he buzzed his secretary. "Get me Solomon Cohen straight away. After that, I've got an urgent job for you so don't go anywhere."

§§§

As the door to his office opened, a somewhat confused Solomon Cohen emerged from behind his desk and with genuine warmth shook the hand of the man entering. "Well, this is a surprise Mr Farida," he said slightly bemused. "A very pleasant surprise, but a surprise none-the-less. I thought by now you would be enjoying the delights of retirement in Tehran."

Amu Sultan's smile was an awkward one and he was just a touch out of breath as he had rushed from Isador Barnett's office to Solomon Cohen's — a distance of two hundred and fifty yards. Panting, he slid into his usual chair on the opposite side of the desk, his forehead slightly perspiring.

"Are you alright Mr Farida?" Solomon asked him with some concern.

Amu Sultan tried to smile and catch his breath. "I am very well, thanking you." Solomon automatically poured Amu Sultan a glass of water and handed it to him. A grateful Amu Sultan took a few sips and gradually composed himself.

"A touch of asthma I think," said Amu Sultan artfully punctuating with an artificial cough.

Solomon returned to his chair. "You should really see a doctor Mr Farida."

Amu Sultan smiled politely, "You are as always a gentleman Mr.Cohen, but I am fine thank you."

"Not at all Mr Farida," said Solomon. "Now, if you are sure you are alright. What can I do for you?"

"I changed my mind," Amu Sultan blurted out cryptically.

"About what exactly?" enquired Solomon.

"My business," said Amu Sultan, "I am buying it back."

"Oh I see," said Solomon," Well that's your prerogative Mr Farida. Just exactly what do you require me to do?"

For a few seconds Amu Sultan's smile seemed stuck to his face. "Since I am buying the business back, of course I want you to deal with this matter in your usual and quick way."

Solomon's next question was more one of personal interest than anything else. "And Mr Husseini has agreed to sell it back I take it?"

"I think he has problems," confessed Amu Sultan. "He is in a great rush, and who knows, maybe I get a good price." Nervously, he laughed.

"Mmmm indeed. Well it all seems a little confusing," said Solomon with gentile smile.

"I hope this is not problem for you Mr Cohen."

Solomon now shrugged his shoulders. "Not at all Mr Farida, I simply take your instructions."

It was at that precise moment that Solomon's telephone rang. "If you would excuse me for a moment," Solomon apologised and picked up the phone. "Hello.......yes.....ahhh....yes..... I am with Mr Farida at the moment."

As he spoke on the phone, Solomon was staring rather sceptically in Farida's direction, or so Amu Sultan thought.

Amu Sultan tried to smile but inside he was a growing bag of nerves as he sat watching Solomon on the phone, talking to Barnett, he guessed. Getting one over on a young solicitor who was still wet behind the ears was one thing, but getting one over a man of Solomon Cohen's years and experience was quite another.

"I see....yes....," Solomon continued. "Well just between us, that's not a surprise." Solomon started to laugh.

"Well if you would just give me a moment, I'll ask Mr Farida now." Solomon pressed the mute button on the phone. "Have you agreed a price with Mr Husseini Mr Farida?"

Amu Sultan suddenly swallowed hard. He had been in such a hurry to leave Isador Barnett's office that a question of the price had not even entered his head until now.

"A price?" Amu Sultan unsteadily repeated aloud.

"Yes, Mr Farida a price?" repeated Solomon, "Do you have one in mind?"

Amu Sultan awkwardly laughed aloud. "Of course, yes... yes I have a price."

A few moments passed in embarrassing silence. "Well, what is it Mr Farida?"

Amu Sultan said the first number that came into his head. "One million, yes..yes, one million."

"One million?" Solomon queried. "Are you sure Mr Farida. Mr Husseini has just paid you two-and-half million for the business."

Amu Sultan shrugged his shoulders. "He is in big trouble with money. Tell him take it or leave it," he answered harshly.

Solomon furrowed his brow and took the instruction. He lifted his finger from the mute button. "Hello Mr Barnett.......Yes, I have just spoken to my client and he is offering one million pounds...........Yes, one million pounds. If you could find out if that figure is acceptable to your client we can proceed..... Goodbye Mr Barnett." Solomon put down the phone. "Mr Barnett is going to contact his client forthwith and ring me straight back."

As soon as Solomon finished speaking, Amu Sultan's mobile phone rang. "Hello......?" said Amu Sultan.

It was Isador Barnett on the phone. If looks could have convicted a guilty man, then such a look was on Amu Sultan's face. "Yes....Yes...I accept it. I accept it," he snapped.

"Yes..yes..Goodbye." He snapped the phone shut and gave a nervous cough. "My stockbroker," he told Solomon with an animated laugh.

Solomon stared without expression over his half moon spectacles. "Indeed." And again Solomon's phone came to Amu Sultan's rescue.

"Ahh, hello again Mr Barnett." Solomon was staring again at Amu Sultan as he spoke. "Well that is good news...........Good..........then let's proceed at full speed then, I think my client wishes to move quickly............I can draw up the papers by tomorrow...........Let's say four o'clock tomorrow afternoon...........That's perfect.....Goodbye Mr Barnett."

Solomon replaced the receiver. "Well it is good news Mr Farida."

"Really, how so?" asked Amu Sultan with innocence.

"Well it seems you were right," announced Solomon with a note of surprise, "Mr Husseini it appears is in a great hurry to sell."

Amu Sultan shook his head with an expression of disapproval. "I think perhaps tax man is after him."

§§§

Tony tucked hungrily into his big Mac and fries as he sat waiting in the burger restaurant. He had arranged a meeting with Tom Bradley at the VAT office and was half-an-hour early because he was also waiting for Amu Sultan to see if the events at the solicitor's had panned out. Outside a black cab pulled up and deposited a strident Amu Sultan, his face oozing success. Tony guessed things had gone well. Amu Sultan almost danced his way to Tony's table.

"You are fuckin' genius Ahmed," he said laughing aloud. "Fuckin' genius."

"I take it things went well then?

"Like fuckin' watchwork," answered Amu Sultan mixing up his English.

"You mean clockwork," said Tony.

Amu Sultan sat down. "Who cares what I mean. It worked I think."

"What do you mean, you think?" said Tony.

"You choose that young solicitor well," answered Amu Sultan. "But Solomon Cohen is not a fool. I think he knows something dodgy is going on."

Tony pursed his lips without care. "He's a solicitor Amu Sultan. He does as he is told, you know that. He might know what is going on, but that is not his business. Just so long as he gets paid and he is not compromised, he is not bothered."

"I hope you are right," said Amu Sultan showing crossed fingers.

"I know I'm right," said Tony emphatically.

"Just something in his face, when it came to the price," said Amu Sultan.

Tony suddenly leered across the table at Amu Sultan. "I hope you didn't do anything stupid did you," he said staring at him.

Amu Sultan made an innocent gesture with his hands, and it was enough for Tony to know that he had.

"Come on," said Tony dragging it out of him, "what did you do?"

Amu Sultan was looking at Tony and the words just would not come, but Tony had already guessed. "How much did you offer you greedy old bastard," he asked with anticipation in his voice.

Amu Sultan's arms were waving about all over the place before he spoke, as if already trying to explain. "Why should I pay more than I have to?" was his reticent answer.

Tony started to laugh. "Come on then, how much?"

Amu Sultan shrugged a little. "A million," he said in sort of whisper.

Tony fell back in his chair laughing. "And I take it he accepted?"

The joke went over Amu Sultan's head. "Of course it was accepted. I accepted it, silly bastard."

"Yes, I know that...but..." Tony started and then shook his head. "Never mind."

"You have problem?" said Amu Sultan.

"It doesn't matter how much you offer for the business," Tony tried to explain. "The amount the VAT want stays the same." He looked at Amu Sultan and paused for a second. "Don't you understand that?"

Amu Sultan's face was suddenly angry. "Of course I understand this thing," he snapped back him.

"Then why did you offer a million?" retorted Tony.

Amu Sultan gritted his teeth and glared back at Tony. "Because I tell you why. Husseini, Rashar and Yunis have been having good laugh at my expense," explained Amu Sultan. "I know these people, they tell everyone they have fucked me to make themselves clever." Amu Sultan started pointing at himself. "Well when they find out I get all my business back for a million, all will know that I fucked them. And I will be laughing. You should understand Ahmed, these things are important. I will be clever bastard then and for this I will get respect and some will fear me."

"You mean you want your vengeance?" said Tony in a low voice.

"You are English Ahmed," said Amu Sultan intently. "You do not understand these things. To be made a fool in my culture is a very bad thing."

Tony took an envelope from his pocket and slid it across the to Amu Sultan. "Maybe you are right," he said heavily. "I got this in the post this morning.

Amu Sultan slipped out the letter inside. The heading on the letter said it all in big black bold letters, **INLAND REVENUE HUMBER AREA COMPLIANCE OFFICE**. He took a few moments to read the letter and slowly folded it closed. "Bastard!" he cursed aloud. "They want a lot of money from you." Amu Sultan had a surprise for Tony as he too took a letter out of his pocket, unfolded it and handed it to Tony. The letter had the same big bold heading as Tony had on his. **INLAND REVENUE HUMBER AREA COMPLIANCE OFFICE.** Only it had Amu Sultan's name on it.

Tony's laugh was bitter. "So they got you too?"

Amu Sultan gestured with a contemptuous hand gesture. "Don't worry Ahmed, me and you sort it."

Tony shook his head with a hard grimace. "I'm not worried," said Tony. "And now I'm like you Amu Sultan. This whole thing is pissing me off now." He pointed at himself, "I too want my vengeance now." He picked up both the letters angrily, tore them into pieces, then threw them into a nearby waste bin. "For this, I am going to fuck Rashar and Yunis so hard they won't know if they want a shit or a haircut."

From the corner of his eye Amu Sultan saw Tom Bradley and Angela Carrick enter the restaurant. "Your friends are here," said Amu Sultan in low voice.

"I have to speak alone with them. I hope you understand," said Tony. "They will not want witnesses for what I have to say to them."

"Don't worry Ahmed," said Amu Sultan smiling. "I trust you."

Tony now smiled back and knew that he meant those words. "I hope so."

Amu Sultan was up and out of the exit before Bradley and Carrick got to the table.

"And where's Ali Baba going?" said Bradley sarcastically.

Tony looked up at Bradley angrily. "Don't call him that again." It sounded like a warning. "His name is Sultan."

Bradley slid into the opposite seat. "Go get us something to eat and two coffees," he instructed Angela.

"Do you want anything?" Angela asked Tony coldly.

Tony looked her over with a suggestive smile. "I could be tempted," he answered cheekily.

"Tea or coffee?" she snapped back unamused.

"Coffee, white, no sugar," said Tony.

"So what do you want to talk about?" Bradley asked him.

"You want your money don't you?" said Tony with a curious smile.

"And have you got it?" asked Bradley slowly.

"Three-and-a-half million is too much," Tony said flatly. "Considering that I don't have to give you anything, I think maybe two million is more than satisfactory."

Bradley sneered with contempt. "Now how did I know that was coming."

"I haven't finished yet," said Tony. "Two million is just what you get to wipe out mine and Sultan's debt." Tony and Bradley stared silently into each other's eyes both knowing what was coming next.

Angela Carrick returned to the table with tray of burgers and drinks and slid into the seat next to Tom.

"Go on," said Bradley slowly.

Tony started to explain carefully, "Effectively there are two more partners from whom you need to collect the other one-and-a-half million."

Bradley shook his head and smiled with disgust in anticipation of what was coming next. "Rashar you mean?" Bradley answered for him.

"Rashar and Yunis," Tony answered through gritted teeth, "I want them both. They started this whole thing. Why should they be left to just walk away?"

This whole thing was getting more complicated and dangerous by the minute and Bradley was beginning to feel that he should never have gotten involved in the first place. In the beginning he had thought of this as an easy way to get himself promoted. But breaking this massive VAT scam was turning into a nightmare. A nightmare where his future job prospects diminished with every word that left Tony's mouth. He had the feeling that Tony knew exactly what he was doing, and was doing it deliberately. He was being used as a tool in some personal vendetta, and there was not a damn thing he could do to get out of it, other than be led by the nose.

Bradley swallowed hard, trying not to show his growing anguish. He decided to go on the offensive, "As far as I'm concerned I don't give a fuck about your personal beefs and your sleazy goings on," he said ferociously. "We're VAT officers and somehow you have managed to drag us both down into this sewer where you do your business."

"Well look who's getting on their fucking high horse." Tony leaned across the table to whisper some home truths to Bradley. "You thought you were just going to help Husseni, Rashar and Yunis, fuck over me and Sultan, and just walk away with three-and-a-half million quid in VAT and get yourself a nice little feather in your cap, mainly at my expense. And now ya' crying in ya beer because I won't rollover and play dead. You started this game Bradley!! Only you're on my side now whether you like it or not. And as for Rashar and Yunis." Tony started to laugh. "Well, you let me worry about them. All you have to do is to just do as I tell you and you get three million pounds back VAT money and a big slap on the back from your boss." Tony lightened his voice and smiled, "And who knows, you might even get promoted."

Bradley turned to Angela. She looked just as worried as he did and felt just as cornered. Without a word she raised her eyebrows as if conceding they had no choice.

Bradley turned back to Tony. "You said three million just now."

"We'll give you two-and-a-half," said Tony, "and the other half you get out of Rashar and Yunis."

"And just how do we do that?" asked Angela.

"Ten percent of two-and-a-half million is two hundred and fifty thousand pounds," Tony started to explain. "That's how much of the company Rashar owned."

"But how do we get our hands on the money?"

"You get yourself a warrant to search his house just like you did mine," Tony answered simply, "And that's where you will find the money." Tony shrugged his shoulders, "Who knows you might even find more."

"But we can't just enforce against Rashar without enforcing against you and Sultan as well," said Angela, "...it will look too suspicious. We just won't get away with it."

"God you people amaze me sometimes," answered Tony almost mocking them. "You enforce against all of us, and me and Sultan will simply give you what we owe you."

"And Yunis?" asked Bradley, "We ain't got nothing on him."

"Oh don't worry about Yunis," said Tony softly. "With what I give you on him you'll have enough to put him away for five years."

"What do you mean?"

Tony smiled. "You think he just did the till rolls for us?"

"You mean there's more?" asked Bradley.

"I'll tell you where, when, and how," said Tony emphatically. "You'll both be fuckin' heroes by the time this is over. Just make sure that if you arrest Rashar he doesn't go to prison."

Bradley and Angela looked at each other. "Why?" asked Angela.

"Once you get your money, its over," Tony answered. Tony was looking at them both without an expression. "Just leave Rashar alone."

Before Angela could ask again, a light came on in Bradley's head and told him that it was better that they didn't know. "Okay!!" he interrupted over Angela's impending question, "We leave Rashar alone."

Pizza Wars

"So that's settled," said Tony finally.

"Just the matter of Yunis then?" said Bradley carefully.

Tony looked at them both for second. "Get your pen and paper out, ya gonna need them."

FOURTEEN

"Well Mr Farida," said Solomon Cohen pointing to an area of a legal document, "…if you would just sign here." With a big smile Amu Sultan scribbled his name across the document and passed it back to Solomon.

"Excellent," said Solomon, "that just leaves the matter of Mr Husseinali's signature and you are once again the proud owner of thirty pizza parlours."

Amu Sultan unceremoniously lifted the suitcase and placed it onto the middle of Solomon's desk. Solomon was amused since it was the same suitcase Farida had taken away with him only a week or so ago but in a reverse transaction. It had been a strange turn of events these past few days but Solomon knew better than to let his curiosity get the better of him. Whatever Mr Farida was up to was his affair. The legal profession came across all sorts of people in its line of work and Mr Farida was by no means the dodgiest. He was courteous, humble, well mannered and always paid his accounts on time. As far as Solomon was concerned, he was a model client. Solomon opened the suitcase to inspect the contents. He allowed himself a gentle sigh as he eyed the money packed inside. "Well, I suppose we had better have it counted it Mr Farida."

§§§

"If you would just sign here Mr Husseinali," said Isador Barnett, "that will complete the exchange of contracts. Mr Farida signed an hour ago."

Amu Sultan smiled as he obligingly forged the name Reza Husseinali across the contract. Isador lifted the document for a final inspection. "Well that's it Mr Husseinali. All contracts signed, sealed and delivered. I just have to fax this to Solomon Cohen and the money, which I understand is in cash, will be brought across."

Amu Sultan stood up to leave. "Thank you most kindly for your good work Mr Barnett," said Amu Sultan as he shook Isador's hand. "If you would put the money somewhere safe for an hour, I will have it collected."

"I'm afraid there will of course, be a counting fee Mr Farida," said Isador.

Amu Sultan smiled. "I will leave all things you Mr Barnett and please feel free to settle your full account once the money has been counted. Now if you would forgive me."

§§§

It was almost two thirty in the morning; Rashar Nuraman was stark naked and fast asleep when a relentless pounding on his front door jolted him awake. His first thought was to go straight for the baseball bat he kept under his bed. His second thought was to sneak to the window and peak through the closed curtains. In front of his house he could see two police cars and three unmarked cars. "What the hell is going on?" he whispered aloud to himself in Arabic. Quickly he flung on his bath robe, put back the baseball bat, and went downstairs to answer his door. "Alright!! Alright!! I'm coming," he shouted. He opened the door.

"Are you Rashar Nuraman?"

"Do you know what time it is?" protested Rashar.

Without asking a second time, Tom Bradley and a few other officers pushed their way into the house. "What the hell is going on!!" Rashar now shouted at the top of his voice. Bradley stuck his warrant card under Rashar's nose and the words Customs and Excise were clear. "I have a warrant to search theses premises Mr Al Arash."

"But....but you can't do that," said Rashar almost in shock. The worst was yet to come as Bradley automatically reeled off his next statement. "Rashar Nuraman I am arresting you on conspiracy to defraud Her Majesty's Customs and Excise. You are not obliged to say anything..."

Rashar could feel nervous sweat beginning to run down his face and the next thing he knew his hands where behind his back and he was being led away in hand cuffs as nosey neighbours watched through their windows.

§§§

The noise inside the large bedroom was almost as unbearable as the pungent odour of sweat. So cramped was the room that those working were almost shoulder to shoulder as they sat squat on the threadbare carpet toiling away into the night. This was the nerve centre of Sheik Yunis's secret cottage industry of fraudulent till rolls. Scattered around the floor of the room like some colourful glossy mosaic were menus from what must have been hundreds of takeaways ranging from one end of the country to the other. In near twenty-four hour shifts they worked non-stop with few breaks at wages less than one pound an hour. With cheap illegal labour in plentiful supply, few complained.

Sheik Yunis had returned early as was his habit of being unpredictable. It was his trick to keep those who worked for him on their toes. He dropped in freely and often to ensure the wheels of commerce were turning speedily and efficiently. Anyone caught slacking was beaten and swiftly thrown out into the street—no second chances, no appeals. Tonight Sheik Yunis was happy and content man as he observed, with a smile, the hive of industry before him. He was just turning to leave when the front door almost flew off its hinges as police in full body gear rushed into the room.

"EVERBODY JUST STAY WHERE YOU ARE!!" a loud English voice commanded. Then the command was shouted over and over again in other languages. The noise in the room fell into sudden silence as people looked up from their work, some in shock and some in fear.

Sheik Yunis was in handcuffs before he knew what hit him.

"What is the meaning of this!!" he shouted indignantly in Arabic.

"Ishmael Mohamed Yunis," one of the officers addressed him, "I am an officer of the Customs and Excise. I am arresting you for conspiracy to defraud Her Majesty's Customs and Excise. You do not have to say anything…"

Sheik Yunis' eyes were wide open with rage as once again his rights were read out to him. This time in Arabic so they would be no mistake.

§§§

It was a Spartan place where no man or devil would wish to find himself in this world. The odour of fear, death and pain had been left behind by those lost souls who had passed through this place before and left the pungent aroma of their horror impregnated into the bare brick walls like some phantom testimony. The invisible evil spirits screamed at the broken wretch in the chair and hid behind the blinding light of the halogen lamp that beamed its hot rays across Husseini's bleeding lumpy face with eyes so bruised they could hardly open. Again the voices screamed in the blackness beyond the light. In the chair Husseini was aware of nothing but this nightmare reality or dream he prayed to awaken from. His mind wondered from vague reality to the escape of dreams and Husseini knew that his deeds had finally caught up with him as fate and Allah always did. Calling on what little strength remained in his body, he cried out against shadows that tortured him beyond the light.

"My brothers, my brothers," he whimpered, "…what have I done?"

Mocking laughter and a confusion of voices came out of the darkness at him. Husseini was weeping now for mercy in place where such a thing would be an alien. And then he was aware of a single figure towering over him.

"What have I done?" he wept aloud once more.

The figure grasped Husseini by the hair and dragged his head backwards with a jerk of such violence that Husseini's body arched over the chair. Husseini was suddenly aware that the features of this man were so close he could feel his hot breath on his own face. The man started to laugh. "You ask such a question then I will tell you what you have done," he whispered into his face. "You trusted an Iraqi."

Husseini's eyes suddenly defied medical physics and opened wide as he screamed in hatred a word that echoed forlornly around the cell. "Rashar!!!"

§§§

It was two o'clock in the morning at the Customs and Excise building on King George Dock in Hull. At the nearby dockside the North Sea ferry ship, The Norland, blasted its horn as it came to tie up. The waiting night shift of Duty Customs, Immigration, and plain-clothed Special Branch took up their positions to await yet another rush of embarking passengers.

Inside the deserted Customs building Bradley and Angela sat impatiently drinking coffee at their desks. Bradley lit his fourth straight cigarette and did not have to say a word for Angela to know that he was not a happy bunny. While so far they had gotten a good result with the arrest of Sheik Yunis and Rashar, she knew that Bradley hated the thought of being stitched up by Tony despite the fact that the department would be getting a good portion of the VAT owed. It was a personal thing now between the two of them.

Bradley sneered to himself as he pulled on his cigarette. "So our clever little rag- head friend thinks he's just going to walk in here, give us what he thinks he owes and walk then just walk away."

"We've got a good result so far," said Angela beginning to get concerned, "We are getting almost two-thirds of what we are owed and we can put the whole mess quietly behind us."

Bradley glared back at her. "Well maybe you can," he snapped back, "...but I can't."

"I don't like this as much as you," Angela started to reason with him. "But we screwed it up remember." She then paused. "We also made a deal," she added emphatically.

"I don't make deals with people like him, greasy half-wogs who think they can do what they like and walk over the law." Bradley mused at his cleverness. "Well he's in for a shock."

"What are you going to do?" asked Angela, the concern

obvious in her voice.

"Oh don't you worry your pretty little head," said Bradley. "I'll take what's on offer tonight. Then I'll give it a couple of months till things die down."

"Then what?"

"Then," said Bradley with a clever smile, "I'm going to restart the whole investigation. Only this time they'll be no fuckin' mistakes and that smarmy Arab mongrel freak will be behind bars where he belongs."

"I think you're making a mistake," said Angela carefully. "They won't go for it upstairs anyway."

"Oh won't they?" he countered sarcastically. "Well I've already put the idea upstairs and they've given full approval. In fact, they want him banged up as much as I do."

It was clearly no use arguing with Bradley and with this new revelation totally pointless. She was tired of the whole thing.

§§§

After parking his car in the nearby car park, Tony climbed out into the cold sea air of the Humber night, pulled a suitcase from the boot, and walked into the Customs building for a pre-arranged meeting with Bradley and Angela. They retreated to a private back office and closed the door was quietly behind them. Inside, Toni threw the large blue suitcase onto the desk with contempt. On the other side of the room Bradley and Angela stared at each and then at the suitcase. Toni threw open the lid. The wads of plastic covered notes stared back at them.

Tony smiled sourly. "Two million," he said aloud, "Just like we agreed."

"Should we count it?" asked Angela.

"You do what you like with it," said Tony. "The slate is clean now. You get what you want, and so do I." But something in Angela's eyes set off alarm bells for Tony; he had the feeling he knew what it was. After a couple of seconds he turned to leave, but looked back to say, "Give my regards to Yunis and Rashar."

"Just out of interest," Bradley called after him, "what happened to Husseini in all this?"

"I thought you were never going to ask," said Tony with a

broad smile. "He's in prison," he answered flatly.

"Prison?" queried Bradley. "What for?"

Tony deliberately paused before answering. "Spying."

"Jesus Christ," retorted Bradley. "Spying!! What prison is he in?"

"Ovin Prison," Tony answered him.

Bradley shook head. "Never heard of it. Where's that?"

"It's in Tehran," Tony said watching the colour drain from Bradley's face.

"Tehran?" repeated Bradley unsteadily.

"That's right, Tehran," said Tony and added almost mockingly, "Oh, you thought he was an Iranian spy?" Tony shook his head. "No, he was a British spy."

Bradley was almost too reluctant to ask the next question, but he knew he had to. "Did you have something to do with this?"

"Of course," said Tony with an obvious laugh. "And if it wasn't for you Mr Bradley, I would never have guessed."

"Me!!" Bradley shouted back. "What did I do?"

Tony stared at Bradley coldly, "You let him get away with too much. Police, Immigration, Dole office; I knew something was going on. Then when you two came on the scene and you spilled the beans on Husseini…"

"—But you already knew it was Husseini who came to us," protested Bradley.

Again Tony shook his head. "No, I didn't. I guessed it was him and that night in the motorway café you confirmed it."

"You bastard," said Bradley with growing anger. "You tricked us."

"Yes, I tricked you," said Tony. "And I am going to walk out that fuckin' door and I never want to see your face again. If you have any idea of coming after me when things have quietened down; well," said Tony making his intentions obvious, "…if I go down I take you with me. That's a fuckin' promise. I don't think the local spooks will be too pleased with you Mr Bradley, spragging up one of their boys. It'll look real bad for Customs in the newspapers."

Across the room Bradley swallowed hard and had suddenly lost his voice. Next to him Angela bit her lip trying to contain a grin. Tony had already guessed Bradley's intentions towards him. He was just sticking to two golden rules of the political game. One: The word of a Lord is worthless to a lesser. Two: Never do anything without taking out an insurance policy.

He knew men like Tom Bradley, he had met them and shit on them a hundred times. White, black, brown or green, they were all the same. Their predictability for the double deal was just part of the endless game that these men played. Tony lingered for a moment, staring down at his defeated and sullen opponent. Tony's expression was contemptuous. "See ya Mr Bradley." As Tony left, the office door slammed behind him sending a ringing echo throughout the empty office block.

FIFTEEN
Six months later

The university lecture theatre was almost full. As the droll voice of the bearded lecturer rambled on at his captured audience some of the studious scribbled, some yawned and some just listened or pretended to listen.

"So what do we understand is meant by the term Development of Social Policy?" the lecturer asked his bewildered audience. With a smile to encourage the coy, he waited for an answer from the sea of silent faces staring at him. For a few moments the question lingered in the silence until a lone hand raised itself into the air.

"Yes?" said the lecturer.

"The development of social policy," said Tony confidently, "...as a national strategy, is about the considered intellectual wisdom of planning and management of society for the ultimate benefit of society as a whole."

The lecturer smiled with bewilderment. "I have never heard it defined quite like that before," he answered, "And I never heard it described so accurately before." He took a moment to think. "I think on that thoughtful note, we'll take this subject further next week." And the lecture broke up.

Outside the university, Tony along with a group of newly found friends made their way for a liquid lunch and a sandwich along the tree-lined road. He paid no attention to the old, battered, red and rusting Ford Escort that had pulled alongside until an unmistakable voice called after him in his Arabic name.

"Ahmed!!"

Before Tony even turned round he knew who the voice belonged to. Staring back at him through the lowered window and wearing that irrepressible smile, was Rashar. Tony bade those with him to go on and he walked to the car with a smile of his own now growing on his face. He stared down at an uncertain Rashar.

"*Salem alicome achee* – Hello my brother," said Rashar awkwardly.

Tony's response was without enthusiasm but certainly not without amusement. "Hello Rashar."

"So you have your wish," said Rashar, "you are an Englishman now, eh?" He chuckled. "You look well Ahmed."

Rashar seemed to have fallen on hard times. The road tax on the car had run out by five months and even his clothes, which he always took so much pride in, appeared unkempt and dishevelled.

"Which is more than I can say for your car," answered Tony.

"Mine is in the garage being repaired," he lied badly. "A friend lent me this one."

"Then your friend does you no favours Rashar," commented Tony harshly.

The smile was then gone from Rashar's face. "I need your help Ahmed," Rashar suddenly blurted out.

The irony of the request was not lost on Tony. "I am not in that business anymore Rashar," said Tony.

"Not that sort of help," Rashar answered.

Tony shook his head and laughed. "Rashar!" he started emphatically, "I don't do any sort of help, *anta tefhan*? – you understand?"

"You still hold things against me then?" asked Rashar.

"And what things would I hold against you Rashar?" Tony asked him to explain what they both knew, and Rashar dared not answer.

"We were always friends Ahmed," said Rashar groping for words. "And I need you as a friend again."

"I told you once before Rashar," Tony reminded him. "Business and friendship cannot be mixed. You are either one or the other, and please don't take this personally Rashar, but such a friend as you I do not need."

Rashar's finger was pointing accusingly at Tony and there was desperation now on his face and in his voice. "I know it was you Ahmed," he said at him. "And I understand what you did. In business you have to do these things."

"And what things are those Rashar?" Tony snapped back at him. "You mean fuckin' the people you call friends for a man like Husseini?"

"I know it was you Ahmed," Rashar said again, "and I swear I will say nothing. But you have to help me."

"And *what* do you know Rashar?" Tony scoffed. "Fuck-all, that's what you know."

"I know Husseini is in prison in Tehran," said Rashar flatly. "His family are very angry." It was a statement with all the usual implications of threat masquerading innocence.

Tony threw up his hands in a gesture of supreme indifference. "Do what the fuck you want Rashar. Your threats don't bother me."

Rashar quickly backtracked. "I am not threatening you Ahmed," he answered with sudden innocence. "I am just saying, that's all."

Tony was now looking at him with impatience and his words came out in demanding staccato."Rashar!! What..do..you..want?"

Gradually Rashar turned to pleading. "Ahmed I made mistake. I always liked you. I ask you this one favour, and as God is my witness, I swear I will never say anything again."

Now Tony cared little about Rashar's threats, but the reason for his desperation was making him more curious by the minute. And there was always the slight chance that he might learn something useful. After all, there was nothing to be lost in just listening and perhaps an advantage to be gained.

"Alright, alright Rashar," Tony pretended to relent. "What favour?"

Rashar's sighed with relief. "Please Ahmed, you have to speak with Sheik Yunis for me. He is out of prison now and he is blaming me for everything. He thinks that because I did not go to prison that I made a deal. Husseini, the bastard, sold the business. I lost everything and so did the Sheik. He thinks I was in with Husseini to set him up and his people are looking for me. I know if you speak with him on my behalf he will listen to you. He always spoke highly of you and trusted you." Rashar paused and pleaded again with his eyes. "I know he will kill me if you do not speak with him. Please Ahmed, use your silver tongue to speak for me and I will always be in your debt."

There was justice after all Tony thought smugly to himself. It hadn't been kindness that had kept Tony from letting Bradley to lock up Rashar. In fact, it was the opposite. With the certain knowledge that Sheik Yunis would get banged up in the clink, he knew that when he came out he would be looking for somone on whom to take vengeance. With Rashar getting off scott-free, it would look to Sheik Yunis like Rashar had made a deal with the VAT and had spilled the beans to save his own neck. It was all good Machiavellian stuff to ensure that if Sheik Yunis came looking for anyone after his holiday in Her Majesty's Prison, it would be Rashar and not Tony.

Just as he had anticipated, the thieves had turned on each other, though he could hardly believe that after all Rashar had done to try and screw him, he had the gall to grovel and now ask for his help. Maybe Rashar believed that because he was basically English, he was instilled with some sort of fair play. He was also well aware that if he was stupid enough to get Rashar off the hook with Sheik Yunis, he too, would have to watch his back. Sheik Yunis would want revenge and had probably allied himself with Husseini's family.

Tony suddenly had an idea. Rashar was offering him an opportunity to get rid him for good. Taking out his mobile phone he feigned a look of exaggerated reluctance. "This is the last time Rashar."

"I swear it Ahmed, I swear it."

Tony keyed in Sheik Yunis's number.

§§§

In the flat above his takeaway in Sheffield, Sheik Yunis was fast asleep after his long journey from Ranby Prison in Nottinghamshire where he had served six months of a one year sentence. It was his young daughter Samina who woke him to tell him that Tony was on the phone.

"How are you my old friend?" began Tony deliberately speaking in English.

"Ahmed it is good to hear your voice," answered the Sheik.

"I am sorry I did not call you before," said Tony, "...but I have been busy."

"I have heard Ahmed, and you should not concern yourself," said the Sheik. "You go to the University now. This was always in your heart I think, to do good things. Not like that son-of-a-dog Rashar."

Tony feigned a smile at Rashar as he spoke with the Sheik. "It is on the very matter of Rashar that I am calling you now my old friend."

The Sheik sat bolt upright in bed suddenly attentive. "If you know where he is then you should tell me. I am going to slit his throat from ear to ear when I find him. His body I shall feed it to the crows."

The Arabic rant went on for some time with Tony trying without success to squeeze in a word.

"What is he saying?" whispered Rashar's intently.

"He asking how you are," Tony lied.

Rashar's face light up with sudden hope. "Really?"

"Do you know what the pig did to me?" the Sheik's tirade continued. "He robbed me and put me in prison. He came to me in prison and blamed it all on you Ahmed. Do you know that Ahmed? He wanted me to kill you Ahmed."

Tony stared at Rashar with the mask of a smile still on his face. "Really. *That's* interesting."

"This I warn you because I look on you like a son."

"Look Sheik," said Tony, "I must be honest with you so that we remain friends. Your friendship is an honour to have and I treasure it greatly."

"Then speak Ahmed, I am listening my son."

"I am with Rashar now....," the language and profanity coming down the phone only Tony could hear, and with a pleasant smile for Rashar, Tony continued to speak over the rant. Two very different conversations were being had simultaneously.

"I think you have to talk with Rashar Sheik," said Tony. "I know you are a forgiving man."

"I am going cut off his hands and feet!!!" screamed the Sheik.

"That is so kind of you Sheik," answered Tony. "So you are willing to see him?"

"I am going to tear his heart and brains out."

Tony covered the phone with his hand and gave a big smile to Rashar. "He will see you," said Tony. "When can you go?"

"I'll go now," Rashar panted, "I'll go now."

Tony returned to his conversation with the Sheik still spewing insults and threatening to kill Rashar.

"He is coming to see you now Sheik...........You are a good man Sheik to offer this forgiveness."

"I kill the bastard son of bitch!!!" the Sheik shouted back.

Tony shook his head with a warm smile that made Rashar smile too. "*Ma salama* Sheik and God keep you." Tony closed his phone.

Rashar was elated. "Ahmed you did it!!" he shouted. "What can I say? You saved my life."

"Just forget it Rashar," Tony answered him. "Now get going and sort it out with Sheik Yunis."

"You know Ahmed," said Rashar starting his car. "You are like my own brother Ahmed." He wound up his window and drove away. In his rearview mirror Rashar looked back at Tony as he stood waving on the pavement. Another expression now filled his face and thoughts of vengeance were already in his mind. "I'll be back soon Ahmed," he whispered ominously to himself.

Tony stood watching as Rashar's car disappeared into the distance. "And you are like my brother too Rashar." He shook his head to himself thinking that maybe he had sunk too low this time. "You have to do these things," he said aloud to himself.

§§§

In the public bar of the Three Nuns Hotel in Whiten, Amu Sultan slammed two pints of Tetley cask bitter onto the pub table and sat down still laughing to himself. "Sometimes Ahmed you are bastard," he said after swilling down half his pint in one gulp.

Tony sat across the table and followed suit, but this time guzzled his complete pint in one gulp and unsubtley slammed down his now empty glass in front of Amu Sultan.

"Alright, alright," said Amu Sultan, taking the hint and getting up to go to the bar again.

Tony looked at his watch with a thoughtful expression. "He should be there right about now."

"You are *cuss um muck* – a motherfucker. Allah has said I may take your hands off. This is the law and the judgement of God for a thief.!" Sheik Yunis screamed at the man in the chair.

The battered and bruised face of Rashar Nuraman tied to a chair in the centre of black cellar tried to plead, but the Sheik's answer came with a swift nod of the head and a thousand blows rained out of the darkness. The cellar filled with a thunderous panic of flapping wings from other caged prisoners who awaited the same fate as the screaming human.

§§§

It took the forceful tongue of Brian, the pub landlord, to finally persuade Amu Sultan and Tony that it was long past closing time and that they had had enough. Like two drunken cavaliers they staggered across an empty Whiton Square towards a takeaway, once again owned by Amu Sultan. They were as drunk as two skunks and jabbering so incoherently that neither had a clue what the other was saying.

§§§

A battered and rusting ford pick-up trundled through the gates of the factory on the decaying industrial estate. But for the dimly illuminated sign that barely lit up the factory name over the gates, the surrounding factory units were in darkness. The name on the sign could just be seen: MADJID'S MINCE AND DONNER KEBAB MAKERS OF NEWCASTLE UPON TYNE.

A smiling Madjid stood waiting for his midnight delivery with happy thoughts of vengeance. The pick-truck pulled up in the darkness and two men garbed in the headdress of Yemeni Kafiyahs climbed out of the cab.

"Quickly now!!" Madjid told them harshly, "I haven't got all night."

The two men dropped down the back flap of the pick-up and struggling to hold its weight, dragged out a long bundle of rolled up carpet. Madjid, still smiling, pulled back a bit of the rug to look inside, a slow smile of satisfaction crept across his face. "*Inshallah* Ahmed will be soon to travel this path," he said smugly to himself and then bade the men to follow him inside.

§§§

By the time Tony and Amu Sultan made it back to the takeaway it was packed with drunken revellers creating the usual nuisance as they ordered, and waited for their food. On the other side of - the counter Tony stood drunkenly swaying as he watched an equally drunk Amu Sultan trying to show off in attempt to shave the revolving donner kebab on the gas fire spit with the electric knife.

"You see," said Amu Sultan with drunken pride as neatly cut slices peeled off the roasting donner. "I can still do it." He picked up a newly cut slice pulled it in two and offered one half to Tony. "Madjid is making some good donner lately. Here try."

Tony looked straight at Amu Sultan and cringed.

Amu Sultan looked at the donner and then back at Tony with the same thoughts. "Maybe you are right I think." He threw down the slice of donner.

§§§

It was difficult enough for the two Arabs struggling with the bundle to get it up the narrow metal stairway that led to the top of the giant mincer without the harassing voice of Madjid hurrying them in the unlit factory interior.

"Come on, come on, and now hurry," Madjid ordered them. "You are like two old camels."

The heaving groans of the men suddenly relented as their bundle finally toppled into the top of the mincing tank with a loud metallic gong as the bundle hit the tank floor. Madjid was beside himself with mischievous laughter as his finger poised with enthusiasm over the green start button. "You bastard Rashar," he shouted with an evil laugh, "You don't cost me money now." And his finger came down on the button. The whir of the electronic blades started up like a jet engine. Madjid was almost jumping about in the darkness like some mad Professor in his laboratory. His pleasure did not lat long as sudden harsh metallic grinding brought the mincer to an abrupt halt with a loud crunch. Madjid's face was in agony and he screamed at the two Arabs like a man in great pain."You stupid sons of bitches!!.....YOU FORGET TO TAKE OFF HIS SHOES!!!"

******